THE DARK
AND OTHER
LOVE STORIES

ALSO BY DEBORAH WILLIS

Vanishing and Other Stories

THE DARK AND OTHER LOVE STORIES

BY DEBORAH WILLIS

W. W. NORTON & COMPANY

Independent Publishers Since 1923 • NEW YORK • LONDON

For information about permission to reproduce selections from
this book, write to Permissions, W. W. Norton & Company, Inc.,
500 Fifth Avenue, New York, NY 10110

For information about special discounts for bulk purchases,
please contact W. W. Norton Special Sales at
specialsales@wwnorton.com or 800-233-4830

Manufacturing by Berryville Graphics
Book design by Brooke Koven
Production manager: Anna Oler

ISBN 978-0-393-28589-5

W. W. Norton & Company, Inc.
500 Fifth Avenue, New York, N.Y. 10110
www.wwnorton.com

W. W. Norton & Company Ltd.
15 Carlisle Street, London W1D 3BS

1 2 3 4 5 6 7 8 9 0

*In memory of
my grandparents
and the
love stories they lived*

CONTENTS

THE DARK
AND OTHER
LOVE STORIES

The Dark

Were like Betty and Veronica in those comics we read endlessly—practically identical, except for our hair. Andrea's was dark and I was blond. Her skin tanned easily and I worried about sunburns, but we were the same height and our bodies were lean and undeveloped.

We met when we were assigned to the same canoe at summer camp. Andrea took the stern and I was in the bow. As we drifted on the placid lake, she said, "If we paddled hard, how far do you think we'd get? Before anyone caught us?"

It was the closest thing to love at first sight I've ever found. At summer camp, the days are long and friendships are quick and intense. After that canoe ride, Andrea and I sat beside each other at meals, played on the same sports teams, and slept in adjacent top bunks. And we were always the last to fall asleep. If I closed my eyes, Andrea would stretch out one of her legs and kick something over on my shelf: my flashlight, or the bottle of calamine lotion my mom had packed for me. Something to knock me awake.

"Jess," she whispered. "Wake up." Her voice was quiet but

demanding, and it forced me to open my eyes, to focus in the dark, to stay in our private world of wakefulness.

During the day, we participated. That's what we called it—*participating*—imitating our counselor, Lisa, and her sunny way of speaking. In the past I'd enjoyed participating, but that summer, I hated everything: swim lessons, nature walks, dodgeball, arts and crafts, tennis, basketball, canoeing. Most of all, I hated horseback riding, which involved getting saddle burn as your horse walked listlessly around a ring. The horses were so tired and used to their work that we could drop the reins and they would continue at the same pace, retracing the same circuit. Andrea said riding one of those horses was like having sex with a dead person. She'd never had sex with anyone, living or dead, but she had a gift for a memorable turn of phrase. She kicked uselessly at the horse's sides, flicked the reins, yelled, "*Vamos! Caballo!*" She always got in trouble for that.

Other girls fawned over the horses—brushed their manes, fed them apples, kissed their noses—but I didn't like to touch those big, sad animals. The camp rented them from a rancher who provided horses that were too old to be of any use to him. Some had sagging bellies from bearing foals, others were scarred with bug bites. Sometimes they would sweat so much that a white lather foamed along their necks. And they weren't gentle like the horses in books. They kicked and bit each other furtively, the way children abuse each other when their parents aren't watching.

What I mean is, Andrea and I were thirteen and beginning to outgrow this daylight world of lessons and games and sing-alongs. We were sick of having our days parsed into hour-long blocks, sick of being led from one activity to the next. We were hungry for feral time. That's why we loved the dark.

We remained awake until long after the other girls had finished brushing their teeth, trying on each other's clothes, and talking about which boys they liked. We stayed up even after Lisa had flicked off the light and left the cabin, on her way to plan the next day's activities. Andrea and I stayed up until the sky was so black that each star was outlined against it, sharp and bright like scraps of metal. That's how we knew it was time.

We changed from our pastel pajamas into jeans and hooded sweatshirts, and put on running shoes that we'd turned from white to black with a permanent marker—my mom would freak out when I got home. We dressed quietly so none of the other girls would hear us—those girls were our friends during the day, but we didn't want them to know what we did at night. They might tell on us. Or worse, they might want to join us.

We opened the cabin door and ducked out, careful to keep close to the small wooden building. We couldn't let ourselves be seen by any of the counselors who sat on benches outside with flashlights and first-aid kits and boxes of Kleenex, ready to deal with bleeding noses, stomachaches, homesickness. We slipped through the night as silently as fish through water, skidding between cabins until we were far from where the other kids slept. In the dark, we felt brave. We were no longer part of that camp world. Or rather, at night, the camp itself changed to accommodate us. It ceased to be an ordered, regimented place, where we ate at the same time every day, where we sang songs after lunch, where we played sports after singing. At night, the infrastructure for these activities—the dining hall, the soccer field, the lake—seemed mysterious.

Our favorite place to go was the horses' field. We crawled along the barbed-wire fence of the camp's perimeter, rolled down a steep hill past the boys' cabins, and came to the corral: a locked tack shed and a ring of close-clipped grass used for riding lessons. The horses were kept here during the day, but each night, when the lessons and trail rides were done, they were let out—*set free!* we called it—into an open field, where they grazed and slept. There was nothing romantic about this field during the day: it buzzed with mosquitoes, and smelled of the overflowing septic tank. But at night, these things could be ignored. At night, the field was full of moon.

To get there, we passed the corral and went through a small patch of forest. We followed trails the horses had made through the trees, and, because we never brought flashlights, had to feel our way, our hands gripping rough branches, our feet moving slowly over dirt and rocks. I've never thought that I have good hearing, but on those nights, I heard everything: distant coyotes, insects circling my body, my own breath.

I was only scared once. Andrea and I moved through the densest part of the forest, along a path so narrow that branches scraped my face. No moonlight could reach us, and I couldn't see anything. I followed the sounds of twigs cracking under Andrea's shoes. I felt the thrill of my heart in my chest.

Then there was silence. I couldn't hear Andrea's breathing or her steps.

"Andrea?" I figured this was a joke. "Andy?" I whispered, using the nickname she hated.

There was no reply. I held my breath and tried to quiet my body, but my heart seemed lodged between my ears.

"Andrea!" I screamed, and that's when she grabbed me from behind and put her hand over my mouth.

"You chickenshit." She laughed. "Do you want us to get caught?"

I could feel her heart against my back. "You're a bitch."

"Shh." She still had her arms around me. "Look."

She turned my head toward the outlines of the horses, ghostly and elegant against the black sky. At night, it was easy to forget how ordinary they were. Or rather, at night, we could see the beauty of their flawed bodies. They stood together, some of them asleep, some eating, and we could see the breath from their wide nostrils. They looked like shadows, not entirely real.

We approached the horses quietly, with the single-mindedness of lovers. It was as though Andrea and I had created them, as though they were our secret, a gift we'd given each other. They had a quiet kind of bravery, a grace I've rarely seen since. The only thing that comes close is the dignity of some old women—the ones who remember being beautiful, the ones who know they still are.

The hour-long Rest Period was the only time we had to ourselves during the day. That's when our counselor would throw on her bikini and lie in the sun. She arranged her limbs on a red towel, closed her eyes behind her sunglasses, and drifted into a silent, more grown-up world. We envied the way she looked, so pretty and still.

All the girls in our cabin followed Lisa, dragging their towels out onto the grass beside hers. Andrea and I did the same, but we laid down our towels away from the others and spent the hour reading from Andrea's extensive *Archie* collection. We adored the swerving of Archie's affection from Betty to Veronica and back, the way competition pervaded the friendship between the blonde and the brunette. These things seemed subtle and full of meaning.

"Veronica is his beast-lover." Andrea sounded wise and resigned, using a term she'd picked up from her older sister. "Once a person finds their beast-lover, that's it. They can never escape."

Neither of us had any experience with any kind of lover. Some of the other girls in our cabin—Lena Bindman and Nicky

Jmaeff—had kissed boys, then described the experience in detail for us. But we weren't interested in the boys our age. They were as thin as we were, their voices sounded like our own, and they traveled in packs like stray dogs. Instead, we liked the older boys, the ones we saw talking to Lisa. They were tall and muscular and wore the timeless uniform of camp counselors: bandannas tied around their heads, T-shirts tucked in the back pockets of their baggy shorts. They had a pale line of skin at their hips where the sun had not reached, and, if their shorts hung low enough, this paleness could be glimpsed.

Once we saw Zack, the most beautiful guy at camp, throw his arm over Lisa's shoulder and say, "Hey, you." After that, Andrea and I lay on our towels—comic books scattered around us, the sun forcing us to squint—and imitated them.

"Hey, you. Hey, you," we'd say, switching roles, practicing for when it was our turn.

At first, the horses didn't like our nightly visits. They sidestepped away from us when we approached, and each kept a wide, dark eye on us. But we didn't mind. We never felt we owned them, or that they owed us. It was enough to be outside, to be awake. To be free to watch them move through the tall grass. To listen to their knees crack as they took long, gorgeous steps.

After about a week, they didn't mind if we touched their flanks, their heavy bellies, the ridge of bone along their backs. We cupped their rough chins in our palms, and felt the softness of their noses. Putting my hands against their warm skin made me feel like a thief, stealing something I didn't deserve.

This was all we were doing when we were caught. Andrea and I were running our fingers through the mane of a horse we called Hell Bitch, though her real name was something less memorable.

We were pulling burrs from her hair when a flashlight shone in our eyes.

Someone yelled, "Who is that?" and I recognized the voice. It was Lisa, but she didn't sound like her usual, sunny self. Andrea and I froze. We stood perfectly still, as though we could pretend we were horses, asleep standing up. Then, in the same instant, we ran. It spooked the horses and they bolted too, kicking up dirt.

We heard Lisa and someone else screaming at us to stop, but instinct drove us toward the forest. We were fast and I thought we'd make it, but then I felt someone grab my hood and a handful of my hair. The sweatshirt choked me and Lisa shone her flashlight in my face. "Hey, you," she said.

"Look at this," said another familiar voice—it belonged to a redheaded counselor named Dahlia, one of the camp beauties. She held Andrea by the wrist. "Two sneak-outs."

"I didn't think you'd do something like this, Jessie." Lisa's face was so close to mine that I could smell the stale hot chocolate on her breath. "Andrea, maybe, but not you."

"Sorry."

"Sorry's not good enough. Sneaking out is illegal."

"We're going to have to call the police," said Dahlia. "We'll have to inform the RCMP."

I was almost sure that wasn't true. I was almost sure they were making it up. But somehow, at night, it seemed harder to distinguish the truth from everything else.

"No. Let's not be too hard on them." Lisa still held me by the hair. "We won't call the police."

"Yeah, we'll go easy on you," said Dahlia, and it occurred to me that they were enjoying themselves. It occurred to me that Andrea and I had only done what was expected of us.

"We won't soak you with the fire hose," said Dahlia. "We won't even make you run laps around the soccer field."

Lisa let go of my hair and threw her arm around my shoulder. "Where were you going, anyway? Who were you going to visit?"

I didn't understand the question. "No one."

"You can tell me." Lisa pulled me toward her and spoke into my ear. "Which boys were you going to see?"

"Was it Jason Lazarick?" said Dahlia. "That kid's hot."

Lisa and Dahlia laughed, which didn't surprise me. What was alarming was that Andrea laughed along with them.

"So it *was* Jason." Lisa shook me. "What were you going to say to him? What were you going to do?"

"I know what they wanted to do." Dahlia's voice had a malice she would never have exhibited during the day. "I think these girls should crawl back to their cabin. I think these little sluts should lick the ground."

I thought it was a joke, until Lisa shoved my back and almost knocked me over.

"We weren't going to visit Jason," I said, facing away from her.

"Shut up, Jess," Andrea hissed at me. She was on her hands and knees.

"We weren't going to see anyone." My voice sounded loud against the soft noise of the forest—the creak of tree branches and rustling of leaves. "We just wanted to see the horses," I said. "We just wanted to be together."

"*We just wanted to be together,*" Dahlia imitated me. "That's fucking sick."

Then one of them—I think it was Lisa—kicked the back of my knees and I fell to the ground.

"Come on," she said. "Crawl."

After we were caught, we stopped going to see the horses. Andrea seemed to get over it.

"It's not like they're dead." She put her arm around me. "We could go to the corral right now."

But watching the horses during the day wasn't the same, and she knew it. She rested her head on my shoulder. "I have an idea."

We decided to sneak out to the lake, where we'd met, drifting in that canoe. The lake was easy to reach from our cabin—we had only to go down a grassy slope to arrive at the waterfront. But if we were caught there, we'd be in real trouble. No one was allowed near the water without supervision. There were stories about a boy who'd drowned years ago, and who haunted the lake now. They said he was half human and half fish, and if you went near the water at night, he would drag you to the bottom. They said he was lonely and wanted company.

But Andrea and I had outgrown that kind of story, so we came up with a plan. The lakefront was blocked off at night by a metal fence with a gate that was locked each evening. We inspected it during the day, and determined that if we lay flat on the ground, we could just fit under the gate.

The first night we tried it, I slid on my stomach, making myself lithe and long as a cat. Andrea waited for me, already on the other side. I could feel the sharp edges of the fence catch my clothes, but I made it. That locked gate meant that if anyone noticed we were missing from our bunks, no one would expect to find us here. On the other side, we felt safe and alone.

We sat on the dock and looked out at the lake. It was not as striking as watching a herd of horses—nothing was like coming upon that wildness. But it was something. The water was calm and black and lapped gently at the wood, made a sucking sound as it hit the tires that ran along the edges of the dock. Lights from cottages and campgrounds along the shore seemed to rest on the water's surface.

Andrea untied a blackened running shoe and peeled off her

sock to reveal a slim, pale foot. Then she took off her other shoe, rolled up her pant hems, and let her legs dangle over the edge of the dock. "Hey." She turned to me. "The water's warm."

"Not really. It just feels that way 'cause the air is cold."

She stood up on the dock, water dripping from her feet to the wood, and began to take off her clothes. She pulled her sweatshirt over her head, and took off her layers of shirts with it. The skin of her arms, chest, and stomach seemed to pick up the light of the moon. She unbuttoned her jeans and kicked them off. Her cotton underwear came off last, and she tossed it onto the pile of her clothes. She looked white and fragile against the sky.

Once, years later, I began to tell this story to my husband, but stopped at this point.

"Okay," he said. "So you're at the lake. She takes off her clothes. Then what?"

"Nothing," I replied. "That's it."

I didn't trust him with this story. I worried he would read it as only sexual.

In truth, I noticed Andrea's body, but mostly to compare it with my own. I watched as she stepped to the edge of the dock, and wondered which one of us would later be considered beautiful.

When she dived, her body shattered the glassy surface. The water was so dark that for a few seconds I couldn't see her. I was alone. I held my breath until her head burst through the surface, a ghost returned from the other side.

"Jess!" She was out of breath and loud and laughing. "Come on!"

I was already pulling my arms out of my sweatshirt and I left my clothes in a pile beside hers. I didn't dive, but slid off the dock and splashed in. The water was *good*. It felt as though the lake had been waiting for us, had stored the sun's warmth inside itself in expectation of our visit.

I put my head under for as long as I could, and when I came up for air, Andrea said, "You're a fish."

I knew what she meant. Our pale bodies moving through the black water shimmered like they were covered with scales. Her dark hair was pasted to her head, and I said, "You're an eel."

During the day, there were reasons to avoid swimming: the algae in the water, the imagined threat of leeches, and the boys who splashed us and assessed our bodies in our swimsuits. But at night, even the algae didn't bother me. I liked when the soft, green arms wrapped themselves around my legs. And I wasn't afraid of the possibility that a fish might glide past me, its cold body brushing against mine. At night, I was a fish. I was made to swim. Andrea and I dived under the surface again and again and counted the seconds we managed to stay underwater—*twelve Mississippi, thirteen Mississippi*—then burst above the surface and shouted our best time. We swam out as far as we could, as fast as we could, to where the water was deep. Andrea wrapped her arms around me, tugging me farther. We held each other, laughing, our skin slick, our hearts pounding in time with each other.

That night, nothing bad happened to us. We swam until we were tired, then dog-paddled lazily back to the dock. We climbed out of the water, shivering, and got dressed. Then we slipped back into our cabin and changed into pajamas. We were exhausted and happy. We fell asleep with our hair still wet, leaving stains on our pillows.

Every night we sneaked down to the lake, and every night we took off our clothes and swam. I got up the courage to dive in, and felt the water hit my face. We didn't care about making noise—we felt we were safe—so we played tag in the water. Andrea started the game by pushing me and yelling, "You're it!"

I swam toward her and smacked her shoulder. "No, you're it!"

It was stupid to play with only two people, but we didn't care. We liked swimming and the fact that we weren't supposed to be swimming. Andrea splashed toward me, and I kicked away from her, and that's when we heard it.

"You're it! You're it!"

It was a voice that imitated ours but didn't belong to us. I couldn't see where it came from.

"No, you're it," said another voice, deeper this time, and I turned toward the sound. I had been looking at the shore, expecting to see one of the camp's staff members, but these voices came from the water. From a small metal fishing boat, about fifteen feet away. There were two men in the boat, one at the stern and one at the bow. One of them held oars and rowed toward us.

"Who is that?" Andrea managed to steady her voice.

"Just a couple drunken sailors," said the rower. "A couple lonesome fishermen."

I wanted to get out of the water. There was no ladder to climb onto the dock, but Andrea and I could have hoisted ourselves up. Or we could have swum in toward the shore, where it was shallow enough to stand, and simply walked out of the water. We could have done that, except that we were naked.

As the boat neared, the aluminum sides picked up light from the moon. The boat had no motor and the man who rowed had to face away from us in order to move toward us. The first thing I noticed was his thin back and bony profile when he turned his head to ask, "And who are you?"

We didn't answer. We watched as they drew closer. Neither Andrea nor I appeared to move, though under the surface we kicked furiously.

The men looked about twenty or twenty-one, maybe older. They wore shorts and T-shirts, despite the cold night air. One of them drank from a bottle of something. I'd never had a drink in my life, so I couldn't tell by the color or even the label what was in the bottle.

"Come on, ladies," said the one with the oars. He had high cheekbones and eyes set deep in his face. "You're not going to tell us your names?"

"You haven't told us yours," said Andrea.

"I'm Scott." He pointed with the end of the oar toward his companion. "And this is my brother, Gareth."

They didn't look like brothers. Gareth had a face wide like a moon, hair cut close to his head, and muscles bunched along his arms and neck. He was the one holding the bottle, and he raised it to salute us. The liquid sloshed inside.

"Hi, Scott. Hi, Gareth." Andrea was beginning to take on the flirty, confident tone Lisa used when she talked to the guys her age. "I'm Andrea."

"Your friend isn't very friendly," said Scott, smiling at me and leaning his elbow on the boat's misshapen gunnel.

"Her name's Jessie," said Andrea. "And she's shy."

"That's okay." Gareth's voice was deeper and softer than his brother's. "Shy's all right."

"Maybe you can help us, 'cause we have a bit of a problem," said Scott. "Show them your problem, Gare."

Gareth seemed to lunge at us, faster than I expected his big body to move. I splashed away from him like a skittish animal, until I realized he was only stretching out his arm. He held his hand out, palm up, and a fishhook was embedded in his first two fingers. There was no blood, but the hook was lodged deep in his flesh, fastening his fingers together.

"Accident," said Gareth, as though that explained it.

"My brother's an idiot," added Scott.

"Maybe we could get the nurse," I said, even though I knew that was a bad idea.

"This is our nurse." Scott nodded to the bottle. "He's going to drink the whole thing and then we're going to rip that hook right out."

Gareth pulled his hand away from us and rested it in his lap, as though it were something he'd stolen from the bottom of the lake, a treasure he wanted to keep safe.

Scott kept smiling. "But we're willing to share, aren't we, Gareth? You girls want to join us? You care for a drink?"

Andrea's eyes were on Scott's face. "I don't know."

"We're not even supposed to be awake now," I said.

"Who says?" Scott laughed. "You're grown-ups. You can do what you want."

He couldn't have seriously believed this. Andrea and I were thirteen, and we looked it.

"And you're probably cold." Gareth dropped his gaze to my bare shoulders. "We got towels in the boat. You can dry off."

"It's warm." My throat was dry. "The water's warm."

"Not really." He kept his eyes on me. "It just feels that way."

"Who wants to row around in a boat all night?" said Andrea. "That sounds boring."

"We're not just rowing around." Scott pointed across the lake, toward blackness. "We're going to the reeds."

Andrea put one hand on the boat's metal edge. "What's that?"

"You've never been there?" Scott leaned toward her. "The reeds are really tall. You take a boat through and it's like being in a jungle."

"If we did go with you," she said, "we'd have to be back soon. Before it gets light."

"That's cool," said Scott.

Andrea looked at me and there was brightness, a visible excitement, leaping from her face. Then she held the boat's metal sides with both hands and said, "You guys have to close your eyes."

Neither of them did. They watched as she pulled herself, naked and dripping, into the boat. Gareth handed her a towel and she wrapped it around her body. She was shivering. "Come here," said Scott, and she sat beside him. He put his arm around her and whispered something in her ear that made her laugh.

I was used to following Andrea, so I swam toward the boat. I wanted to climb in, to be with her. I also wanted to row through the reeds. I imagined reaching out my hand to touch them, and I wanted to hear the dry clicking sound they'd make as the boat passed through. And I was curious about something else too. I had no desire to try whatever they were drinking from that bottle, but I wondered how Gareth's mouth tasted.

He leaned toward me, his pale face reflecting the feeble light. "What's your name again?"

"Jessie." I could smell the liquor on his breath. "Jessica."

"You want a hand, Jessica?" He stretched out his arm and I would have taken it, if he hadn't offered the hand with the fishhook. The metal piercing his skin, the hook ready to bite into mine.

"Come on," he said. "You scared?"

"Jess." Andrea waved to me as though she were far away. "Come on."

"Come here, little miss shy," said Scott. "Little miss scaredy-cat."

Everyone in the boat laughed, but I watched only Andrea's face. In the darkness, I could almost see how she would look as an adult, how her features would shift and age. She already seemed older than me, ready to go wherever these guys would take her.

My voice came out too loud and absurdly polite. "No, thank you."

"Hey." Andrea sounded more angry than afraid. "Don't just fucking ditch me."

"You don't have to go."

"What's up with your friend?" Scott spoke into her wet hair. "What's her problem?"

Gareth shrugged and took another drink. He said nothing and I was grateful for his silence. I turned and swam toward the shore. I could hear the boat creak as it moved away, the wooden oars knocking against its sides. I glided past the dock, and when the water became shallow enough, I stood up. I could hear Andrea laughing, but the sound was distant and I didn't turn around. I wondered if Gareth could see my pale back as I emerged from the water. I hoped he could.

I want to say that I was concerned over Andrea's safety. I want to say that I did the smart thing, and woke Lisa, and asked for help. I want to say that I spent the rest of the night awake and anxious. But I didn't. I put on my clothes and felt them stick to my wet skin. Then I crawled back to the cabin, and climbed onto my bunk. I was so tired that I fell asleep in seconds and I slept until morning. I don't know what time Andrea got in, but she was in bed when Lisa woke us for breakfast. And I don't know what happened in that boat after I abandoned it. Andrea never told me.

Our friendship didn't end. She and I continued to spend every day together—suntanning with the other girls, participating in basketball and nature walks and arts and crafts. The next summer, we were again in the same cabin, but we each made a new best friend. The summer after that, we got boyfriends.

I think of her only occasionally now, the few times I allow myself to see a man I know. This man and I, we meet at night, at the edge of our ever-expanding city. We meet away from our daylight lives of jobs and spouses and children. We meet where suburban development bleeds into countryside. Out there, the houses are half built, and the city has yet to put in streetlights. We park on a road without sidewalks, on pavement that crumbles away to gravel. When we turn off our car engines, everything goes dark and we find each other through sound alone. I walk toward the click of his car door closing and he moves toward the jangle of my keys. We reach each other through the noise of our shoes on the pavement, and through habit, and through long friendship. Finding his familiar smell out there is like coming upon those horses at night: a moment of stolen grace, of beauty we don't deserve. I slip my hands under his jacket, his shirt—my hands swim toward his skin. Then we hold each other, this man and I. We press our chests together and feel the identical thrum of our dark hearts.

Girlfriend on Mars

Amber Kivinen—drug dealer, lapsed Evangelical Christian, my girlfriend of twelve years—is going to Mars.

This is real. This is what I've been told.

Amber, three months ago: "Hey? Kev?" Sitting beside me on the Voyager, tucking a blond curl behind her ear. "You busy?"

Me, clearly not busy, wondering if I looked as stoned as I felt: "What's up?"

That curl bounced into her face again; she tucked it again. "I have to tell you something."

I expected the *something* to be that she wanted to adopt a cat, or that she wished I would find a real job, or that she had made out with a guitarist or a guy who writes graphic novels. I did not expect her to say that she would soon be on television in a *Survivor*–meets–*Star Trek* amalgam, where she would compete for one of two seats on the MarsNow™ mission. I did not expect her to say that within the year she would ("hopefully") strap herself into a rocket and blast into deep space, where she would float for nine months like a fetus in a womb before landing on the iron-rich red dirt of Mars. That she would then use the frozen water in the planet's crust to grow her own food and produce her own oxygen. And she would stay on Mars forever, because the technology to come home doesn't exist yet. And even if it did. Even if the technology existed, even if she wanted to come back, she couldn't—her muscle and bone density would have decreased so drastically that Earth's gravity would crush her to powder.

She confessed all this while sitting next to me on our green IKEA Beddinge couch, in our basement suite off Commercial Drive. She used the same voice as when she told me, last year, about hooking up with a guy we sometimes sell to, a computer programmer/skateboarder named Brayden. (She "accidentally" went down on him on that green couch, one of our first purchases together—the couch we named the Voyager, because we've taken our best trips on it.)

"So." She spoke quietly and looked at the constellation of confusion that was my face. "This is probably a bit weird for you."

I wondered if I was more stoned than I thought. I waited for her to laugh. But she hadn't been joking about Brayden, and she wasn't joking about this.

"I mean," she chattered, "it's not dangerous or anything. Mostly the ship will be remote-controlled by people in Houston. It's sort of like a drone."

"Aren't drones notoriously inaccurate?" I said. "And what about aerobraking? What about solar radiation?"

How did I even know those words? From hours of sitting on this very couch, watching *Star Trek: The Next Generation*.

"Will you do something for me?" Amber took my head in her hands. "Will you be a little bit happy for me? For, like, one second? 'Cause I made it to the third round and that's kind of a big deal."

"Since when were you in the first round?" I said. "Do they know you're a drug dealer?"

"We're not *drug dealers*. We specialize in hydroponics. Which, by the way, will be the technology used to grow food on Mars."

"*By the way*," I said, "we sell drugs."

"To family and friends."

I thought of when we were kids and she went away to summer camp, then mailed me letters addressed to:

> *Kevin Watkins*
> *105 Boulevard Lake Road*
> *Thunder Bay*
> *Ontario*
> *Canada*
> *The Earth*
> *The Milky Way*
> *The Universe*

"Remember when your parents sent you to that weird Bible camp?" I said.

"Kevin." She shut her eyes, then opened them. "Are you even listening?"

"Is this like that time you made out with Marcus?" I said. "Just to see what I'd do?"

When she shook her head, her hair bounced like it was already on Mars, like her hair already existed in low gravity. "No," she said. "This is real."

Amber applied to go to Mars, without telling me, one year and three months ago. She read about the competition online, then sent in a résumé and a two-minute video of herself. The video was filmed in our kitchen—I must have been out buying groceries or picking up chai lattes from Waves or hanging out with Marcus, and it must have been summer because her hair in the video catches the sunlight and haloes around her face.

I've now watched the video over and over, in the obsessive way a man might watch pornography that he happens to find on the Internet and that also happens to star his wife. Our laptop is ancient so the video is grainy and slightly distorted—Amber appears as though she's looking out through the curved glass of a space helmet. You can see a hint of the sequoia-tree tattoo that wraps itself around her bicep, and there's chipped green polish on her thumb. Her lip ring glints in the light, and calls even more attention to her shimmery mouth.

"I believe that discovery is a universal human drive." She leans forward, showing just enough cleavage. "And I am sure that my athleticism, expertise in the field of hydroponics, and thirst for spiritual meaning will serve me well on the first manned mission to Mars!"

The panel of MarsNow™ shareholders and venture capitalists and scientists must have liked what they saw, because Amber beat out over 150,000 other candidates such as Laurie Kalyniuk, housewife in Iowa, and Dr. Christopher Gelt, Germanic literature professor living in Guatemala City.

Round two involved writing a placement exam that tested your basic math skills, and a thousand-word essay about your motivations/ambitions. Amber must have composed the essay when I was having naps or showers or something, because if I'd seen her writing anything, I would have worried. When Amber writes—always in one of those overpriced Moleskine notebooks—it usually means that she has a secret she can barely keep. Like that she bought a single flight to Chile using our joint airline points, or applied to work in a fire tower, or ate pulled-pork poutine every day on her lunch break even though we were vegans at the time and I was subsisting on peanut butter and rice cakes. Writing is often followed by surreptitious texting, generalized anxiety, and finally by the relief—for both of us—of confession or discovery.

But this time she didn't want to get caught. This time she quietly composed her essay and submitted it. This time she told me she was going to meet friends for coffee, when in fact she was being checked by a MarsNow™-hired team of medical specialists: cardiac, psychology, osteopathy, and kinesiology.

Of course, I noticed that she'd joined a gym and lifted weights, enrolled in spin and boot-camp classes, hiked the Grouse Grind every Wednesday with her "Active and Out There!" Meet-Up Group, practiced yoga and meditation for mental/psychological well-being, and talked a lot about *maintaining muscle mass*. I also noticed that she started taking a cocktail of supplements—vitamin D, curcumin for inflammation, CoQ10, and cal-mag (same stuff we fed the plants). I noticed that she lost weight and became ropy with muscle. I noticed that she stopped getting her period and her boxes of different-absorbency-level tampons sat unopened in the cupboard under the bathroom sink.

I noticed, but didn't notice. I lived in my own world, existing mostly in a limited, indoor orbit. (This metaphor only works if you think of me as a small and insignificant planet and our pot plants—glowing under nine thousand lumens of LEDs—as the sun.) And even when she told me—the day before the MarsNow™ team was set to send out a press release—that she was one of 143 MarsNow™ applicants worldwide who'd moved on to round three, I didn't believe it. Mars just didn't seem real.

Here's what's real: Amber and I are twenty-eight years old, born one month apart in Thunder Bay, Ontario, but currently living in Vancouver, BC. She works part-time as a receptionist at the conference center downtown and I work as an extra on film sets (I once met Jennifer Love Hewitt) but we generate most of our income from selling the high-THC-content weed we grow in our bedroom.

Here's what else is real: we've known each other since grade three. At first, I thought nothing of her—she was just the tall girl who stood at the back in class photos. Then we were briefly friends, paired up as pen pals in grade five. We had to write each other weekly letters and she sealed her envelopes with stickers of cats wearing mittens. Then I got shy around girls for a few years and didn't talk to her, barely knew her—she was just one of the Christian kids who had to leave the room during sex-ed classes. Then she was the girl known for being the gymnastics champ of eastern Canada, particularly impressive in the vault event. The local paper had pictures of Amber shooting off the springboard like a rocket, pirouetting through the air. Then she was the girl whose Olympic ambitions were dashed when she injured her shoulder. The girl who started drinking too much and hanging out at parties with guys like me and Marcus. The girl who stood with me outside in perfect silence, in -42°, when we were in grade eleven.

We lost our virginity to each other two months after that, on her single bed, under a canopy of glow-in-the-dark stars she'd stuck to the ceiling. Afterward she pressed her body against mine and said she hadn't been able to breathe properly since losing her chance at the Olympics, said she felt nauseated all the time because now she didn't know what to do with her life—she was only seventeen but already fully heartbroken. She said she liked me because I calmed her down, because I didn't seem to have expectations of her. I said that was true: I loved her for no reason at all. (It came out sounding dumb, but I meant it in a good way.)

We are officially the only people we have slept with. Unofficially, during the 2.5 weeks we broke up in 2004, Amber had sex with a video-store clerk and I technically had sex (for about two seconds, in and out) with Tanya Vargas at a bonfire. But other than those 2.5 weeks, we have been together every day for the past nine years. We live in a suite as hot as a sauna, are vegetarians, and like to cuddle on the couch and look at LOLcats. I call her Slammer (she once spent a night in jail) and she calls me Tater-Toter (don't want to talk about it) and we have a life together. We own one of those $300 blenders that can probably pulverize your skull, and the entire six seasons of *The Sopranos*. And we have our plants.

We started with a few seeds that we sprouted between wet sheets of paper towel, then planted like an herb garden on our windowsill. We transplanted those into bigger pots that we kept beside our bed like babies in basinets. We fed them molasses and they grew past our knees, and that's when we started selling. Just to Marcus and Amber's sister and our former friend Brayden and some people I worked with on-set.

It was Amber's idea to go hydro. She had a master's in environmental sciences (thesis: "Pacific Northwest Ferns and the Traditional Food Technologies of the Coast Salish People") but couldn't find work doing anything but waitressing or answering phones. We could have moved to Alberta where Amber would write dodgy environmental reports for oil companies. Or we could have moved to Chilliwack or Prince George, where minimum wages would stretch further. These were our options, and two years ago we sat on the couch and considered them.

Amber packed the small pipe I'd bought for her birthday. The glass used to be pale orange with swirls of gold, the same color as her hair, but years of smoke passing through had darkened it to a burnished red. We passed it back and forth, and that's when Amber said, "Or we could stay here and do this."

She said we'd probably produce more marijuana, using less space, if we grew hydroponically.

"Dealing drugs," she said, leaning against my chest, her eyes half closed. "It's the best idea so far, right?"

First we cleared it with our upstairs neighbor, Norm, who works nights stocking medical supplies at the hospital. He said our secret was safe with him so long as he got to partake in the product—marijuana helps him sleep when he gets home from work in the mornings. So we bought a pH and PPM meter. We bought a water pump, lights, nutrients. We went to a pet store and bought six kitty-litter boxes to use as reservoirs. We set up in the bathroom because it has good ventilation, but opening and closing the door and using the shower kept messing with the ambient temperature. We moved our operation into the bedroom.

It's not ideal to live where you grow. We keep the heat at twenty-eight degrees Celsius, and when the plants are in a vegetative state, we have to leave the lights on for eighteen hours a day. And there's that skunky, sticky smell that coats your skin, your throat. But this has become my habitat. I'm used to the heat, the humidity, the stillness, the silence. It's like the garden of Eden, except better than the original. Every plant here is the Tree of Knowledge, and you can eat from it whenever you want.

So I don't get why Amber would want to go anywhere else, especially to a red, dead rock. I thought we had an understanding. We're not married; we don't have kids; we don't have pets. But we have our plants and we have each other. And we're committed to this kind of noncommitment: growing weed in our bedroom, ordering pizza from the gluten-free place up the street, watching whole seasons of *Arrested Development* all at

once. We sat on this couch and made a decision. We were—
I believed—committed to going nowhere. Going nowhere
together.

Why? I asked. Why Mars? Why now?

Because I want to see the Earth from above!

Because it's an amazing opportunity!

Because it's the first mission of its kind!

Amber sounded like a convert to a new religion. Still, I wasn't
super worried because I knew this: her parents were coming to
visit the following week, and her father—this freaky, alcoholic
Finn—would never allow his daughter to go to Mars.

When we were growing up, her dad coached peewee hockey
and would put me in goal without a helmet, which was supposed
to teach me to be less afraid of the puck. He still addresses me
by my last name, Watkins, and it still scares me. My fear is made
worse by the fact that I'm in love with his daughter and have a
crush on his wife. (This might be the only secret I've kept from
Amber, the fact that when her blond, big-boned mom sat in the
bleachers, it made me play harder, skate faster, flinch less when
the puck flew at my teeth.) What you need to know about Amber's
father is that he hates our cannabis business and blames me for
his daughter's life going nowhere. But now he was my savior. He
would come to town, and he would bring his vodka and his disap-
proval.

And then here they were, in Vancouver, after driving for a
week straight from Thunder Bay because Amber's mother has a
fear of heights. (She is unlike her daughter in this regard—in fact,
everything in Amber's life, from gymnastics to weed to Mars, can
be read as one long attempt to be nothing like her sweet mother.)

We all went to a pub that served burgers and craft beer, and Amber told her parents about her plans to move to Mars.

"Mars," said her father. "You mean the planet."

"The planet." Amber shifted in her chair. "Fourth from the sun."

"The planet." His accent sounded dangerous. He crossed his arms, leaned back, and I had never loved him until that moment. "Mars."

But then he raised his glass. He was the kind of man who gave speeches when he drank, and he gave one then. He talked about moving from Finland to Canada, knowing that he may never see his homeland again. He compared the winter in Thunder Bay to the inhospitable atmosphere of Mars. He mentioned the Shackleton expedition but didn't seem aware of how it had turned out. He said he was proud that his daughter was an adventurer and that she came from a long line of explorers.

"We are Vikings." He drank, then slammed his pint glass on the table. "And we will die as Vikings."

Then he looked over at me and asked if I was still standing around in the background of movies he'd never seen.

"No," I said. "I mean, yes."

I wasn't hungry; I didn't finish my chickpea burger. And when we got home and her parents went to the hotel they'd booked— they couldn't stand the heat in our place—I rolled a joint as thick as my finger. I wanted to be brain-dead, body-stoned, obliterated. I wanted the kind of high that tears you right out of your skin.

I lit the joint, listened to the paper crackle, inhaled. Amber didn't join me. She did crunches and push-ups and I watched as beads of sweat rose on her freckled skin like blisters.

"Can I come?" I said, holding the smoke in my lungs.

"Where?" She wasn't even breathing hard.

"Mars." I exhaled, toked again. "Fourth from the sun."

"You missed the deadline." Her body moved up and down, up and down. "You didn't apply in time."

"We could have applied together. They probably want couples."

"I didn't think you'd be into it."

"They probably want people to, you know. Propagate." I giggled. "Name the animals, that sort of thing."

Amber finished her push-ups, sat back on her heels, looked at me. I didn't like that. I didn't want to see her seeing me. I closed my eyes.

"It's really competitive." She stood and walked past me to the bedroom, her stride cutting the humid air. "So, yeah."

The earliest memory I have of Amber is from grade three. Our class was sitting on the carpet in a semicircle, listening to Madame Potvin read us a story about a frog. My best friend Marcus was beside me, tearing his shoelaces into small, stiff-with-mud pieces. Amber sat cross-legged on my other side. And as Madame Potvin turned a page of the book, the power went out. The fluorescent tubes above us flickered, then the classroom went black. Kids screamed in exaggerated fear of the dark or made spooky, ghostlike sounds. But not me, and not Amber. We sat very quietly, side by side. Madame Potvin raised her voice to tell the rest of the class to stay seated and calm, and Marcus threw his bits of shoelaces at my face because he knew he wouldn't get caught, and a couple of kids started to cry.

Amber and I were a still-point, a star at the center of a galaxy. She turned toward me and smiled. And that smile literally lit the room: the lights buzzed back on.

After her parents' visit, Amber set up a Facebook page ("Send Amber to Mars!") and a Twitter account (@AmbersQuest) and kept a blog where she posted about her training. And she rarely slept at the same time as me—normally we went to sleep when we put the plants to bed, turning off those LEDs, curling up together and drifting off in the pitch-dark of our bedroom, where the windows are blacked out.

But she started staying up at the kitchen table, the laptop open and shining its pale, alien light over her skin. She was chatting with other applicants on the MarsNow™ forum. I know this because I looked at her browser history, clicked through a few pages of her conversations.

> **AmbersQuest:** Anyone out there? Can't stop thinking about life on Mars tonight.
>
> **FirstMan34:** Living on Mars = unimaginable. I think what appeals is that the simplest things will be extraordinary, u know?
>
> **AmbersQuest:** For sure. Eating a meal. Taking a shower!
>
> **FirstMan34:** Going for a walk. Watching the sun set.

I wanted to punch that FirstMan34 guy. But I didn't say anything because I was trying to appreciate having Amber around, even if she was always in another room. Soon I didn't even have that meager comfort. Soon she went off for two months of training at the Los Alamos National Laboratory in New Mexico, best known as the location where the first atomic bomb was created.

There she took workshops in risk-taking, team awareness, nonviolent communication, conflict resolution, and "applied human relationships," i.e.: kindness and love. (The MarsNow™ people are investing eight billion dollars into this project—most raised from donors, broadcasting rights, and advertising—so they would prefer that their two astronauts don't murder each other.) She also took classes in basic medicine: how to reset a broken bone, how to clean a wound, how to suck alien venom out of your own skin using your mouth.

Now she's on TV. Every Thursday at seven p.m. (Pacific Standard). She was one of twenty-four final competitors, two of whom are eliminated every week. The show is filmed in stunning locations around the world, the idea being that the competitors will see the breadth of what Earth has to offer before two of them are chosen to abandon this planet forever. I've watched Amber on live-stream as she drank protein shakes in Latvia, and "shared" during "group" with her fellow companions/competitors in Kenya, and floated in the zero-gravity MarsNow™ training capsule in New Mexico.

She has not been eliminated. Farzad from Iran was eliminated. Talia from New York was eliminated. Fernando from Argentina was eliminated. Even audience-favorite Cawaale Abaaskul from Somalia was eliminated. Engineers and pilates instructors and physiotherapists were eliminated. But Amber Kivinen—drug dealer, former vault champ, onetime president of the Thunder Bay *Calvin and Hobbes* Fan Club—remained. Why? Because she had a story.

Hers is a conversion narrative: she was once just a failed gymnast, an underemployed twenty-something edging into her unmarried thirties, a woman who had been arrested for marijuana possession. And now she's on television; now *People* magazine has published a fluff piece about her diet regimen: *The meal plan that will take Amber into space!* (You guessed it: egg whites, Greek yogurt, oatmeal with hemp hearts, kale smoothies, chicken breasts, and the occasional indulgence—a square or two of dark chocolate.) According to her one-on-one with Ryan Seacrest, before MarsNow™ she was depressed and "going nowhere." Yes, she had a loving family and a boyfriend (that's me), but "something was missing."

Her story might not be any better than yours or mine, but having been raised in her father's church, she knows how to sell it. *I was lost but now am found.*

"This is what I'm meant to do with my life." She speaks breathlessly, in fast-cut TV segments. "This is real. I can feel it."

Never mind that the grow-op was her idea. And never mind that even though she's publicly sworn to focus, to cut all liabilities from her life, she still calls me. Yes, she still calls me. Last night, she phoned from the set because she needed me to look in the medicine cabinet to remind her of what brand of acid inhibitors she uses.

"Won't they have state-of-the-art Tums on Mars?" I said.

"Fuck off, Kev, please. I'm serious."

"You just got the no-name kind from Shoppers," I said. "Extra-strength."

"I can feel my stomach acid all the way up in my throat," she said. "I can feel it in my head. It's burning my eyes."

"Is that even possible?"

"Is it? Do you think it can get into my brain?"

"Slammer, your stomach acid can't reach your brain." I was sitting in the bathtub, which is the place Amber and I go to cool off. The ceramic was cold against my back. "And anyway, you're going to Mars. The landing will kill you first."

She couldn't help but laugh. Just like she couldn't help but call me. She now calls me in the same manner she used to call those other guys, the skateboarder or the video-store clerk—because she can't stop herself. Because I'm the secret she's keeping from everyone on this planet.

"You're fine," I said. "Take a breath, okay?"

"Okay. I'm doing it." She inhaled, exhaled. "I'm breathing."

"And you look hot," I said. "In that little uniform they make you wear."

"Oh, god." She laughed. "Thanks. Thank you."

And it occurred to me that when Amber is on Mars, when we are light-years apart, we'll still watch the same sun set.

During her weeks of competing, I kept the op running. Kept the lights the correct distance from the roots, maintained the water's pH at 5.8, fed the plants with a homemade cocktail of nitrogen, phosphorus, potassium, and magnesium in the form of Epsom salts, along with a teaspoon of a micro-nutrient mix that contained copper, zinc, iron, molybdenum, chloride, and manganese.

I didn't leave the house except to buy groceries and lottery tickets. I kept track of the days only so I'd know how long Amber was gone (five weeks) and how often to change the water (every 1.5 weeks). Four times I switched out the water solution, using tap water that had been aged for three days.

Patience is the key to a successful grow-op. It's tempting to over-fertilize to try to speed the growth process, and it's tempting to harvest early to get at the product faster. But harvesting too early will give a dark, depressing high. And too late will make you feel like you've been brained by an asteroid. I waited for that perfect time because I wanted a Goldilocks high—not too heavy, not too light.

I tapered the nutes, then fed the plants distilled water to get rid of any chemical aftertaste the plants might hang on to. Then I waited. I waited until some of the leaves had curled and fallen off the plant, scattering softly on the floor. I waited until the pistils turned a shade I can only describe as "amber."

A few clients came over to purchase. A girl named Bronwyn who brings me and Amber whatever raw-vegan desserts she's made recently—this time it was coconut-almond macaroons.

Brayden, that graphic designer/skateboarder who once had his cock in my girlfriend's mouth but thinks I don't know about that and who now gets charged triple. And Marcus, who also moved to Vancouver after graduating and who has suggested that I followed him out here. (Not true.) (I followed Amber.)

When I told Marcus that my girlfriend was in training to go to Mars, he said, "Shit, dude." He is exactly the same as he was in high school. The apelike arms, the studied nonchalance. "*Mars?*"

"The plan is to launch from Earth and then land on Olympus Mons." I have spent too much time on the Internet researching Mars, the way you might flip through guidebooks to plan your next vacation. "It has this huge, red impact crater. Twice the size of the Grand Canyon."

"Olympus Mons," said my oldest and stupidest friend. "Like the biggest, warmest vagina in the universe."

I understood, for a moment, why some people think getting stoned is boring.

Then Marcus said, "Why do you stay with her, man?"

There are formations on Mars that resemble volcanoes, valleys, deserts, and polar ice caps. I say "resemble" because the surface of Mars is geologically dead, no volcanic activity to recycle chemicals and minerals from the interior to the exterior. Dust storms cover the entire planet for a month at a time, and only 43 percent of the sunlight that reaches Earth gets to Mars.

If you were awake during a dark Mars night, you might look up and see two small moons. They are believed to be made of the primordial matter of the solar system, the stuff that existed before anything else: water, sticky tars and oils, amino acids. Their names—Phobos and Deimos—mean *fear* and *terror*.

In the thin atmosphere of Mars, hurricane-force winds would

feel like a gentle breeze. This weak atmosphere offers no protection from the sun's radiation, and there isn't enough pressure to keep water in a liquid form—it sublimates into a gaseous state and vanishes.

I fell in love with Amber in an atmosphere like this, during a Thunder Bay February. It was -42° with the windchill, and we were partying at Marcus's place. It was Amber's idea to try to vaporize water—she'd seen it on TV. "You just bring it to a boil," she said, "then toss it."

She put the pot of water on the stove until it boiled, then tried to rally us up off the couch. No one moved. Marcus was playing *Mario Kart*, and the rest of us were too drunk to care. No one wanted to put on boots, tuques, and coats. "Fuck off with your science shit," said Marcus, who was sort of her boyfriend at the time.

"Dickhead," said Amber. "I'll go myself, then."

But I followed her up the stairs. "So what's the deal?" I said. "The water will, like, disappear?"

"It vaporizes." She carried the heavy pot of water, which was still bubbling. "Instantly."

I loved her focus. The intensity on her face, the wrinkle between her eyes.

We didn't bother to put on coats or boots. We opened the door, stepped out onto the porch in our socks. The cold was so sharp in my lungs that I coughed.

"Okay," said Amber. "Three. Two. One!"

She dumped the boiling water from the pot. And instead of landing on our feet, it turned into steam. We said nothing, just stood together, and the water traveled upward like our breath.

Soon they were down to fourteen competitors, then twelve, ten, eight, six. There 's Amber, resident botanist and go-getter.

There's Tamiko Hoshino, thirty-two, from Japan: a medical doctor, yoga instructor, and Ph.D. in astronautical engineering. (She's also super hot, so there are a lot of shots of her doing sun salutations.)

There's Ramesh, twenty-six, from India. He has a good story too, which he illuminates on his website: "I am an IT graduate with experience handling critical computer applications. An orphan, working since age ten to fund my education, I am a mentaly [sic] agile day-dreamer and a scientist who loves finding answers. I can also do stand-up comedy acts."

There's Marion, forty-six, from France. A hairdresser who happens to have a photographic memory and is better than all of the other candidates at remembering flight procedure and physics. She applied for the MarsNow™ experience on a whim, and is always crying with happiness.

Sergey, fifty-one, is a chess champion from Ukraine and the least TV-appropriate of all the contestants—his gray hair sticks up and his accent is ridiculous and he tends to say things that don't quite fit into sound bites. "I would like, on Mars, to create a more logical society, free from judgment and hatred. This will be difficult. This will be the true challenge. Technology cannot help us solve this."

And then there's Adam, from Israel. In his own words: "I am, first and foremost, a medically trained doctor who is also educated in alternative therapies. I served in the Israeli Defence Forces, working with pilot/vehicle interfaces, and am familiar with most aspects of avionics. I believe in every human's right to sovereignty over their body and mind."

Adam, from Israel. Soulful brown eyes and smug cheekbones.

It's him. I know it's him: FirstMan34, from the chat forum. He's the one. I can feel it. The one Amber will be locked up with inside a space capsule for months. The one she'll fall in love with. The one who will fondle her pliant flesh in zero gravity. The one she'll get space-married to. The one who will father her Martian children.

And I'll be here, on a planet that has breathable air and koalas and ballpoint pens.

According to director of marketing and communications Johanna Flinkenflögel, I could make a donation to MarsNow™ via PayPal and receive a small replica of the Lockheed Martin MarsNow™ Lander to show off to my friends. Or I could have my name printed on one of the landing parachutes. Or perhaps I'd like to virtually travel alongside my girlfriend via my own Mars selfie?

No. No, thank you, Johanna Flinkenflögel. Because I know something you don't. I know that Amber will never sit still, never settle. Mars will seem great for a while, and so will FirstMan34. But eventually Mars will be as stifling as this basement suite, and FirstMan will be just like me, the guy who's always around.

And I'll be here, on a distant planet she distantly remembers. I'll be the one she wants. And she'll send me an email from her Settlement Structure. An email that will travel through the ether like smoke, from one satellite to the next. An email that will take between seven and twenty-two minutes to load on my screen. I know this. I can feel it. An email that says: *I miss you.*

Three weeks ago the MarsNow™ competitors were in Scotland and the "challenge" consisted of lifting an entire tree and tossing it through the air like in the Highland Games. Marion, the French hairdresser, couldn't even pick up the tree—sure grounds for elimination.

Amber strained, lifted the tree a few inches, then there was a terrible popping sound. Her right shoulder, the same injury that had cost her a gymnastics career. She dropped the tree and breathed in short gulps, but she didn't cry. I have never seen Amber cry.

I picked up my cell and called her immediately, even though I knew her phone would just ring uselessly in a trailer or a green room somewhere. As her voice mail came on (*You've reached Amber. I'm not living on Mars yet, so leave a message!*), I watched as FirstMan dropped his own tree—abandoning his chances at winning—and ran to help her. I watched as he used his medical training to force her shoulder back into its socket, which caused another horrible *pop*.

"Looks like an alliance has formed," said Bridget, the host of the show, a woman whose only qualifications seem to be breasts that defy gravity.

Then the camera was tight on Amber's face. "I'll never get there," she said. "I'll never get there now."

"Look at me, Amber." FirstMan took her head in his hands. "You're already there. It's not outside of us." He touched her chest, his hand over her beating heart. "Mars is in here."

I said nothing into the phone, letting her voicemail record my silence. Then I hung up.

Why? Why do I stay? Because I want to feel sorry for myself and get high? Because I'm afraid of being alone? And because I thought she would change.

Two days after the Scotland episode, Amber walked in the door of our suite. She'd been sent home to recover during the show's break, all of her travel and physio and massage bills covered.

I had just begun the harvest, and the suite was full of cut buds, which give off an odor that's wet and mulchy and alive. The smell reminds me of Amber's pubic hair, of opening her up and putting my tongue inside her.

"Gross." She dropped her red MarsNow™ duffel bag on the floor. "I forgot how this place gets."

For two days, we ignored each other. I said nothing about her moment with FirstMan and neither did she. Our place no longer felt like a garden—everything was too damp, too muggy. The quiet between us felt wet and heavy, a thing that could drown you.

Amber mostly stayed on the couch, icing her shoulder or sleeping or texting with FirstMan. I did what I would have done anyway: clipped the buds, then laid them out on newspaper to dry. And I was expanding the business, baking the leaves, then soaking them in Bacardi and honey.

She pointed to one of the bottles and said, "What's that?"

I told her my plan to produce a sweet, potent Green Dragon. My plan to sell it hipster-style, in growlers and Mason jars. My entrepreneurial spirit must have impressed her, because she went into the bedroom, rummaged in a drawer, and came back with that small glass pipe.

Then she sat beside me on the floor, filled the bowl with a few of the buds that were laid on the newspaper, lit up, inhaled. Her chest rose and fell; the smoke slid out of her mouth.

"Oh, my god," she said. "Those Mars guys would shit if they saw me right now."

I supposed she meant the producers and CEOs, the guys in suits. The ones who are raking in advertising dollars as our relationship implodes like a dying star. "Fuck them," I said, and Amber laughed in a throaty, raspy way.

She passed me the pipe. It was damp from her lips.

The weed was too wet and the smoke singed my throat, but still, it was good. In fact, it was perfect—not too heavy, not too light. We moved to the Voyager and our spines melted into its cushions.

"I overheard one of the engineers say he hoped we'd find precious metals on Mars," she said. "And carbon compounds. Stuff we can eventually ship back to Earth." Her laugh was cynical this time, the bitter disappointment of the true believer. "*The space economy.* That's what they called it. They want to turn Mars into a garbage dump, just like home."

"Someone always makes money," I said.

It surprised me that Amber, of all people, didn't know this. But she has always believed in absolutes. Right and wrong, good and evil, heaven and hell. She was never satisfied to just grow weed—she had to attend legalization rallies, had to post things on Facebook about the medical benefits of cannabis, had to try to convert the whole world.

"I guess I thought we were going for some grand reason," she said. "For the mystery of it."

The side of her body touched mine, flowing over my skin like honey. I passed her the peace pipe and she sucked smoke into her lungs.

Can you blame me for thinking this meant something? For thinking that since she was willing to get high—to risk that the next MarsNow™-administered drug test would show traces of illegal substances in her blood—it meant she was done with Mars? For thinking it meant she was home?

"There's a face on Mars," she said. "In the Cydonia region. A human face."

Her eyes were closed just like when her dad would say grace around the table when she was growing up.

"Why?" She turned to me. "Why a face? Is it just a random rock formation? Or is it a sign?" She touched my arm. "You know? Why is there something rather than nothing? Why are we here?" She laughed. "God, I sound like I'm stoned."

"That's 'cause you are."

I had my own questions, no less impossible to answer. Why do we love who we love? And why does love die?

Sitting beside her, my body felt light as air. "Maybe this is what it feels like," I said. "Zero gravity."

But Amber shook her head. "No." A smoke ring left her mouth and floated through the living room. It dissipated, disappeared. "Zero gravity is a trip," she said. "Way better than this."

Amber recovered. FirstMan did such a great job of setting her shoulder, and her muscles were firing so quickly, and her physiotherapist was a miracle worker—in two weeks, she was back on set. And now there she is, on TV, for the special two-hour finale. Part of it was shot in Dallol, Ethiopia, the hottest place on Earth. The sun scorches down from above and heat bubbles up from the ground through volcanic activity. The earth is covered in bright, swirling mineral deposits—it looks like a different planet than the one I know.

Amber looks different too. They've done something to her hair—it's straighter, shinier, tamer. And they've done something to her face to make it look less open, less natural. *Less*. She's wearing this tight unitard thing with the MarsNow™ logo over her heart. When she runs or jumps through the heat, the unitard thing shows off the slim, hard muscles of her arms and legs. I noticed when she was home that she now waxes those arms and legs, even though the hair that grew there was fine and soft.

There's a dark, raised mole on her left thigh—a perfect circle, a pristine planet in the galaxy of her long leg. I can't see it on TV, but know it's there.

Then the shot changes and we're in the L.A. studio. Marion and Sergey were eliminated last week and the four remaining competitors are onstage, wearing those unitards: Amber, First-Man, Tamiko, and Ramesh. One pair will be chosen to go to Mars. People in the studio audience cheer and hold signs: *Team Tamiko! Adam and Amber Forever!*

I could have been in the audience too. Isn't that what you offered, Johanna Flinkenflögel? I could sit front row, holding an *I [heart] Amber* sign. I could cry in a not-too-ugly way as MarsNow™ steals my girlfriend forever.

But I refused this once-in-a-lifetime opportunity. Amber said she wished I would "support" her.

"Does FirstMan34 support you?" I said.

"Wow," she said. "Have you been spying on my browser history? That's classy, Kev."

"You know what's classier?" I said. "Running away from your problems by moving to another fucking *planet*."

So now I'm here, on the couch where Amber and I used to watch *Guys and Dolls* and hold each other when Marlon Brando and Jean Simmons sang "I'll Know When My Love Comes Along."

"How do you all feel?" asks the host, Bridget. She can't move most of the muscles of her face, but she can widen her eyes in an imitation of human empathy. "Today two of you will be champions. And two of you will be eliminated."

There is ominous, pounding music. There's a montage of scenes from earlier in the season—lots of running and sweating and hugging and weeping.

Ramesh says, "I feel good. I feel ready."

Tamiko is doing some sort of yogic breathing.

Amber and FirstMan are holding hands.

I hit the mute button because I can't stand that music. Then I pick up my phone and dial the 1-900 number that keeps flashing along the bottom of the screen.

"Hello, and welcome to the MarsNow™ hotline," says an automated voice—the pleasant but mechanical voice of a woman. "Please listen carefully to the following options: if you want to purchase MarsNow™ products and memorabilia, please say, 'I want to make a purchase.' If you want to vote for one of our Mars-Now™ contestants, please say, 'I want to vote.'"

"I want to vote."

"Thank you." The voice has a slight accent, and I imagine it belongs to Johanna Flinkenflögel. "Please say the full name of the contestant you wish to vote for."

"Amber," I say. Then, more clearly: "Amber Kivinen."

"I have recorded your vote for: Amber Kivinen." The machine pronounces it *Am-bar Kiv-eye-nen*. "Thank you. And do not forget to visit our website at www.marsnowandforever.com."

"Okay," I say. " 'Bye."

But I stay on the line, and the voice starts up again: "Please listen to the following options." I listen to the following options, but they're the same choices that were available to me before.

"What I'm wondering about is *why*?" I say to Johanna. "Why are we here? Does anyone notice? Does anyone care?"

"I'm sorry," says my automated friend. "I cannot understand your request."

Then I realize this might not be Johanna after all. This might be the voice of God.

"If you would like to return to the main menu," says God, "please say, 'Main menu.'"

I hang up. I reach for that little glass pipe, the one that used to be the color of Amber's hair.

What most people don't understand is that pot isn't a plant or a drug or a habit. It's a location—a place to travel to. A place between waking and dreaming, between living and dying. I could spend the rest of my days there. And I will too, when

Amber goes to Mars. Because who will blame me? And who will stop me?

I pack the pipe, light it, breathe in like it contains the purest form of oxygen.

And on the muted screen, Amber and FirstMan are hugging, near-crying, holding each other—it appears that they've won. They're going to Mars.

I stay on the couch. For days or weeks or months—hard to say because time doesn't exist, not here in the garden. But I do watch. I watch the launch, when the rocket bursts from its chamber and Amber and FirstMan are mashed back into their seats. I watch as they glide through the atmosphere, jettisoning their fuel tank, which will be their final mark on this Earth—the tank falls to the Indian Ocean to rust down there like an old ship.

I watch as they hurtle through space, swimming like fish inside their shuttle. I watch as they eat freeze-dried asparagus and shower with wet wipes and pee in the HAB module's urine receptacle. They do exercises by strapping themselves to a treadmill. They meditate. They play Uno.

There are difficulties: one of the external fuel tanks dislodges, and the MarsNow™ people talk them through the emergency procedure. FirstMan has to do an EVA, as in extravehicular activity, as in space walk. He grips the sides of the module; he reattaches the fuel tank; he survives. Afterward, he and Amber say a prayer, thanking a god they are beginning to invent together.

During a solar storm, they take refuge in a smaller, sheltered area of the rocket, an aluminum tube that is technically called the HUB Tunnel but which they rename "the womb." They curl up together and float in the dark. This is where they share their first kiss.

I watch what Amber watches out the windows, and soon there's nothing she recognizes. No Earth, no moon. The sun is shown for what it is: a star like any other. Space is cold and lonely.

Ratings drop because nothing is happening. They float, and there seems to be no end to it. Space, space, and more space. Then, like a puppy come to greet them, that small moon, Deimos, runs by. And there it is: Mars.

First it is just a disk, then a sphere, then a craggy uneven rock that looks like a potato. They feel the heat of it: the delicate skin of their lips actually blisters.

They land at dusk, in a valley that runs along the equator, a valley that might once have been a lake. There are striated dunes and a giant, extinct volcano. Amber and FirstMan put on their MarsNow™ suits, check their oxygen levels. They hold hands, the way they did during that final episode. They step out onto dust as fine as oxygen. They look up, and so do we, the audience, over three billion of us tuning in to see the first humans to walk on Mars. They look up, and we all look up together. We see a purple sky.

That's when I get up, go to my window, look out at the Vancouver skyline. Amber and I watch the sunset together. And I'm so used to seeing through her eyes that I know she's touching the mystery—it will escape her soon, but she's touching it now.

"Amber?" says FirstMan, all business. "You okay? Your vitals have dropped."

"Hm?" she says. "Yeah. I'm good."

They climb to the top of one of the mesas, and decide to marry. Right then, right there. Because they know that to survive, they will have to be one flesh.

"I do," they say in unison.

Then they set about making this strange place home, or at least making it recognizable. They inflate their MarsNow™ Settlement Structure, which provides them with fifty square feet of private space and two hundred square feet of communal space. Amber begins to grow tomatoes in her hydroponic garden—the first seeds do nothing, but the second batch sprouts. FirstMan spends his days collecting samples, taking pictures, looking for alien life-forms.

Medical issues arise. FirstMan's teeth begin to rot and Amber lovingly pulls several of them out with a pair of pliers. And Amber becomes pregnant. She nearly carries the baby to term, but miscarries in her seventh month—bleeds onto the inflatable floor, whimpering, then gives birth to a stillborn boy who has the same cheekbones as his father and the same curls as his mother. They name him Aleph Innocence—for real—and bury him behind their Settlement Structure, in the place they call the garden even though it's just a barren patch of dirt.

Then Amber gets sick. At first, it's just a lack of energy, and FirstMan quizzes her, wondering if she's depressed. "No," she says. "I'm fine." But she grows thinner and thinner. FirstMan takes her pulse and temperature, takes blood samples, records everything. Then they see it. We all see it. A tumor that protrudes from her back. A tumor that looks like a human face.

FirstMan speaks to the camera. "Amber and I believe she may have contracted cancer from cosmic ray exposure," he says. "Further tests will be needed to confirm the diagnosis."

He wants to use the surgical equipment and anesthetic that the MarsNow™ people provided, but Amber is convinced that the face is a sign of something—a sign that they are not alone. She lets him perform reiki, but won't let him remove the tumor. Soon the cancer has moved through her like water through the veins of a leaf: to her lymph nodes, her blood, her bones.

She becomes smaller and her skin is gray—she looks alien against the bright, swirling mountains of Mars. Ratings have plummeted because there's nothing pretty or exotic about this reality show now, nothing but the kind of pain with which people on Earth are already too familiar. But I still watch. I watch as Amber Kivinen—former drug dealer, former vault champ, former player of strip-Scrabble—dies.

FirstMan and I cry together. We cry in an ugly way. I am on the couch, no longer young; I haven't left the basement in months or maybe years. And he has aged too quickly, his hair white like the Earth's distant moon. He doesn't address the camera; he says nothing. The thing he most feared has happened: he is alone. He has found no evidence of life on Mars, and he will die there with no one to bury him in that red dirt.

I open my eyes and Amber is beside me.

"Hey." She's wearing a MarsNow™ hoodie and leggings. "How long has it been since you took a shower?"

Amber is here, on the couch, intact. This is real.

"I thought you were dead," I say.

"You're stoned again." She closes her eyes. "You're always stoned again."

"Are you staying?" My mouth is dry and stale. "When did you get here?"

"It was rigged the whole time." She slouches into the couch cushions. Without the makeup, her face now looks terribly naked. "That's Adam's theory. The Japanese put in, like, two billion. So of course Tamiko gets to go."

"Tamiko's going to Mars?"

"Did you even watch the show?"

I still feel fuzzy. I can't remember how much I smoked last night, or the night before, and maybe there was a night before that too.

"I voted for you," I say.

"Thanks. I guess."

I want her gone again. I also want to touch her hair. "You're here."

"I'm here," she says, but I can see that she's lying. That she's doing that thing where you float outside yourself, looking down at your own life. My girlfriend is on Mars.

"I'm here," she says again. Then she cries—silently, quickly wiping her eyes with the back of her hand.

I put my arm around her and she's as familiar as always— more familiar, even, because I sort of understand her. The desire to escape, to see the Earth from above. To see what God sees.

But we're here, on this planet of breathable air and koalas and ballpoint pens. We're here in this room, on this couch. It's soft as mud and it roots us to the earth. We're in the garden, and gravity crushes us to powder.

The Passage Bird

When Shiri was growing up, her family lived so close to the airport that the bones of the house shivered when planes passed overhead. From her bedroom window, she saw the Fraser River; from the living room, the runways. She could tell time by rumbles in the walls.

The year was 1971, her father worked as an airline mechanic for Boeing, and they lived in one of the small, identical houses built for company employees. Two parents, two children: a family constructed to fit the house. Like every other dwelling on that block, it had three bedrooms, one bathroom, an unfinished basement, and a front yard with a young cedar tree. Her parents appreciated the uniformity of the street. It confirmed that Canada was a new, safe, clean continent.

As a child in Germany, her father had seen an Allied pilot drop from a burning plane, graceful as a diver until the parachute failed to open. Hirsch was six years old, the same age as Shiri now, and never forgot the sight of the pilot's body crumpled on the ground, both arms bent at unnatural angles. That's when

Hirsch decided that the world needed competent mechanics and engineers, men who could fix problems, save lives. Now he came home each evening smelling of exhaust, his hands smeared with grease that could never be scrubbed clean. When he picked Shiri up, she buried her face in his overalls and smelled the sour odor of fumes, of flight. She'd never been on a plane but when her father lifted her in his arms, she imagined taxiing down the runway and rising smoothly into the air.

"She's meant to fly," said the Hawk Man. "I can tell."

He too worked at the airport, flying his hawks and falcons on the runway to keep smaller birds away from the planes' engines and windows. And though her parents didn't observe Shabbat after moving to North America—they kept their heritage to themselves—the Hawk Man's Friday evening visits were a kind of ritual. His truck pulled up in front of the house, the engine cut out, and Shiri and her brother, Dann, ran to the window. *The Hawk Man! The Hawk Man!* they shouted as he strode, lean and confident, toward the house. He always had a bird with him, perched on his gloved hand. A leather hood covered its eyes.

"Good evening, Hirsch." The Hawk Man shook her father's hand. When sober, the two men were formal with each other. Standing on the porch, their differences were clear. Hirsch could block a doorway with his chest and there was a physicality to his commands. *Leave that alone*, he'd say, and snatch the comic book from Dann's hands. *Get down from there*, and he'd wrap one of his thick arms around Shiri's waist, pull her from the branches of a tree. The Hawk Man—much younger than Hirsch—looked like he never told anyone what to do, and probably no one ever bossed him either. He had an unkempt amber beard, suntanned skin, and two gold fillings, one in each eyetooth.

Unlikely friends, as Shiri's mother put it. Not that any of them, other than Dann, had many friends. They didn't fit in this town. Other families went to church, Shiri noticed; no one else's parents had accents; and other girls had straight hair that she envied, hair that hung prettily down their backs.

The two men spent Friday evenings on the porch, drinking the beer Shiri's father made in the basement and smoking cigarettes the Hawk Man rolled himself. Her father rested his hands on his hard stomach and the Hawk Man propped one long leg on the railing, leaned back in his chair, his bird's talons wrapped around his wrist.

Shiri's mother brought them cheese and crackers and a bowl of pickles—Ruth didn't bother to cook dinner because she wouldn't allow the bird in the house. Shiri and Dann hovered in the doorway, behind the screen, staring. Dann was two years older than her, and braver, so he would talk to the men. "Can I have some beer?" he'd ask, and sometimes Hirsch would let his son taste the bitter, golden liquid.

Shiri kept quiet and watched the bird shift its weight, or pick at the Hawk Man's sleeve, or nip the hair at his temple. Every once in a while, he gave a gentle tug on the bird's beak. "How are you, love?" he whispered. Or, "Ready to go, my dear?"

The Hawk Man spoke directly to Shiri only once, when her father went into the house to use the washroom and her brother was sent to the basement to bring up more beer.

"Come on out here." He nodded toward the bird, a small brown thing with a sharp and curving beak. "She won't bite."

Shiri wasn't sure if she was more afraid of the bird or of him. Her brother knew things she didn't and had told her stories. He said the Hawk Man always wore that glove because it had magic powers. What kind of powers? she wanted to know, and her brother said the Hawk Man could bring dead birds back to life, and that he could turn himself into a bird of prey—a hawk, of course, or a falcon or an eagle—that would swallow you whole. Can not, she said. Can too, he replied. "Sometimes people disappear," Dann told her, "and everyone knows it's 'cause they went to the Hawk Man's house."

"She's a sky hawk." The Hawk Man unsnapped the leather hood and peeled it off to reveal the bird's hard eyes. "Also known as a red-tailed hawk. But you can call her Rose."

Shiri thought of the gold chain her mother wore, with a delicate pendant in the shape of a rose—the only thing she'd managed to save from before the war. But there was nothing delicate about the hawk. Rose had a broad, cream-colored belly, yellow feet scaled like a snake, and a curved beak that ended in a knife's point.

"Don't be scared," said the Hawk Man.

Shiri stepped onto the porch but the hawk turned with such a fierce, jealous glare that she looked down at her socked feet. When Shiri glanced up, the bird stared past her. Cold, superior.

"Don't mind her," said the Hawk Man. "She doesn't mean it."

"Where did you get her?"

He took one of Shiri's hands and stretched out her arm like a wing. "I turn little girls like you into birds." He smiled and showed his gold teeth, two tiny suns in his mouth. "Would you like that? Would you like to fly?"

She was about to say *yes* when her father gripped her arm and tugged her away. "That's enough. Back inside." He didn't want his children near the birds, said they'd get their eyes plucked out.

"She's just making friends," said the Hawk Man. "They're both daughters of the air."

That's when he said Shiri was meant to fly.

But her father opened a fresh bottle of beer and said that no child of his would ever get on a plane; it was too dangerous. "Too much can go wrong." He took a swig. "And I should know."

"What could go wrong?" said the Hawk Man, giving Shiri a wink.

Her father shook his head. "Everything."

Everything did go wrong, though not in the ways her father predicted. Shiri and Dann didn't break bones or lose an eye or get kidnapped by strangers. They grew, their changing heights recorded on a corner of the living room wall, until Dann was so tall that their mother couldn't reach to make a pencil mark above his head. He could do fifty-six push-ups without stopping and was captain of the swim and debate teams. At school, when he bothered to talk to Shiri, he called her *Shitty*. But at home, he asked her to walk on his back to crack it, and he let her eat all the chocolate from the brick of Neapolitan ice cream. And even though they were too old for it, sometimes he helped her climb the tree in the front yard, gripping her hand so she could reach the tallest branch.

Up there, they talked. He still knew things she didn't: he taught her the cosine rule, told her which boys to stay away from, and explained matter-of-factly that their parents had probably never been in love.

"Maybe they were," she said. "But a long time ago."

"Yeah. And they're friends, at least." Dann picked up an insect from one of the tree's needles. "I'll pay you a dollar to eat this ladybug."

"No, thanks."

Then he swallowed it himself, just to watch her face. "There." He coughed. "Not bad."

He was like that sometimes, needing to prove something. Maybe that was why, on his sixteenth birthday, he got drunk and, on a dare, dove off the Moray Bridge. He fell into the Fraser and never came up.

Shiri was fourteen and hadn't been invited to join Dann and his friends, so she was asleep when it happened. But she could imagine the way he must have stood, brave and foolish in the cool air. She imagined that last breath he must have taken, filling his lungs. She imagined his friends cheering him on, whooping and laughing while they waited for him to surface. Then waiting longer, too long, their cheers dying out.

Then she decided to imagine that he hadn't drowned. She'd once seen a raven near the river, so she imagined that Dann turned himself into one as he fell. That he hadn't hit the water but had soared away from it, invisible, as black as the sky.

His body was found two days later, bloated with river water.

He was so transformed that the funeral required a closed casket. They didn't sit shiva—who would visit them, asked Shiri's mother, they had no family outside the thin walls of this house. But they did sit at the kitchen table, watching the Fraser flow past. The house was quiet without Dann to slam doors, to whistle while he made a mustard-and-chicken sandwich, to tell his little sister that she smelled like dirt. The only sound was the thunder of engines overhead. Shiri's mother stood and closed the curtains so they wouldn't see the water. Now only the runways were visible from the house—smooth, clean stretches of concrete.

"There," she said. "That's better."

Ruth was a *survivor*—that was the word Shiri learned in school for people who'd lived through the Holocaust camps—and she understood that what was important was to live, to get through. She did not dwell. Even in summer, she wore long sleeves to hide the numbers tattooed on her arm.

As a boy, Shiri's father had seen his parents carried off in a train to the camps while he hid in the neighbors' cellar. And when his son died, he did the same thing he'd done then: he went into hiding. He started sleeping in the basement, on the old, dusty couch with its protruding springs. Soon he refused to come up for meals, or to take a shower, or to go to work.

"Will he stay down there forever?" Shiri asked her mother.

"How can I know?" said Ruth, who seemed to have grown heavier overnight, her ankles thick with fluid and her skin sagging from the bones of her face.

Shiri watched the closed basement door. Her father was so quiet you'd never know he was down there.

At six years old, he'd spent weeks in the cramped earthen room under his neighbors' house, playing with a faded deck of cards and reading any books they could spare by the light of one small, smudged window. He heard life above him—footsteps, muted speech—but saw no one and ate only what the neighbors brought him. *They were so good to me*, was all he ever said of it.

Shiri knew almost nothing about this time in his life, except for the stories he told, stories he used to invent for his children before bed. About a boy who could turn himself into a mouse and burrow into the earth. The mouse dug deeper and deeper until he found an underground river.

"Like the Fraser?" Dann asked, and Shiri used to imagine underground log booms and hauls of yellow sulfur.

Like the Fraser, her father said with a nod. Except the water flows like tar, and the boats are steered by blind men, and the fish don't have eyes.

Because Hirsch no longer went to work, Shiri's mother got a job in a clothing store called Eve's Fashion Shop. It was in the Richmond Square Mall and catered to women who worked as secretaries and receptionists, women who needed suits and blouses and fake pearl earrings.

Her mother worked until the store closed, so it was Shiri's job to cook dinner and care for her father. She made tuna sandwiches, rice with stewed tomatoes and ground beef, or soup from a can that formed a gluey skin as it cooled in the pot. She left some on the stove for her mother, then made up a tray and carried it down to the basement.

Her father kept the room dark. Once, her mother had flicked on the light and Shiri saw him, vulnerable and startled, blink into the brightness. She preferred that their interactions remained blind, so stepped slowly down the dark stairs, the tray gripped tightly in her hands. The basement was cooler than the rest of the house and smelled of mildew and of her father's unclean body. She held her breath as she took one step, then another. She could see his outline on the couch. She breathed through her mouth. "Dinner's ready."

"Thank you, sweetheart." He sat up, heaving his own weight. "You're so good to me."

He liked when she sat beside him on the couch and told him what she'd learned in school. She had trouble remembering anything—each school hour felt slow and blurry—so she invented stories the way he had once done at bedtime. She mentioned books she hadn't actually read; projects she hadn't actually completed; tests she hadn't actually passed. She didn't mind telling lies, but hated that he believed them.

"That's wonderful." He patted her knee. "That's my girl."

Anything he left on the tray she carried up and ate herself. She was eating the rest of a cold grilled-cheese sandwich, dipping it in ketchup, when the Hawk Man showed up.

She hadn't seen him in years, not since she was a child—her father and the Hawk Man, she supposed, had simply drifted apart. But she recognized his truck when it pulled up in front of the house, then that lanky gait as he walked toward the door. His beard had thinned and darkened to a burnished gold. He didn't seem as tall as she remembered, but he still carried a bird on his arm.

"Shiri." He spoke to her through the screen door, as he'd always done. "Is Hirsch in?"

"He's downstairs." She stared at him. "He doesn't want to see anyone."

"I heard about your brother."

She pointed to the bird. "What's that?"

"You've already met." He looked down as though he'd only just noticed the hawk's presence. "This is Rose."

Even with the leather hood covering her eyes, the bird looked proud and stubborn.

"If you took off her blindfold," said Shiri, "would she kill us?"

"She wouldn't bother." He laughed. "She finds us absurd at best."

"What does she eat?"

"Insects. Rodents. Small birds. Tears the wings off those and tosses them on the ground." He winked at Shiri. "They eat the way we'd eat, if we were allowed."

She smiled at that.

"You should come by sometime," he said. "Meet the others. You'd like the owl. She looks like she's made of snow."

Shiri looked at his leather glove and remembered the stories Dann used to tell about the Hawk Man. "Maybe," she said.

He shrugged as if to say, *Do what you want,* and she liked that. Since her brother died, people watched her too closely. Teachers at school gave her concerned looks and other students stared like she was somehow changed. Even her best friend, Marla, acted shy around her.

"Give my best to your parents." He didn't pat her shoulder or try to tell her that time heals all or that Dann was in a better place now or that everything would be okay. He turned and strode back to his truck.

She next saw him when she sat on the curb outside Eve's Fashion Shop. She'd trailed around touching the clothes—slippery polyester, staticky acrylic—until her mother slapped her wrist and said, "Hands off."

"Can I have two bucks for a snack?" Shiri wanted to sit at one of the plastic tables in the Copper Grill and eat fries with gravy, looking at the tiles the way some people watch clouds.

"Do you think we're made of money?" Her mother whispered so customers wouldn't hear. "There's food in the fridge at home."

And now Shiri was on the sidewalk, staring at the pavement, nearly crying. She was bored and hungry and wished she had money to buy a hair dryer—she wanted soft, shaggy waves instead of the dark curls that frizzed around her face.

The Hawk Man pulled up and rolled down the window of his truck. He had a hawk perched on the back of the bench seat. "Hey, Shiri. You need a ride?"

She hated him for seeing her like this. "Why are you here?" She gestured to the mall, the parking lot. "I thought you liked nature."

He pointed to three women on their smoke break outside Fields Department Store. "You don't call this nature?"

The women looked at him like he was a predator, and at Shiri like she was something worse.

"Come on," he said. "I'll take you home."

She would have to sit right in front of the bird, its talons near her head. "Will that thing claw my eyes out?"

"You're just like your dad, you know? 'That thing' has a name."

"Rose," said Shiri. "I don't like her."

"I'm sure she can live with that."

Shiri lifted her bike into the bed of his truck, then climbed into the cab. The vinyl bench, warmed by the winter sun, felt soft and sticky and intimate under her thighs. It struck her that no one knew she'd gotten into this truck, that she could disappear.

"You said I'd like the owl," she said. "Maybe I want to see it."

"Maybe you do? Or you do?"

She turned to look at him, his sun-beaten face and the glint of gold in his mouth. He had mud splattered up the legs of his pants and there seemed to be dirt—later, she would learn it was blood—under his nails.

"Yes," she said. "I do."

He lived in a place he'd built himself, on a soggy property near a patch of trees. It was more cottage than house, with wood beams and a simple porch. That's where he left her, standing on the porch while he went inside to tidy up.

"It doesn't matter." She'd never made a man nervous before. "I don't care if it's not clean."

"You might care," he said, "if you saw the place."

He disappeared into the house and she could hear him walking on what must have been a wooden floor. She didn't feel like waiting.

"You're not as shy as you used to be," he said when she stepped inside.

The house was as dim as a basement, the walls and floor bare of paint or varnish. She was in the kitchen now and it had a table, two chairs, a stove, fridge, and an upright freezer. Rose-mary and mint were drying on the counter, laid out on sheets of newspaper.

Dead birds were mounted on every wall. Robins, starlings, falcons, and other kinds she didn't recognize. They stared, dead-eyed and caught, forever in mid-flight. And on the table there was a taxidermy-in-progress: the feathered skin of a headless bird, its flesh scooped out, wire jutting from its neck. Beside it were a knife, a needle and thread, cotton balls, antiseptic. A chipped jar full of glass eyes.

He followed her gaze. "A grouse. Found him on the road. If I'd known you were coming—" He pushed the knife and wire cutters to one side of the table.

So her brother had been right: the Hawk Man could bring dead birds back to life.

She crossed her arms and leaned against the doorjamb, tried to adopt the tough, indifferent stance she and Marla perfected in front of mirrors. "Where's the owl?"

"The birds are outside. Their quarters are much more comfortable than mine."

He brought her to the aviaries behind the house, large wire-mesh cages. Inside were branches for perches and plastic pans filled with water for baths. He first introduced her to the vultures, Hansel and Gretel. Hunched together on the same branch, they looked like old men in overcoats, but the Hawk Man said they were, in fact, both female. Their heads were covered in rough, red skin that looked like a bright scab.

"Wonderful creatures," he said. "I thought I'd become a better man if I owned vultures. Reminders of mortality and all that." He carried a shoulder bag full of raw meat and took a chunk out, opened the cage, and fed them from his gloved hand. "What's bad for us is manna for them. They can digest arsenic. It's almost enough to make you believe in God. Do you believe in God?"

"I don't know."

"Good answer. It's the only truthful one."

"Do you?"

"Almost." He squinted and leaned against the wire mesh of the cage. "I often wonder, a god in man's image? Why would God want to be like us when He could be a turkey vulture?"

"Are you kidding?"

"If you could soar through the air or crawl around like a grub in the dirt, which would you choose?"

"I guess—"

"Exactly. You would fly. Who wouldn't?"

Rose was in the next cage, on the ground in a patch of sun, her wings spread.

"She likes to suntan. Belongs in Malibu." He squatted down so he was eye-level with the hawk. "Isn't that right, love?"

She made a growling, coughing noise, rolled her eyes toward the back of her head, then regurgitated what looked like a large wet pebble.

"She has no manners," said the Hawk Man. Then he picked up the soft pellet and crushed it between his finger and thumb. Inside was part of a skeleton, a small backbone. "This used to be a bat," he said.

Next he showed Shiri the noisy dovecote, where he had five mourning doves. Last week there had been six, he said, but doves were less peaceable than their reputation suggested; yesterday he found Victoria pecked to death in a corner. The doves' coos sounded like laments, and a fine gray powder from their feathers silted the air.

Lastly, he showed her the owl, putting on his glove and opening the cage. "A barn owl. Or a heart owl, because of the shape of her face."

He held out his arm and the owl stepped onto his wrist. He

clipped leather straps—he called them jesses—onto her legs, then tied a thin leash to his glove's metal loop.

"This is Eugenie."

The owl turned her flat, open face toward Shiri.

"You can touch her if you want. Here——" He took her hand and placed it on the soft tips of the owl's feathers. Her wing felt like a fraying hem of silk.

"No oils on the feathers. Helps her fly more quietly." The Hawk Man untied the leash. "Listen."

Then the owl flew from his arm, edging into the stand of trees, and Shiri heard exactly nothing.

When he drove her home, he didn't bring any of the birds. They were alone in the truck and Shiri searched for something to say, more questions to ask. "Is Rose your favorite? It's like you're married or something."

"We've known each other the longest. We're used to each other." He was quiet for a moment, and Shiri listened to the rattle of the truck's engine. "I had a goshawk once," he said. "A passage bird. She was probably my favorite. She was terrifying."

"Passage?"

"From the wild. I was in love with her. Helen. I could admire her all day." He turned onto the Sea Island Bridge. "She had gold eyes. And she was totally indifferent to me. 'Musée des Beaux Arts.' The Auden poem—do you know it?"

Shiri shook her head.

"You'd like it. A boy falls out of the sky but no one pays attention. *The white legs disappearing into the green | Water.* We need that sort of reminder. Of how unimportant we are. Helen was my reminder."

"How did you get her?"

"Same way I met you. By chance. By luck."

"What happened to her?"

"You ask a lot of questions. Shows you're clever." He had one hand on the wheel, the other dangling out the window. "She might still be around somewhere. Every time I see a hawk overhead, I wonder if it's her."

"She escaped?" That pleased Shiri.

"I released her. Fed her and set her free."

They pulled up in front of Shiri's house, and she felt like she was in two places at once. She was here, in the truck, fourteen years old. And she was still six, inside the house with her brother, their hands pressed to the window. *The Hawk Man! The Hawk Man!*

She turned to face him. "You just let her go?"

"She was done with me, that's all."

"She didn't like you?"

"I'm not sure any of them like me. I'm not sure that's how their minds work. The best you can hope for is that they tolerate you and get used to you."

"They don't love you?"

"Love is something humans impose on them." He shrugged. "You never really own birds. Just get to be their companion for a while."

"That's dumb." Shiri crossed her arms. "I would have kept her."

He laughed, showing his gold teeth. "You're clever and you're honest," he said. "But who knows?" He reached past Shiri to open the passenger door, his arm brushing against hers. "Maybe she'll come back to me."

The next week, Shiri made pasta covered in a can of mushroom soup and egg-salad sandwiches. She fed her father, herself, and left the rest on the stove for when her mother got in. She couldn't focus on her schoolwork and didn't feel like going to Marla's. Everything they used to do—choreographing dances to David Cassidy or smoking filched cigarettes in the basement—seemed uninteresting. But she couldn't stay in this too-quiet house.

She thought of going to see her mother at the store, but knew she'd just be in the way. Eve's Fashion Shop was her mother's first job, unless you counted doing labor at Ravensbrück, and Ruth treated the work like it was her key to life. Maybe it was the racks of skirts and blouses, organized by color and size, or the mirrors wiped spotless—the clean predictability of retail. Ruth worked split shifts and overtime and never complained about being on her feet all day. Tough bones, a strong heart—those had helped her to survive before, and would get the family through now.

So Shiri rode her bike until it got dark, even in the rain. Raced as fast as she could, then raised her feet off the pedals and soared down hills, wind sweeping her hair from her face.

She ended up at the Hawk Man's house. It was dusk and she could tell he was home by the light through the window and smoke from the chimney—his rooms were heated by an old potbelly stove he'd found at an estate sale.

She rested her bike on the grass and heard the plaints of the doves, the owl's haunted and hollowed-out voice. She stepped onto the porch and the Hawk Man opened the door before she knocked. "Shiri. This is a surprise," he said, though he didn't seem surprised.

He wasn't wearing a shirt. His skin was tanned and hair grew over his chest and down his stomach, toward his belt.

"Are you hungry?" He gestured for her to come in. "I'm just about to eat."

There was a good smell coming from inside and she saw a pot

bubbling on his gas stove. Lentil soup. The Hawk Man, she learned over dinner, was a vegetarian. "Well," he corrected, "I only eat the meat my birds catch." He drank his soup from a metal cup. "So sometimes I literally eat crow."

She looked at him and blinked. "You're insane."

"You are not the first woman to point that out."

After dinner, he worked on the grouse. He told her that he'd used a knife to scrape the innards out, then sprinkled the skin with a mixture of borax and cornstarch to dry it. Now he wired the wings so they stayed open as if in flight.

"Made of the same stuff as human hair." He held one bent feather to show her. The grouse had probably run into a car's windshield, he said. Some of its feathers needed repair.

"Have you ever been on a plane?" Her mind was drifting. "I'd like to go somewhere. To Europe, maybe."

He seemed not to hear her—she would get used to the way his focus was always to the side of her, on the birds. One of his hand-rolled cigarettes dangled from his mouth and he explained that each feather locked into the next, each one was necessary. A perfect architecture of flight.

"It's enough to make you believe in God," he said.

"Almost," she corrected him.

She started spending every evening with the Hawk Man, riding to his place after she'd prepared a meal for her father. It didn't take long to get used to the wooden walls, the fridge full of exotic cheeses and leafy vegetables, and the stand-up freezer where he kept food for the birds. Raw turkey necks, frozen mice, bags of yellow chicks.

And she became familiar with his face. The scar along his jaw where his beard didn't grow, the cluster of wrinkles that spread like sun rays from his eyes, a jagged tear in his left earlobe. The scar and the torn earlobe were gifts from Rose, he said. "She likes to remind me of who's in charge."

Shiri wondered how old he was. Older than her brother, younger than her parents.

She went with him when he flew his birds, releasing them and luring them back with raw meat that he held in his glove. The birds got smaller and smaller in the sky, the chime of the bells on their legs fading. Sometimes they disappeared and she thought they were gone for good. Then, as if by magic, they swooped toward him and landed magnificently on his arm.

"Beautiful," he always said when they alighted, and she pretended he was talking about her. It was possible—he'd started talking to her in the same gentle voice he used to address the birds. And sometimes he let her wear his glove, so it was easy to imagine she'd slipped her hand into his.

He taught her to tie a falconer's knot: hitch the loop, under, over, through, and tight. She used her right hand to secure a leash to the glove, and soon the birds would perch on her wrist. The owl was lighter than seemed possible, a cloud of cotton. But Shiri spent the most time with Rose, the two of them sitting on the grass, the hawk spreading her wings to warm herself. Then she practiced flying the bird on a creance, whistling to call her from a close perch. Each time the bird landed on her glove—*twack*—Shiri rewarded Rose with food. Soon the hawk flew to her from twenty feet, then thirty, then fifty.

Soon, she stopped eating lunch with Marla, then stopped going to class altogether. She rode to the Hawk Man's place in the morning and stayed there all day, even when he worked at the airport. Then she went home to make dinner and returned as soon as she'd brought her father a tray of food.

She was browned from the spring sun and she wore a necklace the Hawk Man had made her out of wire and one of the hawk's tough feathers. Her sneakers were dirty; her clothes hardly got washed; the powder from the doves' feathers left a pearly film over her hair.

The Hawk Man seemed to enjoy her presence, but didn't seem to require it. In the evenings, he smoked and worked on his taxidermy projects, and she read his books. She liked Ovid's *Metamorphoses*, cheerful stories of girls avoiding grief or rape by turning themselves into cows or laurels or birds. She also flipped through his tattered copy of the *Whole Earth Catalog*, a book that had instructions on how to build a bomb, how to raise chickens, how to give cunnilingus. It seemed akin to a book of spells and she thought it must be illegal. "Where did you get this?" she whispered, but the Hawk Man only laughed at her.

He never touched her. He drove her home each evening, dropped her off, and never made plans for the following day. He seemed confident she'd return to him.

Her mother must have seen his truck idling outside the house, but she didn't mention it. She was exhausted after her shifts at the store and Shiri found her in front of the TV, her feet propped on the coffee table. She hardly seemed to be watching whatever show played in front of her, though she always turned up the volume when the weatherman came on. She stared at the map of Canada, the highs and lows marked over each province, and when she talked to Shiri, it was like from across time zones. "How was school today?" she asked, even though she must have been getting calls about Shiri's truancy.

"Fine." Shiri clenched her fists, dug her nails so deep that her palms almost bled. She wanted to scream, to fill this house with sound. To rage and lament like one of the doves. "I'm going upstairs," she said.

Then she lay on her bed and looked at the glittering stucco on the ceiling. Its gold flecks reminded her of the Hawk Man's teeth and she pressed her hand to her mouth, practicing. She wanted to be kissed so hard it left an imprint on her skin. She slipped her hand under her jeans, touched herself the way she'd learned to do from the *Whole Earth Catalog*, then fell asleep on top of the sheets.

Once she woke in the night and saw a bird's golden eyes—two small suns that burned in the dark. A goshawk. A passage bird.

"Dann?" she tried, but the hawk didn't answer to her brother's name. It perched on her belly, eyes fixed, crest gray like ash from the Hawk Man's cigarettes. Its talons dug into her skin, cramping, releasing.

In the morning it was gone. The only evidence was blood that ran down her leg and onto the sheet.

"We should go for a hunt," the Hawk Man said that evening. "You'll fly Rose this time."

"Me?"

He gave her a wink. "You."

It was nearly sunset when they reached a wide, empty field in Delta. The Hawk Man pulled off the road, cut the engine, and Shiri climbed down from the truck. She put on the glove and Rose stepped lightly onto her hand. Just as she'd been taught, Shiri tied the jesses to the glove's metal loop, then slipped the hood off the bird's eyes. "Hello, love," she said.

There had been rain earlier in the day, and as she followed the Hawk Man through the grass, her sneakers got soaked through. They stopped near a stand of fir and pine.

"You know what to do," said the Hawk Man. It was true. She'd watched him enough times that it felt easy to walk toward the trees, the bird on her arm—Shiri's muscles, like the bird's, were taut, her eyes hard and expectant. Then she heard something—a rustle, movement in the tall grass—and cast the bird off her arm. Rose flapped her wings, bells ringing sharply.

"There she goes," said the Hawk Man.

To be seen through his eyes—that's what Shiri wanted. But she was heavy and plain, feet on the ground.

Rose edged into the trees, and they ran to follow. They found her crouched in the grass, her feathers mantled over the kill.

"Do the trade," said the Hawk Man. "Like we practiced."

Shiri held out a piece of raw steak on the glove, whistled, and the hawk flew to her arm. There was no time to be squeamish— she crouched beside the kill, grabbed it before the hawk went back for it. A mouse. The bird's talons had punctured one of its eyes— blood poured from the socket—but it was still alive. Shiri felt the throb of its small heart. And she felt pride, adrenaline, ambition fulfilled. She wasn't sure if these were her feelings or those of the bird, transmuted to her through the glove.

Then the heartbeat stopped. The mouse lay dead in her hand.

She was supposed to tuck the kill into the Hawk Man's bag to be eaten later—that's how you taught a bird to be your hunting partner. But instead she offered it to the bird right then, still warm. She wanted it gone.

"You're spoiling her," said the Hawk Man.

And Shiri knew she should hood the bird now. But that would blind and subdue her, turn the hawk into a harmless and decorative thing. Instead, Shiri released the jesses and let the bird go. Watched her fly into the air, wings flaring.

"My god." The Hawk Man was already running. "Rose!"

The bird climbed higher, leveled and soared, circling the field. Shiri squinted into the sun.

"Call her back." The Hawk Man took a piece of meat from his bag, tore it open so it would shine with blood. "Hold this up so she can see."

But Shiri couldn't move, couldn't push air from her lungs to form the sweet, two-toned whistle he'd taught her. Because the bird was high now, too high, only a smudge against the blue sky. If she didn't come back, would the Hawk Man want Shiri instead?

"Shiri," said the Hawk Man. "Now."

She took a breath, whistled.

Nothing. The bird was gone. What had she done? Rose would die out here—bells and jesses weighing her down, tangling her feet. Shiri whistled again. Took a few steps, raised her arm. Closed her eyes to keep the tears back, whistled and whistled.

Then she heard metal bells—faint and tinny and far-off. The sound grew louder, brighter. Shiri kept her eyes shut until she heard the hiss of air through stiff feathers, a whistle that answered her own. The bird slammed into her arm.

"Beautiful!" The Hawk Man was laughing. "Amazing. But don't ever do that again."

Shiri laughed too, tears streaking her face, her legs weak. She sat in the wet grass and the bird perched on her arm, devouring the dead thing in her hand.

"Not quite as planned," the Hawk Man said when he drove her home. "But you'll be a falconer soon enough." He pulled up outside her house, reached across her, and opened the truck's door. Shiri didn't move.

"You should hurry," he said. "You're probably expected."

"I'm not going in there." She stared at her hands, at the blood that had dried under her nails. "I'm staying with you."

"Your parents wouldn't like that. It would break their hearts."

She almost laughed. "What do you care about their hearts?"

She wanted him to say it. To expose his hunger so she could

hate and pity and love him for it. She wanted him to grip her hand the way the hawk had.

"I'll live with you and Rose and Eugenie," she said. "Rose likes me now."

"You know that's not true. She doesn't like anyone."

"Almost," said Shiri. "She almost likes me."

"You have to understand something." He turned toward her so their knees almost touched. "I tend toward fanaticism, Shiri. That must be obvious by now."

"So?"

"So I'm your father's friend." He whispered now, as though Hirsch might hear them from the basement. "And you're fourteen years old."

"Fifteen. My birthday was two months ago but everyone forgot."

"Do you know I can remember a time before these houses existed? No sidewalks, no yards. Just open fields and forest." He pointed toward her house. "I trapped Helen here, my passage bird."

"What does it matter? Who cares how old you are?"

"You'd tire of us. Of me and Rose and the others."

"I even like the vultures. They make us better, don't they? They do."

"Shiri, listen to me. You'll finish school. You'll get a boyfriend. You have an entire life to live."

When she pictured the rest of her life, she always unintentionally imagined herself working at Eve's Fashion Shop. She was prone, that year, to confusing herself with her mother. Even her body looked more like Ruth's—it had gone from being slim like her brother's to being full and soft. She missed feeling light and nimble, climbing the cedar tree.

She looked him in the eye, kept her gaze steady as a hawk's. "I want to be with you."

She knew what that meant. She remembered the way he'd held out her arm when she was a child, stretching it like a wing. *I turn little girls like you into birds*, he'd said, and even then she knew he was telling the truth.

"Come on, Shiri. You're too smart for this."

"Or maybe I'm insane like you are."

She could still feel that mouse, its heart beating itself out in her hand. She never wanted to see the ground again.

"A raven," He touched her dark hair. "Something clever. Did you know ravens are also called 'ravishers'?"

She knew that ravens were birds of mountains and tall trees. She saw herself in high, silent places.

"I'm told that once you have one," he said, "all your other birds seem uninteresting."

She imagined herself soaring, catching a current of air. She saw herself hooded and leashed.

She slipped her hand into his.

He looked at her, pupils expanding to take her in. "You're sure?"

She thought of her mother in that store, on her feet all day, wearing orthopedic shoes. Her father underground: he hadn't seen the sky in months. She wouldn't be like them.

"You have to be sure," said the Hawk Man. "You have to say *yes*."

Her father, heaving himself up to sit beside her. *You're so good to me*. And her mother, trying to believe in a story, trying to survive. *How was school today?*

"Shiri?" said the Hawk Man. "Yes?" And air from his lungs swooped into hers.

She didn't go inside the house. She climbed the tree and sat on the highest branch she could reach. She wished her brother were with her—wished they could live here, between the basement and sky.

Maybe everything would happen the way the Hawk Man said it would. Maybe she would finish school and get a boyfriend. She wanted to go somewhere—fly to Europe, walk along the Danube all the way to the Black Sea. She'd read about it in one of his books. There were red-footed falcons there, and herons, even pelicans.

A bird's shadow passed over her. She looked up, hoping for a hawk or a falcon—she would have even accepted a vulture—with a message for her. There was nothing but the setting sun, and she watched it plunge into the water, bleed along the horizon. She would go inside when it got dark. But for now she perched in the branches, tying and untying a falconer's knot in her own hair.

Hard Currency

The last time Alexei paid for sex, he was eighteen years old. It had been his birthday, only weeks before he and his parents left for the United States. And now, twenty-eight years later, everything is different: the city is named Saint Petersburg and its crumbling facades are being rebuilt and repainted. But walking down the street at midnight, the northern sun turning the canals pink, it's as if Alexei is a teenager again, as if he never left. He's no longer in touch with the friends he grew up with, but it's as if they are beside him, drunk and singing as they lead Alexei down Leningrad's bright streets. On his birthday, they'd laughed, collapsing against each other, saying, "Good luck!" as they pushed him toward an apartment block. It overlooked the Neva, and though the apartments were communal, the building was grand. Alexei felt dizzy and warm as he rang the doorbell.

The woman who answered was older than him by at least twenty years and wore her graying hair tied back. This was not what he'd imagined. He figured it was a joke, and waited for his friends to reappear, doubled over and laughing. But they were gone, and he was left in front of this woman with broad hips and a tired face. She said her name was Oksana. "Please come in." Her voice was softer than expected.

When she led him to her room, he could hear voices belonging to the apartment's other tenants. The hallway was littered with boots and coats, and smelled like his own family's apartment: tea and dust and sweat. Alexei had to lean against the wall to keep steady as he followed her. He watched Oksana's back as she walked. Her black sweater was rough and pilled, and her skirt made a scratching sound against her legs. Had he been less drunk—or less timid—he would have left.

"Excuse me. I'm not sure—" Alexei didn't finish the sentence, and Oksana didn't acknowledge that he had spoken. She led him to her bedroom, and closed the door quietly behind them. There was a narrow cot against the wall, and a lamp beside it. She stood with her arms hanging at her sides, and seemed to see his disappointment. "Please." She pointed to the bed. "Be comfortable."

Then she took off her shoes. She unbuttoned the coarse sweater, then undid the zipper of her skirt and slid it off her hips. She folded both the skirt and the sweater, and placed them on a chair. She reached behind her to unclasp her bra, then slipped her tights and underwear down her thighs. He had seen his neighbor, Yadviga, coming out of the bathroom in only a towel. But he had never seen this: a woman entirely naked.

Oksana's body was more pleasing than he'd expected: full breasts, pale skin, a small round stomach. She appeared tough and capable, but not without vulnerability. Without clothing, she looked cold. She had goose bumps on her arms, and her nipples puckered.

She sat on the single bed and the springs made a sound that reminded him of loneliness. "Don't be shy," she said.

He got down on his knees in front of her, and put his mouth to one of her breasts.

Now it's his forty-sixth birthday and the street along the Fontanka, the one he stumbled down with his singing friends, is full of entrepreneurs advertising boat rides to tourists. His friends—those young men he studied with, who understood loyalty better than anyone he has met since—must still live in this city, but Alexei probably wouldn't recognize them if they passed on Nevsky.

And the prostitute he has hired is nothing like Oksana. She is young and thin and wears a purple dress made of thick, glistening material. The dress has thin straps and no back, leaving the bones of her spine exposed. She speaks proficient English and tells him that her name is Svetlana and she is from Novgorod.

"A nice city," he says. "Do you miss it?"

"No," she replies.

They are at a bar made to resemble a beach, in an empty courtyard where sand has been poured onto the pavement. They sit at a plastic table, under a wide umbrella, and drink glasses of bad wine. From this table, Alexei can see the bright domes of the Church of the Savior on Spilled Blood.

He is trying to get drunk as quickly as possible, so that he doesn't have to think about the fact that he has bought a woman. He never planned to do this, and if his friends or his ex-wife found out, they would be appalled. North Americans, especially the educated, liberal type he associates with, don't look kindly upon men who pay for sex. They are idealists. They don't seem to understand that nearly every touch that passes between a man and a woman is exchanged on the most costly and devastating black market.

Besides, Alexei has been in Russia for two weeks now, and the women of Saint Petersburg—those exquisite creatures in stiletto heels—have got to him. Their faces are as cold as this climate in winter, and their eyes the same blue-gray as the northern sky. They scare him even more than New York women do, and he knows that the only way to tame his fear is to buy one of them.

And there's also this: he is lonely. He'll admit it. It's his birthday, he is in a country that is no longer his, and he is alone.

"In Novgorod, we have a beautiful monastery where monks still live," says Svetlana. There is a false rhythm to her voice that reminds him of a tour guide. "I think you would like it."

"I've been there," he says in Russian. "It was years ago. The church was being used to store grain."

"You would prefer it now," she replies in English. "It is very beautiful. Just the way it was in the twelfth century."

An acquaintance of Alexei's, an elderly professor at the state university, arranged this meeting. He guaranteed that Svetlana was clean and high-class, that she was within Alexei's price range, and that she was beautiful. This last part is not exactly true. She has stunning cheekbones, but there is something strange about her face. Her eyes are too far apart, and her chin is too sharp. It's a face like those of the feral cats that roam the streets at night. Also Alexei is no longer used to women who wear this much makeup: her eyes are rimmed with black and her cheeks shimmer. Hers is an artificial beauty that reminds him of the city's impenetrable architecture, its false facades.

"How long have you lived in Petersburg?" he asks her.

"Three years. I came with my sister."

Alexei had been nervous and had arrived at the bar early to meet her. He'd heard the click of her shoes—purple heels that match her dress—when she came in. She walked purposefully, carrying a gold purse that seemed to have many superfluous buckles.

She recognized him right away. Though he spent nearly half

his life in this country, locals immediately pick him out as foreign. Maybe it's his clothing: he wears a linen shirt, pants that are wrinkled from being in a suitcase, and soft leather shoes. Svetlana walked to the table and held out an anemic hand for him to shake.

"You're Vladimir," she said, because he'd given a fake name over the phone. He'd bestowed Nabokov's moniker on himself and this seemed fitting, not extravagant at all. Many reviewers had already made the comparison.

She sat down across from him, lit a thin Vogue cigarette, and he bought them both a drink. Since then, she has seemed anxious to leave, to get her work over with, and twice she's checked her phone for messages. It's obvious that she doesn't like him, and he isn't sure why he insists on conversation.

He swallows the last of his wine. "I suppose we should go."

"Of course." She smiles in a deliberate, disdainful way, stretching her perfectly painted lips.

Alexei would have hated that smile if it weren't for her crowded, cigarette-stained teeth. Most of the young American women he meets would have them straightened and bleached. Alexei hasn't seen such lovely imperfection in a long time.

Since he arrived, nothing has gone as planned. For one thing, he'd hoped to stay in the Astoria. This would have been a triumphant gesture—to return to this country and be treated like a success in the place that makes him most crave recognition. But money is tight right now. His investments aren't healthy, books don't sell the way they used to, and divorce is more expensive than he'd predicted.

So Alexei rented an apartment from a woman named Galina. He'd been impressed with the ad she'd placed on the Internet:

she lived near the Fontanka, in a stately building where Tolstoy once resided. But Galina lived at the back of the apartment block, past a courtyard so narrow and dark that to walk through it was like wading through a well. A pack of half-starved cats crowded around the door, and inside, the stairway was something out of Dostoyevsky—dank stone steps, mosquitoes, peeling paint.

Inside, there was a mattress on the floor, covered in flowery sheets. Thick, dusty curtains hung over the windows. The shower ran only cold, and the tiles smelled as though something was rotting behind them. Worst of all, Galina had not tidied any of her possessions before she let her apartment. Her clothing filled the closet. The fridge was full of her food: yogurt, cottage cheese, and Diet Koka. In the bathroom, her makeup was strewn across the counter and a box of tampons sat on the back of the toilet. This was why he would never live with a woman again. They invaded and spoiled domestic space, the way beer and souvenir kiosks ruined the view of the Kazan Cathedral.

He dropped his suitcase on the bed and looked around the apartment. He had left Manhattan and traveled for twenty hours to arrive here. At home, he owned a small but stunning loft. At home, he was important—one of the best writers alive today, according to the *New York Times*. His modern, spotless apartment constantly acknowledged that fact, reminded him of it, stroked his ego in the way of an attractive, devoted lover.

Looking around Galina's apartment, this haven for cockroaches, he could have wept. Instead, he unbuttoned and removed his shirt, folded it, and placed it on the bed. He wondered briefly about the cleanliness of the sheets, then decided it was best not to consider such things. He went into the bathroom, which had a door that hung off only one hinge. He turned on the tap, leaned down, and put his head under the cool stream of water. Only a few weeks ago in New York, his hairstylist, Sylvia, had washed his hair. She had leaned over him and he had seen down her artfully ripped T-shirt. She talked—probably about a club or a restaurant or her backpacking trip to Thailand—but he didn't listen. With the water running, her words sounded muted and foreign. He'd closed his eyes and let them wash over him.

Here, he felt cold water hit his head, nothing like the comfort of Sylvia's hands. This was how his grandmother had washed his hair when he was a boy. She did this before bed. His shirt off, he would lean over the kitchen sink—a sink that always had a leak, a soft drip that punctuated every day and night he spent at his grandmother's house. The water from the tap was so cold that it made his head hurt and his ears sting, but still, he loved this weekly ritual. She scrubbed his scalp with soap that smelled of wood chips, and he was able to forget the ordeals of his childhood: his loud neighbors, his drunk father, his careworn and silent mother.

And now here he was, years after he had last seen his grandmother, years after his father had received a letter stating that she'd died at age fifty-five. Here he was, with his head under water, waiting for that familiar, comforting ache. And yes, there, he felt it—that pain behind the eyes. Welcome to Russia, he said to himself. Welcome home.

This is not the first time he has returned to this country. He's been back on three previous occasions, and has written six novels set here. These novels have earned him prizes, and have been called *deft*, *profound*, and *full of insight*.

But he has turned his hand now to nonfiction. He took this journey to research his latest book, a biography of his grandmother. She was born in Leningrad in 1929, and lived through the war and Stalin. She organized and paid for his family's exit visa from the USSR, while she stayed behind and died before Alexei had a chance to visit her. She lived through it all, marrying at fifteen, and giving birth to Alexei's father at sixteen. "Everything happens quickly for me," she liked to say, and this turned out to be true of her death. One minute she was boiling potatoes, the next she was dead of a heart attack on her kitchen floor.

When Alexei heard this from his father, he didn't believe it. It was impossible that his grandmother was dead. She had always survived. She'd lived through the blockade by making soup from cattle-horn buttons and the leather of her small shoes. The winter of 1941 gave her such severe frostbite that she lost two fingers on her right hand, but still, she set up traps and caught stray cats to feed herself and her sisters. Once, she'd pulled out her dead grandmother's gold teeth and exchanged them for food.

This is his material: the personal and costly reckoning of history. The quick passing of years. Time itself. He has written nearly the entire manuscript except for the epilogue, wherein he, the author, returns to his childhood home. Not to the communal apartment where he grew up with his parents—that was torn down years ago and replaced with a Pizza Hut. No, to his true home, outside the city center, where his grandmother lived.

He has already imagined it: the older man, the writer, will return to Moskovskaya after a twenty-eight-year absence. The current occupants will embody today's Russia perfectly: they will be young engineers or computer programmers, perhaps newly married. They will be kind and listen to the reason for his visit. Perhaps they will recognize his name, and they will surely recognize his desire. They will understand the simultaneous pull and fear of the past.

They will allow him to walk through the apartment again. He will see the kitchen where he ate blini with his grandmother, and the closet-sized room where she slept. He will smell the same dusty smell that the rooms have always had. He will be offered tea. This ending, the one he can see so clearly, will encapsulate the past and look toward the future.

There is only one problem: he can't do it. He traveled twenty hours by plane—taking a circuitous route through Paris, Frankfurt, and Moscow because he used Air Miles—and now he can't bring himself to get on the Metro and go the seven stops to Moskovskaya. He has been here two weeks, and makes an attempt every day. He enters Nevsky Station. He buys a token, then stands on an escalator that seems endless, descending deep into the belly of the city. Here is where his troubles begin. This far down, the air smells slightly of sulfur, and he has trouble breathing. He can read Cyrillic easily, but the small blue signs confuse him. People push past him and crush themselves onto trains, and the thought of so many bodies next to his own makes him feel ill. Once, last week, he tried to imagine he was in New York, taking the subway to see his agent or his hairstylist, but even that didn't work.

Maybe he's depressed. He has reason to be. His marriage recently crumbled like Saint Petersburg's plaster walls—a marriage that was ignored and badly maintained, abandoned to the elements and given only the occasional coat of paint. You see, he's not himself: even his metaphors are tired. Maybe it's lack of sleep. Here, the constant sunlight and mosquitoes keep him up all night. He has been unable to do anything since he arrived. He avoided bathing in Galina's cold shower until he began to smell like one of the drunks who sleep on the sidewalk. He craved Uzbek mutton and Georgian bread, but the idea of entering restaurants by himself—looking at menus, dealing with slow service, paying exaggerated prices—was too exhausting. So for two weeks, he lived off street food: blini with jam, ice-cream sandwiches, and Fanta. He supplemented this diet with Russian Standard vodka, which he drank by himself in his rented apartment.

Maybe it's the uncertainty. He doesn't know what he'll find at his grandmother's apartment. What if the tenants are drunk or stupid or not home? And what if the apartment has been torn down, or transformed so fully—into luxury condos, say—that he doesn't recognize it? Whatever the reason, he never made it to his grandmother's apartment, and now it's too late. His flight for New York leaves tomorrow morning.

As they walk down Nevsky, Svetlana hooks her arm in his. He understands this gesture means only that she requires support in her high heels, but still. "Would you like to have dinner?" he asks. "I haven't had a good meal in a while."

She shrugs her thin shoulders. "Yes. Fine."

He takes her to a Georgian place, and since it's his first decent meal in two weeks, and his last night in Russia, he orders extravagantly: roasted eggplant stuffed with almonds, pike perch soup, lamb shashlik, bread baked with cheese and egg, and two hundred grams of vodka. The alcohol arrives first. Alexei pours from the small, cold carafe, and watches Svetlana's cheeks and neck flush from the first shot.

The restaurant is perfect: it's so loud they don't have to make conversation. A singer with a microphone, an electric guitar, and a synthesizer croons folk songs. And a group at a table nearby celebrates the birthday of a chubby blonde named Tanya. The singer dedicates all his songs to her, and she dances in front of him unsteadily.

The food arrives, and it too is perfect: fat drips from the lamb skewers and the bread has a bright, raw egg on top. Svetlana and Alexei eat in silence. She serves herself minuscule portions—she must be counting calories—and he wants to tell her of his grandmother, a woman who survived the Siege by making pancakes out of cottonseed and sawdust. But he resists the urge to be didactic; it's one of his major faults, according to his ex-wife. Instead, he watches Tanya dance. The birthday girl sways with her soft arms in the air, her eyes closed. Every few minutes, a friend steadies her and leads her back to the table, where they pour another round of shots and give a toast in her honor.

"These are the happiest people I've seen since I arrived," Alexei calls to Svetlana over the music.

"That woman is not happy." The prostitute waves her fork dismissively. "She is terrified of how old she is becoming. Look. She doesn't wear a wedding ring."

"Wedding rings aren't all they're cracked up to be."

Svetlana leans across the table. "'Cracked up to be?'"

"It's an expression. It means that something isn't as good as it seems." Alexei looks at her as the neck of her purple dress gapes open and exposes part of her bony chest. "How old are you?"

"Older than I look." Her smile—that false thing she flashes like a piece of jewelry—convinces him she's lying.

"It's my birthday today," he says. "I'm turning forty-six."

"What?" She points to the singer. "I can't hear you."

"My birthday," he yells. "It's today."

For the first time, Svetlana laughs. "You and Tanya," she says.

The combination of the vodka, the prostitute's laughter, and the food—so rich in his mouth—gives Alexei courage. "Can I ask you a favor? Will you go somewhere with me?" He speaks loudly and in Russian, to be certain she understands. "I want to see where my grandmother lived before she died."

"You want to fuck in your grandmother's house?" Svetlana seems unfazed.

"No." He pours them both another shot of vodka—it can only help. "I just want to see it. I haven't been back in a long time. And I don't want to go alone."

She puts down her fork. "It will cost more."

"I understand that."

She tilts her head and looks at him as though she finds him curious. She laughs, and it's a laugh he could learn to like.

"Fine." She raises her glass. "Happy birthday."

Here is another secret: he hates Russia. His books have been hailed as *full of genuine affection* for his country and its people, but he has no love for his motherland. And he will never be one of those expatriates who become nostalgic for Soviet life. He is not writing this memoir out of a sense of loss or regret, but to rid himself of this place. His grandmother's is the only memory that ties him to Russia, and once he has paid tribute to her, he'll never return. After this, he'll write books about New York, California, Boston. About anywhere but a country that slowly destroyed his parents, and allowed his grandmother to die alone.

What he hates most is the way this place ignores him. New York might bully you—he experienced this in American high school as well as in reviews of his second book. But at least, for a brief moment, New York takes note. And on occasion, it celebrates you and seems to belong to you. He has written six books and they have received prestigious prizes, but Russian translators, newspapers, reviewers, and publishers—who are so attentive to other, lesser writers—don't seem to care for Alexei. Being here reminds him of being a child, mostly ignored by his parents and the other inhabitants of their apartment.

He hates this place, but like a needy lover, he has worked tirelessly for its attentions. He has chronicled the country's political shifts. He has invented characters that moved through Moscow's overwhelming streets. He has borrowed the people's accents, their pain, their jokes, and transformed them into stories, into something he can almost own. For his efforts, he has won prizes in America; he has made money. And there's nothing wrong with that. It is much better than those young writers, those naive MFAs who spend a month in a place, then decide they are experts, decide they are owed something. He feels sorry for them, poor things, always tourists in their own settings. He has done better than them, and no worse than the politicians, the oligarchs, the police officers, the mail-order brides, the men who sell stolen umbrellas and bubble-blowers and mechanical rabbits in the streets. He only did what he had to do. He only took what was his, and a little bit more. He only used this place, like the sad and glorious hooker that she is.

The Metro lines are so deep below the city's marshy surface that the escalator ride down takes at least four minutes. The station is far below Petersburg's street level of bruising commerce—an underworld of electric light and bad air, a separate city that seems more real than the actual one. The long ride down reminds Alexei of the first minutes of sleep, a slow descent into dreams.

Four minutes is a long time when you have nothing to say to your companion. So Alexei is grateful for the second bottle of vodka, which they'd bought from a store on Nevsky. Svetlana had pointed to what she wanted, then reached into Alexei's pocket and taken out a one-hundred-ruble bill. She must have noticed, earlier, where he kept his wallet.

On the escalator, she tucks the bottle in her purse. She takes it out and sips furtively, careful not to be seen by police. For a woman who can't weigh much over a hundred pounds, she has an impressive tolerance for alcohol. She is utterly unlike the young women he's met in the States, women his ex-wife called "group-ies." The ones who approach him at readings, holding his books against their chests. Those young women are pleasantly surprised when he listens to their youthful literary opinions, when he buys them a glass or two of wine. They seem to feel as though they are breathing a different kind of air when they're with him, and they're flushed and grateful for it.

Svetlana is not grateful. When he tells her that he is a writer, she looks him up and down as though appraising him for value. "Are you a famous writer?" she asks. "Or just a writer?"

"I've done well," he says. "I've worked hard."

"You've been fortunate," she corrects him, then tips vodka into her mouth.

"I've won a National Book Award," he says, before he can stop himself. "And a Pulitzer."

But Svetlana points to a gypsy who stands at the bottom of the escalator, selling live kittens on leashes made of string. "Oh," she says. "So cute."

"Don't touch those. They're probably diseased."

She doesn't seem to hear him. She steps off the escalator and bends toward the cats. Some listlessly lift their noses to smell her hand.

"Good price." The vendor picks up a white kitten by the scruff of its neck.

"This one." Svetlana points to a thin black cat with eyes similar to her own. "I like this one."

"It looks sick," says Alexei. "It'll be dead in two days."

"It's weak." Svetlana reaches to stroke the kitten's head. "I'd feed it milk and sausage."

"It'll grow to be an attractive animal." The vendor slips the collar off its neck and speaks to Alexei. "Like your girlfriend."

Svetlana looks at Alexei with an expression he recognizes. He remembers seeing this same look on his grandmother's face, and it's one he appreciates seeing on his agent's brow.

Svetlana is a negotiator. "If you buy it for me," she says. "I'll name it after you."

"My ego isn't that fragile. I don't need a stray cat named after me."

She touches Alexei's collar. "But what is your name?"

"You don't remember?"

"I mean your real name."

Her casual knowledge of his deception makes him feel as though there's been some intimacy between them—something so quick and subtle that he hadn't noticed it. "Alex," he says, without being able to help it. "Alexei."

"Oh." She looks disappointed. "That's not a good name." She lifts the kitten to see its underside. "Anyway, it's a girl."

"Fine." Alexei pulls out his wallet. "I'll get it for you." In his wallet, he finds only a five-hundred-ruble bill in with his American dollars. The vendor insists he doesn't have change, and in the end, Alexei hands over the five hundred. There isn't time to argue; Svetlana has already walked off with the cat.

Alexei runs after her, and is out of breath when he steps on the train. These facts—his aging, fallible body and the way the vendor ripped him off—have made him irritable. And the kitten does seem sick; it's too docile, and its eyelids are heavy.

"You should say thank you," says Alexei.

Svetlana looks at him, then blinks—her eyelashes dropping and lifting like theater curtains. "You seem like a nice person," she says, without sounding impressed.

This was not what he'd wanted. He'd hoped for a sweet girl, someone willing to be charmed, or at least to fake it. And he doesn't understand why she insists on speaking English, as though to make him feel even more like a stranger here. They stand beside each other in silence, and as the tracks curve, she tilts toward him. Their hips touch, but he doesn't put his arm out to steady her.

"What about you?" he says, as they approach Frunzenskaya. "What's your real name?"

"I don't tell men that."

"It's only fair now."

"No, it's not the same for me to know your name. I meet so many people. I'll forget your name by tomorrow."

"That's comforting."

"If you want, you can call me Lana. It's what I like."

"Sure." The train speeds up and air whistles through the windows. "Lana."

She isn't listening. She buries her face in the scruff of her nameless kitten's neck, and whispers to it in Russian.

"I love you," she tells it. "I love you, my dear one."

It's one in the morning when they reach their stop, and Moscow Square is nearly empty. There are only a group of teenagers drinking beer and performing skateboard tricks, and a woman selling dahlias from a plastic bucket. She entreats Alexei to buy a flower for his "princess," but he speaks a resolute, "*Nyet*," and walks toward Lenin.

The statue is not as big as he remembers, but still, it presides over the setting sun. Lenin looks handsome and dapper in a three-piece suit, like a businessman ready for the office. He still has dignity, despite the teenagers drinking beer in his shadow. Despite Alexei himself, the prostitute beside him, and the kitten she holds in her arms.

"I used to love this place," says Alexei. "I used to play here."

"This is what you wanted to see?" Lana taps a nail, painted with glittery polish, against the side of the vodka bottle. "You could have bought a postcard."

The more she drinks, he notices, the more she hates him.

"Were you alive then?" He points to the House of Soviets. "Do you remember any of this?"

"I'm not a child."

"You could have fooled me."

"I don't like the expressions you use."

"Here." He takes out his wallet and hands her five hundred American dollars. Far too much. "Here's some money for a cab."

She stares at the bill as though she's never seen cash before. "What for?"

"This was a mistake."

"You want me to go?"

"For one thing, I'm still officially married."

"Are you joking or are you serious? I can never tell with Americans."

"Please leave."

"You don't like me?"

"That's not it."

"You're too famous for me?" Her voice has a simpering, insulting edge. "Too famous in America?"

"Go home," he says. "Go home to your mother or your pimp or whoever buys you that ridiculous perfume."

She grabs the money, and he turns and walks the way he knows by heart.

"I buy it!" she yells. "I buy my ridiculous perfume!"

As a boy, he took the Metro every Saturday. He counted the seven stops on his fingers, then got off the train by pushing past strangers' legs. He walked up the station's staircase into the bright outdoor light, and crossed Moscow Square. He stopped to salute Lenin, then marched down Demonstration Street, humming military songs and imagining he was the leader of a great parade.

When he reached his grandmother's courtyard, he began to run. He ran up the stairway, then knocked on her door. She always answered with her arms crossed and a smile on her face. "What's this?" she said when she saw him. "What's this precious thing on my doorstep?" Right then, his love for her threatened to make his heart explode. He'd throw himself against her legs and hold on to her skirt.

This is why he needs to return to his grandmother's house, because he hasn't felt anything like that since. He loved his grandmother so dearly. He loved the pancakes she served him, covered in condensed milk. He loved the way she boiled water on her gas stove and served tea in china cups—cups she wrapped in newspaper and hid under her bed, so the neighbors wouldn't see that she kept such beautiful things. He loved how she poured milk into those cups and how the milk formed clouds in the tea, clouds that moved quickly like those over Palace Square. He loved how the china felt hot in his hands and the way his grandmother crushed half a lemon into the bottom of her cup.

He never understood how his grandmother acquired her own apartment, not to mention the tea, the lemons, and the good flour to make pancakes. She always knew which store had goods on which day, and was always one of the first in line. He never questioned this. He only knew that in his grandmother's apartment, he never felt alone and always felt safe. He has lived in the United States for twenty-eight years, and has traveled extensively—Amsterdam, Paris, Prague—but never again has he found such a place.

What he loved most were his grandmother's stories. After lunch, over the sound of hot water dripping inside the radiator, she told him of talking wolves, women who turned into crows, and winter that appeared in the shape of a man, wearing a long fur coat and a beard. He was in love with those stories. Is that possible? Can a boy be in love with his grandmother's words? If we expand that frail little word—love—if we breathe into it and stretch it like a balloon, fill it like a lung, then yes. Yes, it is possible. A boy can be in love with his grandmother's stories, with his grandmother herself, in her apartment off Moskovskaya, eight floors up. Because when his grandmother talked, ghosts appeared, witches had teeth of iron, and geese could lift and carry little boys away in their beaks.

He had worried that he wouldn't remember the way, but finds it easily. He turns left down Demonstration, then takes another right. There is one long block before he reaches his grand-mother's apartment. He passes a small pink church that—since his acquaintance with American pastries—reminds him of a cupcake. Everything has changed. This is now a nice neighborhood. The trees, which had been thin when he was a boy, are tall and leafy. There is grass in front of the buildings, and it appears as though someone waters it, someone mows it. There are BMWs parked on the streets. Somewhere nearby, a car alarm rings.

Only the apartment buildings themselves haven't improved. They're made of the same cinder blocks, with iron bars on the windows and small balconies. They're all identical, but still, he recognizes his grandmother's. He walks into the courtyard, where there's now a swing set and a teeter-totter.

Alexei doesn't do what he'd planned to do. He doesn't pause to look up at his grandmother's window, eight stories up. He doesn't even stop to consider the lucky accident that the building's heavy metal door has been left unlocked. He doesn't climb the stairs slowly, noticing the smell of cooking from the apartments. He takes them two at a time, the way he did as a child. If he had slowed down, he would have had time to be angry with himself, angry that he had come back like this: drunk, taking the train with a hooker on his arm, without dignity. The dignity he treasures. The dignity he's worked his whole life to acquire, the same way some people work to buy a house or a car.

He reaches the eighth floor and doesn't wait to catch his breath. He walks straight to his grandmother's apartment, number thirty-one. And without pausing to take this moment in, without stopping to check his watch—which would have reminded him that it was nearly two in the morning—he knocks on the door.

Alexei isn't so drunk that he expects his grandmother to answer. So when she does—when his grandmother opens the door and whispers, "Who's there?"—he can hardly breathe.

"Babushka," he whispers. "My little grandmother."

The hallway is dark—only a dim light comes from within the apartment behind her—and she has opened the door just a few inches. But Alexei knows it's her. She wears her same white night-shirt that reaches to the floor. And she still has those fierce, intelligent eyes. She does not look surprised to see him.

"It's me," he says, then reaches out to take her hand. "It's Alexei."

A man appears beside her, opening the door all the way. "What's going on?" He wears track pants, a green terry-cloth robe, and slippers. The robe is undone and shows his wide, sunburned chest. His hair is thinning, and there's gray stubble on his face. He looks the way Alexei might, if he'd never left Russia. "Who are you?" he says.

Alexei's grandmother speaks in a stranger's voice. "It's just some fool," she says. "He's drunk."

"I'm sorry," says Alexei. "I've made a mistake."

"Yes, you have," says the man. "You've disturbed my family."

"I'm sorry." Suddenly Alexei is sober. "I forgot about the time. I got confused."

"You woke my mother up."

"Who cares?" says the woman. "I was awake anyway."

How could he have mistaken her for his grandmother? It's true that the white nightgown and the shadowy light make her look like a ghost. But this woman has the harsh voice of a lifelong smoker, a sneering expression, and bad posture.

"And you frightened my wife," says the man with the red chest—how did he get a sunburn in this climate? He must work outside. He must be shirtless on some scaffolding all day.

"Now you're getting angry," says the woman who is not Alexei's grandmother. "I'm going to bed."

"You woke me up." The man stares at Alexei. "I work in the morning."

"I'm a Russian-American writer." Alexei begins the speech he'd rehearsed for this occasion. "I was born here in 1963. I've returned now because I'm writing a memoir of the past."

"I remember the past too," says the man, switching to thick, accented English. "But I don't wake people up to tell them about it."

"My grandmother lived in your apartment." Alexei tries to keep his voice steady. "That's why I'm here. It's meaningful to me."

A younger woman appears in the doorway; this must be the wife. She puts her hand on her husband's shoulder. "Who is it, Misha?"

The man's eyes don't move from Alexei's face. "He says he used to live here."

"Lucky him." She yawns, covering her mouth with the back of her hand.

"I'm sorry I woke you." It's not just the vodka that's turning Alexei's stomach. There's something familiar about this scene: a man—like himself, about the age he is now—showing up at this apartment in the middle of the night. This has happened before, he's sure of it. "I'm sorry," he says. "I'm sorry."

"He's writing a book." Misha says this without irony. Perhaps he is a person who likes books. A reader. This gives Alexei hope.

"I only wanted to see the apartment for a few minutes," says Alexei. "Would that be all right? I would come back some other time, but I leave for America in six hours."

Misha has stopped looking at him. He is carefully belting his robe so it covers his chest. "You want a tour?"

"I have some money." Alexei takes out his wallet. "I'll pay."

Misha looks at the wallet. "My home," he says, "is not a museum." There is a tired, long-harbored fury in his voice. He reaches out with a slow assurance and grabs Alexei's neck. He grips a tendon hard enough to leave a bruise. "Why don't you go to the Hermitage?" His face is close now, and Alexei can smell onions and tobacco on his breath. "They'll take your money."

"Don't do this." Alexei uses the same hopeless voice he'd used during his first days of high school in America. When he showed up for class with a Russian accent and the wrong clothes, and was kicked to the ground for it. "Please," he says, though he knows it won't do any good. He knows the ending to this story. It has been years, but he remembers the way it felt to be punched in the face. He remembers the taste of blood, and closes his eyes in expectation of it.

It doesn't come. What happens instead is even more humiliating. He hears, in the stairwell, the click of heels on the steps, and the slosh of vodka in a bottle. Then the stairwell's door swings open, and there she is. In her purple dress, with the kitten slung under her arm. She looks at Misha, his wife, then at Alexei. She smiles, showing those teeth. Then she laughs.

"I knew he'd get in trouble," she says.

"Who are you?" Misha still holds Alexei by the neck, making it difficult to breathe. "Are you a friend of his?"

"He says he's famous in America," says Lana. "But I've never heard of him."

Misha lets go of Alexei's neck and looks at him as though perhaps this man is simply what his mother said: a fool, bothersome and insane. Alexei leans against the wall to regain his balance and what remains of his dignity.

"You followed me?" he whispers to her. Was she listening from the staircase? Did she hear him embarrass himself?

"I'm rescuing you," she says. "You should say thank you."

Then, to Misha and his wife, she says, "Do you want a drink?" She holds up the half-full bottle. "And maybe you could give my cat some milk? She's hungry."

The older woman appears in the hallway, silent in her bare feet and her ghostly nightgown. She takes the kitten from Lana's arms. "Look at this," she says. "Look at this precious thing."

Everything has changed. A wall has been knocked down and the apartment is twice the size it used to be. The bedroom where Alexei's grandmother slept now belongs to Misha's mother, and she has filled it with Orthodox icons. The kitchen has been modernized: a dishwasher and laundry machine stand side by side. The walls have been painted green and there is linoleum on the floor, but the tap still drips.

Misha leads Alexei and Lana to the table, takes out three shot glasses, and Lana fills them. The kitchen lights are bright and buzz like mosquitoes.

The wife takes out a can of mushrooms to eat with the vodka, and the three of them—Alexei, Lana, Misha—drink the first shot unceremoniously, without even a toast. Lana refills the glasses immediately.

"Drink," she says to Alexei, as though offering medicine. "It's your birthday." Then, to Misha, she holds up the second shot and says, "To your home."

The kitten laps at a dish of milk, and Lana and the couple talk and laugh—Misha is drunk now, and friendly. But Alexei hears them as though they are far away, in distance and in years. He is listening to the slow drip of the kitchen tap, and he is a boy again, six years old. His grandmother stands here—in this kitchen—with a man who has arrived in the middle of the night. A man who seems somewhat older than Alexei is now, wearing a pressed suit and a wool coat. It is always the same man. He looks to be someone high-ranking, and Alexei despises him.

"He's a celebrity in America," says Lana, and Alexei hears her cruel laughter, feels her hand on his leg. "He's very important."

Alexei watches this man and his grandmother from the doorway—they don't see him because they have left the lights off, because they think he is asleep. He climbed from his bed without making a sound. He moved silently to the doorway and he stands there without breathing. He watches as his grandmother and this man whisper as though they are friends. She even laughs at something he says as she accepts payment. He gives her currency, of course, but also marvelous things that she'll share with Alexei the next day: a fresh pineapple, mandarin oranges, or a box of candies.

"He's asleep." Lana touches Alexei's neck, which is still tender from when Misha choked him. "Wake up," she says, without gentleness. "Wake up."

Alexei opens his eyes and drinks what they put in front of him. "Let us live long," he hears them say. "Let us meet again." Alexei thinks of that man, the face he didn't know he remembered, a shadow in his mind, and he feels sick and unsteady in his chair. He has avoided this place for years. He remembers, now, his reasons.

By the time Alexei and Lana leave the apartment, the Metro has stopped running. They negotiate with a driver on his way to an early shift at work, and he agrees to take them as far as the Zagorodny for two hundred rubles. He drives quickly, blasting ABBA's "Mamma Mia" from the stereo system. In the backseat, Lana leans against Alexei, her face pressed to his chest as though she is listening to his heartbeat. Her eyes are closed, her mouth open, and Alexei thinks she's asleep until she says, in Russian, "I'm going to throw up."

The driver pulls over near the Obvodny Canal and tells them to get out; he doesn't want anyone being sick inside his Ford. Alexei pulls Lana from the backseat, and watches as she vomits on the road. Then he sits beside her on the curb. She rests her head on her arms, her knees curled to her chest. The kitten seems to sense that she isn't well, and brushes up against her legs and her sides, leaving fur on the stiff lamé of her dress. Alexei tries to flag down another ride, but the few cars that pass don't stop. Lana lifts her face and squints into the morning sun.

"Come on." The makeup around her eyes is smudged and her lipstick has worn away. "We'll have to walk."

She takes off her heels and goes barefoot, watching the ground for broken glass. Alexei carries her purple shoes and her gold handbag, and she holds the kitten. Neither of them speaks, but walking sobers them up.

There is hardly anyone in the streets: they pass only a man collecting garbage and a group of girls who walk tipsily home from a bar. At this hour, in this light, there is something sad and spectacular about the wide, empty avenues. The buildings look worn but proud behind the mesh and scaffolding and advertisements for anti-cellulite cream. They walk slowly, and Alexei has time to read the graffiti. He's especially fond of the words *I love you eternally*, sprayed over a crumbling bit of sidewalk. He sees where plaster has chipped away from walls, where red brick shows through like scabs that have been opened. Without people and cars, the city seems to have generously slipped off her clothes for him. She seems to show him her truest nature, her deepest secret: that she hates him, and everyone else. That she is not meant to be inhabited, only admired.

They pass the Anichkov Bridge, then the circus with its rooftop puppets that bend and shake with the wind. They walk all the way to the Summer Garden, through the lime trees, to the bank of the river. Here, they stop at a kiosk to buy breakfast: two glasses of kvass served in plastic cups, a Twix bar for him and a Bounty for her.

It would have made a better ending if they were somewhere else. There is nothing romantic about this side of the river. The view is of the Samsung building, MegaFon, and a huge advertisement for the Baltika Breweries. The neon signs are reflected in the Neva's dark surface.

For the first time, Alexei wants her. He wants to bring her to his rented apartment, unzip that purple dress, and lay her down on that flowery bed. But sex seems implausible now, and he has a plane to catch. "Where do you live?" he asks her.

"Far away. Near Grazhdansky."

Alexei can't imagine her in the suburbs, living on one of many geometric streets, in a building that resembles every other building. Her clumped eyelashes and shiny dress belong only here, among the exquisite facades of central Petersburg.

"I don't have time to go home," she says. "I have to be at work in an hour."

"Aren't you at work right now?"

"I'm also a tour guide. I have to show the Russian Museum to a group of Canadians." She looks down at the kitten, who stays close to her ankles. "Maybe one of the babushkas will look after her while I do my tour."

"Canadians?"

"They're worse than Americans. So boring and polite." Lana leans on the cement barrier, the only thing between her and a sharp drop to the river. "What was your grandmother's name?"

Alexei leans against the barrier too, and feels the cold granite against his arms. "Anya."

"That's pretty."

"That's what you should name the cat."

"Maybe." Lana straightens her dress. "Is this all right? Will the Canadians think I look fine?"

"The Canadians will love you," he says. "I'll buy you a coffee before you meet them."

"It's okay. This is normal."

Her eyes close slowly, and she leans into him. He feels the jut of her hip against his own. She doesn't smell like perfume anymore, but like her own sweat.

"Lana." He says the name quietly, as though it's hers.

Her eyes remain closed and he wonders if she's asleep. He doesn't mind. And when she reaches into his pocket to pull out his wallet, he doesn't mind that either. She takes some bills, and slips the wallet back into his pants.

"Take more," he says. "Take it all. You saved my life."

She laughs. "That man wouldn't have killed you. And we didn't even consummate."

She says this word—*consummate*—without a hint of irony, and it nearly knocks Alexei over. When was the last time he heard someone use that stunning, antiquated word? It's a word that seems thrilling and magical, like it belongs in a fairy tale. He wants to repeat it over and over. Then he wants to attach it to another word: love. Yes, love. *Lyubov.* A word he uses so rarely.

Is that possible? Has he fallen in love? How stupid—he knows better. This girl doesn't even like him, and she'll forget his name tomorrow. He also knows that his own feelings—so pure, so generous—can only occur when a person is far from home and hasn't slept in weeks. As soon as he gets back to New York, to his deadlines and his ex-wife, he'll get over it. And he will not write about it. This old cliché of a feeling doesn't belong in the kind of books he writes. It is at home in the kind he doesn't allow himself to read, even on airplanes. Books full of false promises and hopeful, misleading logic.

He remembers seeing his grandmother with that man in the kitchen. They were all business in their quiet, breathless proceedings: they never removed any clothing, never kissed. He was too young to fully understand what they were doing. But once, after, he saw them press their bodies together as though money and favors hadn't changed hands. It was summer, and though it was night, light filtered through the kitchen's thick curtains. So Alexei leans against Lana and smells her unclean hair. He lets her reach up and touch his face. She does this gently, as though she means it. And beside the dark, well-used waters of the Neva, he buys it.

Last One to Leave

It was 1961, she was eighteen,
and she took the first realistic means to escape the provincial city of her birth: she answered an ad in the *Colonist* that advertised a job as a copy editor for the Tahsis weekly paper. She wrote a letter to the editor and told him that she read newspapers regularly and had a good grasp of grammar. She was friendly, enthusiastic, willing to work late hours. She signed the letter *S. Lambert*, and didn't mention her age. A month later, she received a letter telling her she was hired and expected in two weeks. *We look forward to meeting you, Mr. Lambert.*

Rather than correct the mistake, she packed her notebook and her warmest tights, but didn't bother with the thin blouses her mother had given her, the cardigans with delicate buttons. Those were meant for a different sort of girl, a girl who planned to wait around for a man to marry her. Sydney would make her own life.

When she arrived in Tahsis, she found she had been misled:

this *we* of the letter—*We have looked over your application and are impressed by your writing samples*—was nonexistent. One person ran the *Tahsis Talk*. Earl had white hair that contrasted with his tanned, weathered skin. He was the paper's publisher, editor, and adman. He also worked at the pulp mill.

He looked her up and down and saw a stout girl in a red slicker. "I guess you'll do."

The town was hours north of Victoria, only accessible by water or by one swerving washboard road. She'd hitched to get there.

He was separated from his mother

but allowed to stay with his father. They slept together on the floor, curled next to other bodies that breathed and wept and coughed. He tucked his head into his father's armpit for warmth. It was Germany, 1942, and they were Jews. But still, his father whispered, "We must be thankful. We must thank G-d. For each other. For our lives. Even for the fleas."

"Not the fleas," said Havryil, scratching the backs of his legs.

"Yes, the fleas. We are thankful, because they allow us privacy. Because if they did not exist, the guards would come and disturb us while we slept. We would not even be allowed to dream in our own language."

Her first memory

was of holding her mother's hand in Water Station, in Vancouver, waiting for her father's train. He was on leave and would be home for three days before going to fight in Europe. This was before her brother existed.

Her mother wore heels and gripped Sydney's hand too tightly. Sydney didn't know what her father looked like and kept asking, "Is that him? Is that him?" Hoping he was one of the tall, handsome soldiers who stepped off the train.

He wasn't tall, but she was relieved he wasn't ugly. He had dark hair like hers, thick legs, crinkles in his nose when he smiled. He knelt in front of her and patted her head like she was a pet. "Hello, little one," he said.

When his father died, falling to his knees

on the hard ground like a man in prayer, Havryil wanted to feel something, anything, other than the ache in his chest. He decided to pull out his own teeth.

They had been festering in his mouth, throbbing for weeks. He used a piece of wire stolen from the factory where he worked. Tied it around each tooth, and yanked.

Afterward, he curled up with his four front teeth clutched in his fist. He forced himself to think like his father. His chest still felt bruised, but he was thankful, at least, that the pain in his mouth was gone.

Her mother drank sherry

from a smudged crystal glass. "Your father," she told Sydney and her younger brother, "is not dead." He'd simply not come home from the war, she explained, because he'd married someone else. He lived in France now. He had a new family, a mirror image of the old family: a wife, a daughter, a son.

"This is a secret," said her mother. "As far as everyone else is concerned, I'm a widow."

Her little brother was too young to understand, but Sydney knew that her mother still had hope. Hope that another man would come along. There was a smear of cranberry lipstick on the glass.

He had a name no one could pronounce

and was from a place no one could pronounce. A Displaced

Person, sent to Canada in 1950 because, after the war, there was nowhere left for him in his own country.

"How old are you, boy?" asked the Canadian doctor who examined him when he arrived.

If Havryil had understood, he would have said, *Eighteen*. But since he couldn't answer, the doctor wrote, *21 years*. The same sort of misunderstanding had led to his name being recorded incorrectly.

The doctor measured Havryil's arms, looked inside his mouth, and said he'd be good at working with trees. Said, "But you should do something about those teeth."

Then he was on a rackety truck, passing a blur of green. He'd never seen so many trees. The truck was met by a man in a blue-buttoned shirt and brown slacks. Probably the boss, from the way he stood straight as a beam. The boss said something Havryil couldn't understand, then took his work stub. "Jim?"

Havryil nodded.

"They don't make you tall over there, do they?" The boss gave him a punch on the arm. "Guess you'll be our whistle punk."

Havryil did not understand these words.

The boss showed him two buildings, one for eating and one for sleeping. Inside the sleeping house, there were sagging mattresses and stinking clothes. He was shown to his bed, a bare mattress with a crumpled comic book where a pillow should be—the last man to sleep there must have left it behind. Havryil looked at the pictures, then the words, trying to decipher this new alphabet. Then he sat on the mattress, wishing he had a bag to unpack, cards to play, someone to talk to. He watched a long-legged spider shimmy up its thread.

She rented a room
in one of the stilted bunkhouses over the river. She ate toast

for breakfast and toast for dinner. She wrote up car crashes and town council meetings and obituaries, getting cramps in her wrists from the heavy typewriter keys. She developed photos in the *Tahsis Talk* bathroom, with a towel shoved under the door to block the light. She did this at night, after Earl had gone home for dinner with his wife. She liked the quiet. She dipped the prints in trays of chemicals—developer, stop-bath, fixer, hypo-clear—then hung them like laundry on a line.

One of those photos was of her. After they put the first issue to bed, Earl had taken her picture. She had a warm beer in her hand, her feet up on her desk, a wide smile on her face.

The other men gambled at night,

betting rolled tens, but he lay on the hill under a million stars.

"Making a wish?" said the boss, finding him there, crouching beside him.

Havryil was sun-drunk from his first days, and half asleep, but still listened as the boss told him about the trees. Pointed to some skinny ones and said, "Those there. Alders. You heard that word ever? *Alder.*"

He explained—and Havryil half understood—that alders are mostly too small to bother chopping, but some grow to a hundred feet. "They take root where the ground's been torn up," said the boss. "Should have leaves with saw edges. See how that one's got no leaves? That one's dead."

The next day, Havryil walked up and touched it. It felt dusty smooth like his skin.

With each paycheck,

she put as much as she could toward buying her own truck. In the evenings, she wrote letters to her mother and brother, told them about the shaved-wood smell that permeated the air and the sound of fast-running creeks. She sent them clippings of the articles she'd written.

Her mother would never admit it—she wanted Sydney to quit this silliness and come home—but was likely thrilled to see her daughter's name in print. *Sydney Lambert.* Her own byline. "Tidal Wave Threatens Coastline." "Garage Sale Attracts 200!"

With his first paycheck,
he went to Vancouver. He stayed in a Gastown hotel, above a flickering sign that advertised a bar named Miranda's. He went there and bought a whiskey and found a girl to take home, a girl who didn't wear nylons over her waxy legs and who kissed him lightly on the mouth and who charged him four dollars for her company.

The next morning, he used the rest of his money to buy some blue jeans, a wool sweater, new socks, and a rifle.

"Whadya need a gun for?" asked the boss when he returned to work. "You plan on hunting your own food?"

Havryil didn't have an answer, at least not one that didn't sound stupid. He had assumed all Canadian men had rifles. Didn't they? Cowboys. Indians.

"Christ almighty." The boss shook his head and laughed. "Next time I'll take you into town, son."

She got a boyfriend, which surprised her—
she hadn't realized she wanted one. He was a mill boy she met while sitting by herself at the marina's outdoor restaurant, waiting for her steak dinner. She'd learned this from her mother: a good way to meet people was to take yourself out for dinner.

The young man fished on the weekends, and was cleaning his catch, slicing salmon and extracting their spines. She saw him notice her. Then he approached and offered her a fish wrapped in newspaper, the way another man might offer a bouquet of roses. "I like a girl with an appetite," he said.

Three weeks later Havryil was back
in Vancouver, the city rain falling down his collar. "First things first," said the boss, opening an umbrella and holding it over them. He took Havryil to a dentist on Granville. "They don't need to cost much," he said. "But the boy needs teeth."

Then they went out for lunch—steak and potatoes, the most food Havryil had ever seen on a plate—and the boss noticed the way he held the menu close to his face, peering at the illustrations of sodas and floats. "One more stop." He gripped the boy by the shoulder and led him to a store that sold glasses.

When they left, Havryil could see the color of women's eyes when he passed them; he could see the leaves on trees. He was thankful, thankful, thankful.

For no reason except that she'd chosen it,
she was more interested in this new town than she'd been in the city where she was raised. So she went to the small museum and read panels about when James Cook first came ashore in 1778.

Cook had been lost—looking for the Northwest Passage—when his ship drifted into this cove. Chief Maquinna sent out canoes of warriors to investigate the strange arrival. The Europeans saw a village of wooden longhouses and more trees than they believed possible. The warriors saw white-skinned men and believed they were dogfish that had turned themselves into human beings.

"Imagine that," she said to the mill boy, as he kissed her in the back of his truck. "Imagine seeing all these pale strangers arrive in your village."

"Sure." The mill boy slipped a hand under her skirt. "I'm imagining."

The name, Nootka Sound, was born out of a misunderstanding. When the Natives explained to Cook that he was on an island, a place you can go around—*itchme nutka*—he believed they were telling him the proper name of the land where he stood.

But eventually the two groups communicated, trading lead and pewter for sea otter pelts. Cook named the place Friendly Cove because the Mowachaht people were so welcoming. By 1920, 90 percent of them were dead.

The boss sat with him each night

and bitched about this suicide show, the price of diesel, that princess of a donkey-puncher. The boss knew a use for everything, knew everything's worth: water hemlock'll kill a guy, cutthroat trout feed him, spruce and cedar make him stink of cash.

"You'll have to tell me about the place you're from sometime," said the boss. "What do they grow over there?"

Havryil shrugged and picked tree-pitch from his clothes. But sometimes, because his accent made the boss laugh, he repeated the names of things: nettle, foxglove, fish hawk.

Mornings were her favorite time.

She liked to sit on the small porch of her house, looking out at the misty sound, a notebook in front of her.

"Aren't you cold out there?" When he stayed over, the mill boy always wanted her to come back to bed, to stay under the covers. But the crisp air, the rising sun. This was when story ideas came.

"Have you heard of that boy who lives out by himself off the Head Bay Road?" she called to him. "Theresa mentioned him at the store yesterday. Said he's mute."

"The DP? Sure, I seen him. He's been lurking around here for years."

"Do you think he can't talk? Or he just doesn't want to?"

"Don't know, sugar pie." The mill boy came out and stood on the porch, stroked her hair. "What do you think? Eggs for breakfast? You'll rot your stomach with all that coffee."

Every morning he had a quiet minute

or two to look down at the steep slide of log pieces, stumps, mud, and chewed rocks. As the whistle punk, he stood in his caulk boots at the top of the skid. His job: to send signals to the engineer by pulling a jerk line attached to the valve of a steam whistle. He'd memorized those signals like a language. A single whistle got the operation going. Three short meant *slow down*. Seven long meant *emergency*.

The mainline hoisted logs, swung them down the slope, and dropped them onto the cold deck pile. The rigging slinger was down there in the gully, dogging the balsam. Fir and cedar slapped down the slope and the rigging slinger's job was to unhook the wire—a half turn to loosen the slip-noose from the log—then send the rigging back up.

That week they were short, so the boss was acting as rigging slinger. That was one way the boss maintained respect. He worked with the men, harder than they did. He stood down there and gave Havryil a wave and a thumbs-up. Havryl had never seen that gesture before arriving here, but gathered that it meant *good job* or *good morning*. Something good.

Earl didn't think it was safe

for Sydney to go there by herself.

"If I were a man, you wouldn't try to stop me," she said.

"What's with this 'if I were a man' business?" Earl's desk was separated from Sydney's by a cardboard partition. They could hear every creak of each other's chairs, but could not see each other's faces. "It's not safe. He lives out there in the trees by himself. We don't know anything about him."

"Exactly."

"It's meant to be light reading, Syd. It's meant to make people laugh."

"But can we agree that he's a Tahsis Personality?" She'd written about Clive and Carla Dell, who ran the bakery. And William Paul, the fishing guide. "Can we agree he fits the criteria?"

"He doesn't talk. Do you get that? He's never said a word to anybody."

"I'll be back in an hour."

"You've been here one month and I'm going to stop concerning myself with you." Earl stood and looked at her over the partition, the lines in his forehead deep as ruts in a gravel road. "From now on, you are your own concern."

He was obviously lying. She appreciated his fatherly attention, but would never admit it.

"That's right." She packed her pen, notebook, camera, and film into her purse. "I always have been."

An alder skidded down the hill.
Underneath the white-blotched bark the tree was a deep golden red, like it bled when sliced from its stump.

Maybe the engineer yarded it too fast, or maybe it was the way it hit that stump, flipping up and over. The boss faced away, still working on the last log, when the alder slammed his wide back and head. The tree threw him like he was light and breakable as a pair of glasses. The boss crumpled to his knees.

Havryil stood still except for his arm that reached for the line—it cut his palm but he didn't feel that until later. *One, two, three, four . . .* after the seventh whistle, he ran, tripped, slid down the skid. He reached the boss's body, saw blood that leaked from a fractured skull.

The engineer had cut the donkey's engine, and everything was quiet except for Havryil's hard breathing.

That evening, he packed his things and walked out of the camp, along the gravel road. He chose a clear, flat patch of forest near some water and figured: good enough. He slept curled up on the ground. His mouth ached as though those infected teeth, the ones he'd ripped out years ago, were back. He decided then to stop speaking. He had nothing to say. Nothing to be thankful for.

She used Earl's truck,
a Ford that was rusted along the bottom, and drove toward the Head Bay Road. The boy, or man—no one knew his age—lived off a small logging road a few kilometers from town. He didn't have a phone, so she couldn't warn him that she was coming.

She felt an edgy excitement. So far all she'd done was write up the tide tables, the results of local sporting competitions, and a few fluff pieces. This would be her first real story.

It rained that day, so no dust rose off the gravel. Instead, she worried about how Earl's bald tires would fare in the mud. The boy's house was set deep in the woods, so far back from the road that it seemed she'd taken the wrong turn. But then the yard appeared. A muddy clearing, a small house near the Leiner River. The house was more of a shack, really: one room built from beams that seemed to have been stolen from a logging site. It was unpainted but did not look precarious. It would withstand storms; every angle was well measured and every board accurately cut. There was a chimney, and it was smoking.

She stepped out of Earl's truck and it rained lightly on the top of her head. Her shoes—a pair of brown Mary Janes she never gave much thought to—squelched through the mud. This deep in the trees, the air was colder.

She'd expected him to hear her engine and to be outside, waiting, when she pulled up. She imagined he didn't get many visitors, so her arrival would merit curiosity. But she was met by silence. She slammed the truck's door as hard as she could, but still there was only the sound of rain drizzling.

She knocked on the wooden door. "Hello? Jim?"

She heard a noise—a gentle cough, a clearing of the throat—and turned. He wore muddy overalls and a pair of gloves that were brown with dirt. He had a metal rake that leaned against one shoulder, and a rifle propped against the other.

Sometimes he still heard that whistle,
the seven long of *emergency*. He couldn't be sure whether it came from a logging camp nearby or if it was just a memory, a shriek that lived in his head. He heard it now, as the stranger stood on his porch, so shrill it made him dizzy.

She put her hands in the air.
"I'm from the paper." She knew from watching her mother deal with customers at the bookshop that the way to calm crazy people was to talk to them like they weren't crazy. "Just wondering if you'd agree to an interview. Have you read our Personalities column?"

His glasses sat crookedly on his nose, looking childish and comic. The lenses were splattered with rain, and maybe this was why he had the posture of someone who was half blind, his chin jutting forward, his body tilting toward her.

From his face, he looked thirty. Thin, with arms that seemed too long. She guessed he was the kind of man who was always hungry, no matter how much he ate. He shifted his weight. He lowered the rifle.

"It's nothing difficult." She took a breath. "Just a few questions. And we take a photo."

He dragged the rake back and forth along the ground, digging furrows into the mud.

"I have everything right here." She reached into her purse to take out her notepad, but saw that her movement startled him. "Just a pen and paper," she said, holding it up.

When he saw it was a girl,
he lowered the gun, picked up his rake. He couldn't see her very well but she was wearing a red coat and had a small, solid body underneath it. She took a few steps toward him, talking fast, and he saw that her brown hair was stuck to her forehead from the rain. That made him shy. Why was she here? Was he supposed to invite her in?

He walked away from her, behind the house.

She followed him, watched as he scraped wet mulch under the apple tree that he hoped would one day produce. She was still talking and he sneaked one or two glances at her. Not at her face—he was too nervous for that—but at her ankles and knees. At the drops of rain darkening her tights.

She stopped talking and watched him. "Well." She shrugged, hands on her hips. "Guess I'll go now."

And it felt like yanking a tooth when he dragged the word up from where it had been buried. "Stay," he answered.

"I've got everything right here."
She flipped open the notepad. "I've got my questions right here."

He nodded but didn't face her, didn't stop his raking.

"Where are you from?" she began.

"Ukraine," he answered. His voice sounded hoarse, as though his throat were torn like a patch of clear-cut. "Lviv."

"How do you spell that?"

When he didn't answer, she moved on to her next question. "What's your profession?" She spoke slowly, so he would understand. "What jobs have you done?"

"I work many places. First for my father. Then German factory for bricks."

She watched his back as he spoke; along his spine, his shirt was yellowed from sweat. She noticed the lean muscles moving under the material.

He was not sure how long he had been in Canada—maybe six or seven years—and for some of those he worked as a logger. "I live here now." He stamped the ground with his boot.

Then she took a photo, directing him to stand beside the apple tree, the rake still in his hand, looking at the camera. "Smile," she said. And he did, showing a plate of shiny metal teeth.

After she left, he took out that old comic book, saved from the logging camp. The paper was yellow and damp, the ink faded, but he bent over it and didn't give up. He used a pocketknife to scratch each letter into the wooden wall of his house.

That evening, the mill boy spoke of his plans. He would work at the mill and offer fishing tours on the weekend. That way he'd have money soon enough for a house. "A place for me and my girl," he said, his arm around her.

She had a perverse desire to offer him up to her mother. Here, she would say, is the nice man you've been waiting for.

"I went to see the guy who lives out there in the forest," she said. "The Displaced Person."

"Why'd you do that?"

"For the paper. For an interview. Did you know that Jim isn't actually his name?"

"Don't like the idea of you going out there." His grip on her tightened. "That guy's a thief. You tell me if you ever see him in town. I'd interview him, all right."

When she came back,
a week later, it was in a red truck.

"It's mine," she said. "Just got it."

He took a few steps toward it and read the word on the side: Dodge. She was still talking and he had to focus on her mouth to keep up. She said she bought the truck from a family in Sayward. Earl had driven her out there, looked under the hood, bargained for her.

Who's Earl? he wondered.

"My boss," she said, as though he'd asked out loud. "He thought a man would get a better deal." Then she passed him a newspaper. "Anyway. You should have a copy," she said. "You're in there. Page four."

He turned to the article and, for the first time in years, saw his own face. Except it wasn't his own face; it was his father's. He felt that old soreness in his chest.

"Well." She seemed not to know what to say. She shifted her weight, looked past him. "I admire your home here, Havryil." She used his real name, pronouncing it as best she could. "Your way of living."

He took a breath. "Thank you."

He surprised her
by asking her to stay for dinner, and she surprised herself by saying yes. He served deer meat, and greens he grew behind the house. He pulled out the only chair for her and said, "You are guest here."

"A guest," she corrected. "You are *a* guest."

"No." He smiled at his own joke. "You are."

After dinner, he showed her the design for the chicken coop he would build, and offered her coffee cake, and asked her to read the article about him aloud while he bent over the paper and tried to follow along. "Sydney," he said, tracking his finger under her byline.

The mill boy was waiting for her
when she got home, leaning against her door. "Working late?" he asked.

"Yeah," she said. "Developing photos."

She leaned in to kiss him but he didn't kiss her back. She took out her key to the door, but he didn't move out of the way.

"Really?" she said. "You're going to do this now?" She could already predict the words he would use: *Where were you? I know you're lying.* "I can't marry you." She crossed her arms. "You should have figured that out by now."

But the words he chose did surprise her. "You're a selfish girl." He stepped away from the door. "Selfish, and not as smart as you think you are."

She couldn't sleep after that, paced her kitchen, then decided to go for a drive. She took the Head Bay Road because she needed the feel of the washboard, the challenge of gravel under her wheels. Then she turned off at the almost-invisible road to Havryil's—it was somewhere to go. Someone to talk to.

"You are back," he said, when he opened the door. "Welcome, Sydney."

She told him that the way he pronounced her name made it sound like a sneeze.

"Sorry." He looked at his shoes. "I practice."

"No." She stepped toward him, touched his arm. "I'm sorry. I shouldn't have said that."

"I am having tea. Do you want?"

He served tea boiled with milk and sugar, so creamy it left a film on her tongue. It was nothing like the thin, bitter drink she'd grown up with. And he was nothing like the mill boy, who prodded with his callused fingers under her skirt. As he unbuttoned her blouse, this man was careful, determined, furrow-browed. She could tell from the way he squinted that his prescription was out of date.

They got married
in the town's A-frame church, a concession to propriety, with Earl and his wife as witnesses. But still her mother was angry, writing that it wasn't proper, it wasn't right. A girl shouldn't get married like a fugitive, without even a good dress. Even so, she mailed her daughter a pair of lace gloves, the same ones she wore at her own wedding. *Something borrowed*, she said.

To tease the newlyweds, Earl wrote up a wedding announcement for the paper:

Sydney Lambert Weds Havryil (Jim) Kohen
   The wedding bells pealed forth joyous music yesterday in the United Church on Maquinna Drive, as Miss Sydney Lambert, of Victoria, married Mr. Havryil Kohen, of Lviv, Ukraine. The nuptuals were performed by Reverend Mr. Bill Howie and witnessed by Earl and Theresa Schuberg. Mrs. Ida Johnson presided at the piano.
   The bride presented a handsome appearance in blue merino, wearing lace gloves, and carrying a bouquet of dogwood. Afterwards, a reception was held at the Tahsis Talk office, where wine and cake were served. The rain did not dampen the celebrations. While walking hand-in-hand from the church, the groom carried an umbrella and the bride wore a red slicker.

Sydney worked at the paper.
Havryil added two rooms onto the house, and a veranda. They had chickens for eggs and a goat for keeping the grass clipped. The apple tree produced small, hard, sweet fruit.

They spent most evenings in front of the woodstove, reading the newspapers Sydney had delivered—they always arrived a week late—from the mainland. Havryil would have preferred not to know anything of the world, but he liked to listen to her voice as she read aloud. She lay tucked under his arm, and he rested one of his hands between her thighs.

Every Sunday, Earl and Theresa invited them for dinner.
All three of the Schuberg children were grown now and had moved away, so Earl and Theresa had more time for guests. They had a smokehouse in their backyard and served a platter of smoked salmon at every meal. Havryil told them about *babka*, a dish made with fish, eggs, milk, onion, and bread. He said his mother used to make it for his birthday. "When's your birthday?" asked Theresa. "You'll come over and show me how to cook it then."

After dinner, they played Scrabble and Havryil always won. He had a knack for memorizing two- and three-letter words, then placing them ingeniously on the board. *Fez. Od. Jig.*

"Are those words?" Earl would have the dictionary out. "Okay, but he doesn't even know what they mean."

Havryil would shrug and grin, showing his lustrous teeth.

A few years later, her mother married
one of the bookstore's regular customers, a divorced lawyer named George Owens. Sydney remembered him from her childhood; her mother had always called him, in a tone that was both admiring and condescending, Mr. George.

Mr. George drove a Lincoln Continental convertible, which he used to bring Sydney's mother to Tahsis. Even along the Head Bay Road, where mists of fog from the river pooled in the gravel's dips and holes, they drove with the roof down. They arrived covered in dust.

"Mom," said Sydney.

"Sydney," said her mother.

Havryil stepped forward. "I am happy to meet you."

Her mother smiled tightly, looked around the small, dim house. "A lovely little room you have here."

"He built it," said Sydney. "Himself."

Mr. George said he'd like to take them all out to dinner. "Come on, Cecilia." He took his wife's hand, led her outside. "We'll wait in the car."

"We have nothing in common," said Sydney, when they were out of earshot. "Nothing to talk about."

But Havryil took her face in his hands. "She is your mother," he said. "You must be thankful to have her."

Sometimes they fought—

Sydney yelling on behalf of both of them, the sound of her voice softened by the wooden walls.

Havryil didn't like when she stayed late at work, had a beer in the office instead of dinner, then drove home along that logging road after dark. And Sydney grew antsy and tired of the forest in the winter. "Sometimes," she admitted, "I just want to go dancing."

So on Fridays he took her to the marina, where the fishermen cleaned their catch while a band played. "Brown-Eyed Girl." "I Heard It Through the Grapevine." They danced close, on wooden boards slick with guts and small, translucent bones.

The town wondered:

Why was he so quiet? Why didn't they have children? And it was strange that she went to work while he stayed home to cook and tend the garden. She would have answered for both of them: *Because we like it this way.*

But the people of the town never bothered to ask her. And

eventually, they grew accustomed to the couple. *Syd-n-Jim*, people called them, eliding the names so they sounded like one word.

Sometimes children from town would visit,

tramping through the trees to see the cabin. Once it was three boys, all siblings, who stood wide-eyed on the periphery of the property. All three had red hair and faces streaked with dirt, and one of them wore thick glasses like Havryil's.

There had been a time when the children of this town taunted him, threw stones at his back, and laughed as he passed them. But she had taught him not to be afraid.

"Come, come." He waved them over. "I'll teach you something. Do you know how to candle eggs?"

Then he lit a candle and placed a punctured tin can over the flame. Each child—they naturally seemed to order themselves from oldest to youngest—placed an egg, still warm, over the top of the can's hole. The flame shone through the shells, lit up the eggs like lanterns.

"This is how we check if there are cracks in the shells," said Havryil. "I sell the good ones and we keep any with flaws."

The boy with glasses placed his egg last. The brown shell became transparent: inside was thick albumen and a yolk that glowed like the sun.

"Do you see any cracks?" said Havryil.

The boy shook his head.

"You're right." Havryil gave him a thumbs-up. "They are good."

When her mother became ill,

Sydney returned to Victoria for the first time in years. Mr. George greeted her at the front door to a house on Rockland Drive with five bedrooms, three bathrooms, and a garden of rhododendrons surrounded by stone walls.

The flowers were like her mother: bright and impractical and resolutely cheerful. Sydney felt a swell of generosity, of gladness that her mother had found herself in the home she'd always wanted.

Her brother was already there, visiting from Vancouver, where he played piano in three or four bands. "Hey, Syd." He looked older than she'd ever imagined he would. "Nice truck. It's so vintage."

Her mother had grown thin, and lost one of her breasts. "Sydney. My little girl." She held her daughter's hand too tightly. "You're home."

Earl retired and moved

with his wife to Courtenay, BC, to be closer to a hospital—Theresa's emphysema was only getting worse. He left Sydney in charge of the paper and she ran it for twelve years. Then the mill closed.

She kept the paper going as long as she could, driving out to Gold River and Campbell River to try to sell ads. But soon Tahsis was down to three hundred people and there was no fighting it. The *Tahsis Talk* died, and she was too ashamed to write Earl to tell him. Havryil made her toast with blackberry jam for dinner, held her under his arm, ran his hand through her gray hair.

Someone put up a sign, just outside the town: *Last one to leave,* it read, *turn out the light!*

He started having dizzy spells.

Twice he collapsed in the garden, that old bruise in his chest flaring up. When he opened his eyes, he looked up at the green canopy and waited for his vision to focus. When his breathing steadied, when he could make out the tree branches and the pale apple blossoms, he stood slowly and brushed the dirt from his clothes.

He was thankful she wasn't home to see this. It would only worry her.

Reading helped—

not newspapers, because even the feel of the paper made her heart ache—but the books Havryil had read to improve his English. *Twenty Thousand Leagues Under the Sea. Great Expectations.*

There was no consolation for how quiet the house was without him. But reading helped, and so did chores, and driving with no destination in mind.

A man visited once.

He wore glasses and carried a briefcase and drove a hatchback. "Hello, Mrs. Kohen."

"Sydney." She shook his hand. "Do I know you?"

He glanced toward the house, the garden. "Amazing," he said. "It looks the same." He claimed to have visited this place as a child.

She shook her head. "There were no families near here."

"My brothers and I came a few times. Your husband gave us apples. We used to fill our pockets."

Her grief had gone quieter over the past few years, but this left her mute—they'd lived together for forty-four years, and still there were things she hadn't known. Children had visited. He'd given them apples.

"Can I interview you?" asked the man, who'd introduced himself as Larry. "I'm putting together a book for the Historical Society. A history of the town."

She understood now: the glasses, the hatchback, the briefcase. He must live in a city now, and be nostalgic for this place.

"I'm trying to capture as much as I can," he said. "Talking to as many people as I can."

"Oh, sure." She nodded. "But you'd better come inside. My knees aren't so good and standing around doesn't help."

She made coffee and they sat at the table where she used to eat dinners with Havryil—she wondered if it all seemed shabby to this man. From the briefcase, he took out a notebook and a cell phone, which he used as a tape recorder.

"What a gizmo," she said, and he smiled. He said he wanted her story, in her own words.

She used to say that during interviews too: *Tell me in your own words*. She used to feel frustrated when people wouldn't just spit it out. But where to start? Her life story. It flickered in her mind like a candle flame, something she couldn't hold and couldn't measure.

She sipped her coffee. "My own words." She looked at the alphabet, each careful letter that Havryil had carved into the walls.

Stay, he'd said,
and she had, for forty-eight years. And still she remained in the house, chopping wood for fires, tending the garden. She'd mostly stopped speaking. Not because she couldn't bear it—he'd shown her that loss can be borne—but because there was no one, now, to talk to.

I Am Optimus Prime

He knocked on the door, a thin guy with pitted skin. Not handsome, except you wouldn't know it from the way he leaned against the doorjamb, confident my mom would let him in. I stood at her side, one finger hooked in her belt loop. I was nine but looked six—one of those fine-boned, fragile boys. "Hey, buddy," he said, giving me a nod. He was probably about the age I am now, twenty-five or so. His pant legs were too short, and even though it was October and there was already snow on the ground, he wore battered sneakers without socks. I could see his bony ankles, red from the cold.

He'd driven eleven hours to get here, he said, in a car with a broken heater. He could see his breath as he drove and had to put his socks on his hands to keep his fingers from going numb. He had the radio on—thank God that still worked—and heard a song that reminded him of my mom.

He told her this in the kitchen while she served him a cup of hot chocolate, the kind I liked, the kind with tiny marshmallows. He put his wool socks back on his hands, and danced my mom around the kitchen with those clumsy mitts on.

He played with me too, using the socks like puppets. He named his left hand Snake and his right Angel, and propelled these characters into a sort of good-cop/bad-cop routine, Snake trying to nip off my nose, Angel giving me woolly kisses on the cheek.

Then he swiveled back to face my mom and said, "I've missed you, angel," apparently forgetting that was the name of one of his socks.

"Right," she said. "Sure you have." But she was pleased.

He told her that he was sober, that he'd been working up north in the tar sands, that he'd driven down just to see her. And now I imagine that was the truth, or part of it. The other part was maybe that he'd been living with a woman up there and things had gone bad with her. Or maybe he'd screwed up at work. Or maybe he'd been staying with his aunt in Cold Lake and had grown tired of her rules. Or maybe, probably, he'd driven from Fort Mac to Calgary, partied for a month, and when he sobered up, realized he couldn't afford to fix the car's heater and couldn't face that cold drive again.

In any case, my mom decided to believe his story. So I still don't know where he'd been or where he went after. I still don't know much more than I knew then, which was only what I'd been told: that he was my dad.

Maybe my mom had boyfriends before—I have vague memories of men in the house, men who were nice to me, one who even fixed up a bike and taught me to ride it—but I'd never understood they were boyfriends. They'd simply been around until they weren't around anymore, and I didn't miss them.

But with my dad, it was different. I couldn't stop staring at him. It was like looking in a mirror, or like someone had shown up wearing my face like a mask. Of course, it was distorted: his cheekbones were more pronounced; his hair was a sandy brown instead of blond; he had purple bags under his eyes that looked like bruises, and the kind of easy smile that wins friends. I couldn't keep my eyes off him and neither could my mom.

She wasn't stupid enough to let him live with us, so he rented a room nearby. She wanted me to get used to having my dad around, and she wanted him to prove himself. To do that, he attended AA meetings every week. He walked east from our place along Bowness Road, to what used to be a storefront and is now one room, almost invisible between the Chinese diner and the CrossFit gym. There's no sign on the front, only white blinds that are always kept closed. Inside it's cold, especially in winter, so people keep their coats on. The walls are covered in posters that remind you of the 12 Steps and the Serenity Prayer, that three-line song you're supposed to sing to yourself.

This is not a place I need to imagine; I know it well. I go there myself now, three times a week.

When my dad wasn't at meetings, he worked at the Safeway down the street, stocking shelves. And when he wasn't working, he and I played *Guitar Hero*, or he helped me with my homework so it would get done faster and we could play more *Guitar Hero*. My mom worked at a doctor's office, doing paperwork and answering phones, and she was good at her job, efficient and appreciated. The doctor she worked for, Carolyn, always said she couldn't live without my mother and so paid her decently and bought me books for Christmas. I had recently started grade four, where I was learning to read in French.

What I mean is, there was a rhythm to our life. We were a family.

In the same way I picked up new words at school—*grenouille, haricot, vêtement*—I collected information about my dad. He liked to watch sitcoms. He did thirty push-ups every morning. He sang all the time—pop or country, any little tune that got stuck in his head. His voice was thin and watery, like mine turned out to be, but still somehow charming.

He taught me how to flip a plate, cradling it on my flat palm, tossing it in the air, then catching it right-side up. He invented stories for me before bed, stories about a boy who had the same name as me but who was much braver and who, each night, *saved the entire world from total destruction*! And when Halloween rolled around, he bought me a Transformers costume from Safeway— how did he know that's what I wanted to be?—and offered to take me trick-or-treating. The past couple of years I'd gone with my friends Justin and Louie, but this year I wanted to go with my dad instead. He said his dad had always taken him out on Halloween and they went house to house until they had so much candy they could hardly carry it home.

"What's your favorite chocolate bar?" he asked.

"Mars," I said. "And Reese's. And Skor."

"Right on." He nodded. "Me too."

The costume was the wrong size. My dad had forgotten that it would be cold at the end of October and I would need to fit my bulky coat and snow pants underneath. Also, he'd been right about me wanting to be a Transformer, but he'd bought me the dark Megatron outfit, and I didn't want to be a bad guy, no matter how powerful the Decepticons were. I wanted the red Optimus Prime costume. So my mom exchanged the suit for a larger size, in red, though it was still too short in the legs.

I looked forward to Halloween with a sense of thrilled fear. Thrill because I'd never been on an outing alone with the guy who was apparently my dad, but more importantly, because I wanted candy. I wanted to carry a gigantic bag of it home. Then I wanted to look at it, sort it, anticipate it. And when I ate it, I wanted to eat it all at once—I wanted my hands and face to be sticky from sugar. I wanted, wanted, wanted.

Fear because I didn't really believe my dad would still be here when Halloween came. It was two weeks away, and two weeks was forever.

In the meantime, he went to meetings the way some people go to church. He had to carry a book around like it was a Bible and he had to walk himself through the 12 Steps. He liked to joke that the first step was easy—all he had to do was admit he was a fuck-up—but he was stuck on number two. "Is there a power greater than myself?" he said, lifting soup cans like dumbbells, pretending to strain his arms. "Seriously, I'm just supposed to believe in God?"

"God as you understand him," said my mom.

"Yeah, yeah." He sniffed at her ear and licked the side of her face like he was a puppy. "Dog as I understand him."

Halloween finally came and my dad was still around. I put on my snowsuit, the costume, the plastic mask, and got my mom to paint the visible part of my face with red face paint. She took pictures and my dad pretended not to recognize me. "Who are you?" he said, spinning around. "Where's Davy?"

And then the two of us were outside, crunching over snow-covered sidewalks. I had an empty pillowcase and was ready to fill it to the top with candy, ready to walk all night if I had to. First we went next door, to the house that belonged to Tracy and Rob and their baby girl. They'd dressed their baby as a bumblebee.

"What are you?" said Tracy, as the bumblebee drooled on her shoulder.

"He is Optimus Prime," said my dad. "Leader of the Autobots." The way he said it made it feel true.

"Aw, so cute!" said Tracy.

"Cool," said Rob, and tossed me a Snickers bar.

We went to a few more houses, and passed other kids—a zombie and a duck, a kid with a bullet hole in his forehead, a group of shivering and giggling Spice Girls who looked too old to be trick-or-treating. My mask kept sliding down my face, making it impossible for me to see. I slipped on the ice a couple of times but my dad caught me before I fell.

"How about I hang on to that for you?" he said.

"But then no one'll know who I am."

"I just don't want you to break your face, buddy."

At the next house, a teenage girl answered the door. "What are you?" she asked, and I waited for my dad to say that thing about me being the leader of the Autobots, but he didn't say it.

"I'm a Transformer," I said.

"Oh. Yeah." She gave me four packages of Twizzlers. "I need this stuff out of the house," she said. "We bought way too much and I'll just eat it all."

I gave my dad one of the Twizzler packs and he ate the whole thing in less than a minute. Then we crossed the bridge and walked along the street that backed onto the river.

"There's more distance between the houses here," my dad explained. "But it's worth it 'cause these people are loaded."

At the first place I got a full-sized Oh Henry! bar, and my dad gave me a nod. "See?" he whispered. Then we went to the next house, a tall modern-looking place where all the windows were dark.

"There's no one home," I said.

My dad rang the doorbell anyway—he was nothing if not hopeful—and we yelled, *Trick or treat!* in unison. We waited but no one came.

And maybe it was that street, or bad luck, or coincidence, but the next three houses we tried, it was the same thing: no one opened the door.

At the third house, a small bungalow set far back from the

street, my dad rang the doorbell three times. Most of the houses here were big, new in-fills, but this place looked like it had sat on that flat stretch of snow for fifty years.

My dad gave up on the bell and knocked hard enough to rattle the door's little moon-shaped window.

"What the hell?" He kicked snow onto the freshly shoveled driveway. "Losers."

"Maybe they're at the mall. I think some kids go 'cause the stores give out candy."

"See, that's just depressing. That's something I wish you hadn't told me."

I didn't understand—the mall seemed fine to me. My toes and the tips of my ears were going numb, my pillowcase was nearly empty, and my dad's face had taken on a dark expression. It's hard to describe what that looked like exactly, only how it made me feel: like my stomach was a sock turning itself inside out.

"Maybe we should try the next place," I said.

"They're probably in there." He put his face against the bungalow's window. "With the fucking lights turned off."

A distorted version of his face, hollowed and skeleton-like, was reflected back in the glass.

"Dad?" I didn't usually call him that—I called him Paul because that's how he'd been introduced. "I'm getting cold."

He stood with his face pressed to the glass and I could tell he wasn't breathing because the window wasn't fogging up. "Hey!" he yelled. "I got my kid out here!"

I expected lights to come on, someone to open the door. I expected to get in trouble. But nothing happened.

"You know what?" he said. "Screw this."

He took my hand and we walked down the middle of the street, me trying to keep up, skidding alongside him in my boots. My mask slipped down again and I nearly fell.

"Jesus Christ." He ripped it off my face. "Give me that."

I thought we were going home but we passed right by our street and headed toward the strip mall, to the warm light of the grocery store where he worked. We slid across the icy parking lot and in through the chugging automatic doors.

The heat inside made my numbed ears sting. One of the cashiers, a young woman with dark hair, waved to my dad and said, "Couldn't stay away, huh?"

He gave her a wink. "Not from you."

Then he led me to what my mom called the "junk aisle," a wonderland she hardly ever let me visit. Rows of two-liter bottles of pop gleamed—cream soda, Orange Crush, Dr Pepper—and beyond that was the special section for Halloween candy. There were my favorites: Mars and Reese's and Skor. And there were Kit Kat, Coffee Crisp, Crunchie. And Rolo, Wonderbar, Bounty, Crispy Crunch, Caramilk, Smarties, Glosettes, Tootsie Rolls, Rockets, Nibs, Nerds, Candy Corn, Zombie Bites, jelly beans, jaw-breakers, Bazooka Joe, Hubba Bubba, Hershey's Kisses, and gum-mies shaped like bears, gummies shaped like skulls, gummies shaped like severed toes. I was in heaven. I was saved.

"What'll it be?" asked my dad. "I'll get you anything you like." He sounded magnanimous, and probably felt it too. He knew that tomorrow all this would be 50 percent off. He swept his arm out like he was in showbiz. "Anything you want."

I looked up at all the glossy packages like someone who'd seen the face of God. "Just one?"

"You little shit." He ruffled my hair like a TV dad. "You can have two if you want. But stay here, okay? I'll be right back."

It didn't cross my mind then that he might go outside through that stuttering automatic door and skid across the parking lot to the Liquor Barn. And anyway, he didn't do that. He just went to the row of fridges at the back of the store and picked up a dozen eggs. Then he must have wandered around picking up other things and putting them in a basket: blackstrap molasses, a liter of milk, a bottle of dish soap, and half a dozen ripe bananas. "You ready?" he said when he returned.

I wasn't even close. I wanted time to weigh my options but I knew there was something girly about hesitating, so I grabbed a bag of Mars Bars and one of Glosettes. I didn't even like Glosettes. Does anyone like Glosettes?

He took my hand again and we went through the till. We were served by Stacy, the girl who'd waved when he came in. "Making a cake?" she asked when my dad unloaded his basket.

"You bet," he said. "I'm good in the kitchen, you know."

"As if." She laughed, brushing our items over her scanner. "Paper or plastic?" She spoke in the pleasant, lilting voice she would have used with a normal customer. "Find everything you were looking for today?"

"Everything I've ever wanted," said my dad.

She turned to me. "I like your costume, honey." She smiled, and there was a small diamond—at the time I thought it was real—glued to one of her front teeth. "What are you?"

Before I could answer, she uttered a little squeal and turned back to my dad. "Oh, my god, is this your son? Oh, my god. He's *so* cute."

"He's a good kid."

"Holy shit, he looks just like you."

When we left the store, I assumed we'd go home—I actually believed he would bake a cake. I ate three Mars Bars as we walked and wondered if I could trade my Glosettes for better stuff the next day at school. But then we passed our street again, crossed the bridge, walked along the river. "Where are we going?" I said.

"Where do you think?"

We stopped in front of that small, dark bungalow.

"They don't like Halloween, they don't give out candy, fuck them," said my dad. He took the carton out of the bag, opened it, and revealed twelve eggs that glowed under the streetlights, white as new snow. "You first."

I fumbled an egg out of the cardboard carton, difficult because of my mitts. I held it for a second, felt its weight in my hand. I wasn't athletic, never played on any sports teams. And I'd never done anything that might get me in trouble before. It's not that I was better than anyone else, just that my mom was on her own and I understood that it was my job to make her life easier.

"What if they're home?" I said.

"They're not home."

"But what if?"

"Did you hear what I just said?"

I shifted my weight from one boot to the other. I didn't want to throw the egg. I wanted to throw the egg.

"Hit the door," said my dad. "So they see it first thing."

They. I wondered who *they* were. An old woman who lived alone with her little dog? A couple like Tracy and Rob? A family? A mom and a dad and a kid?

Fuck them.

I pulled my arm back and threw the egg. But it landed short of the door and splattered on the driveway.

"What the hell was that?" said my dad.

I told myself not to cry. I imagined the yolk would freeze to the cement and stay there all winter, a reminder of my failure. *Don't cry, don't cry.*

My dad took an egg and flung it at the door, hit it square on. I hated him for a second and I also thought he was the coolest guy ever. He picked up another egg, tossed it to me, and I managed to catch it.

"Okay, buddy." He crouched down so our faces were pressed together. "Don't think so hard. Just chuck it."

I threw as hard as I could, made a little grunting noise in my throat. I missed the door but the egg hit the house's siding and my dad let out a whoop. "There you go!" He danced a little jig, kicking his thin legs in the air. "That's my boy!"

He threw another, I threw another—again and again, the eggs cracked against the window, slid down the panes, hit the garage door. One egg I threw landed in a snowdrift and remained intact. "Don't worry!" said my dad, laughing like a lunatic. "That's cool 'cause it'll freeze and crack, then when the snow melts it'll leak all over the grass. A little delayed fuck-you."

When the eggs were gone, he took out the molasses, unscrewed the cap, and we poured it all over the front porch. "They'll never get this stuff off their shoes," he said. We poured the entire liter of milk into the mailbox, then closed the lid. Hopefully it won't freeze, my dad explained, and tomorrow the mail will get soaked. We squeezed the dish soap over the thin layer of frost that covered the walkway, to make it more slippery. Then we dropped the bananas on the driveway and jumped on them. "Bam! Bam!" we yelled as they leapt out of their skins.

I now pictured the people who lived there as Decepticons, dark machinery. "I can take them!" I screamed, stomping through the yard. "I am Optimus Prime!"

I picked up some snow, crushed it into a ball, and threw it at the house. My dad threw some too, but it was my idea to scoop up gravel and rocks from the road to use in our snowballs, it was my idea to aim for that little moon-shaped window, it was me who screamed, *Get them! Kill them!*, and it was me, it was definitely me, who threw the chunk of snow and stones and ice that shattered the window.

I imagine that my parents met at a karaoke bar. I wish it were somewhere else, somewhere that wasn't so dark and stupid, but that's all I can see. I imagine that my dad saw my mom onstage, a woman in a green dress, sweat stains under her arms. And that when she sang "Dust on the Bottle" or "Strawberry Wine," he fell in love. She held the microphone in both her hands, tipsy and nervous, and it seemed to him she would save him. He bought her a drink, they kissed, and they danced to "I Think We're Alone Now" performed by a group of men in business suits. They danced the way I saw them dance in the kitchen, one of his hands in her sweat-dampened hair and the other on the curve of her lower back.

I imagine that's their story, though really it's mine. It happened to me one night, when I was twenty. I went home with the girl in the green dress. She had dark, messy hair and a body that looked strong but wrecked. A faded tattoo around her bicep, freckles on her shoulders from too much sun, fake breasts she must have got years ago and that now hung heavily and incongruously from her frame. She was nothing like my mom, but when I was drinking, I was everything like my dad. Prone to singing, dancing, lying. I pretended to be Elvis, pretended to be a shotput thrower, pretended to be a little kid. The girl in the green dress found me funny. She kept giggling and saying, "You're funny."

When we got to her house, I sat on the couch and she poured us each a glass of wine, then she walked across the room and straddled my lap between her ropy thighs. I reached under her green dress and found she wasn't wearing underwear. It was like going to put your hand on a woman's breast, expecting the lace and wire of a brassiere, and finding instead that you've clasped her bare, beating heart.

I'd asked her name at the bar, but it was Kylie or Kyla, something I'd instantly forgotten. Didn't matter because now I believed she would save me. I felt her coarse hair, the heat between her legs, and I said, "Oh, God," in a voice that sounded like prayer.

When I was nine and I broke that window, I stood there with my mouth open, my breath visible in the cold.

"Holy shit," said my dad. I dropped back into a snowbank and rolled around, snow sticking to my hair. I couldn't stop laughing—I was drunk from the sugar and the destruction. And I was dizzy with love. I loved my dad.

He grabbed me by the shoulders and shook me. "Hey. Hey, hey, hey, buddy. Enough now, okay?"

Then he picked me up, slung me over his shoulder, and ran with me down the street to the riverbank, to the place where families have picnics and teenagers deal drugs. He put me back on the ground, brushed the snow off my costume.

"Listen," he said. "Don't tell your mom, okay?"

"Yeah, I know." And that was true. I already knew there were plenty of things you couldn't tell women, but hadn't yet learned that women always find out anyway. That usually they know even before you do, even before they do.

"You're a good kid, Davy," he said. He had that dark look again. I guess revenge is a lot like addiction—the buzz never lasts.

He walked a few steps away and sat on a bench that faced the river. He leaned back and sang that song that was always stuck in his head. *She was a rare thing, fine as a bee's wing. So fine a breath of wind might blow her away.*

I followed and sat beside him. I wondered who he was singing about—my mom was blond and big-boned, nothing fragile about her. The only fine-boned thing around here was him. And, I suppose, me.

"How do you understand God, Davy?" he said. "What do they teach you about it in school?"

"Nothing." I had no idea what he was talking about. I also wondered if he had ever gone to school.

"They should teach you something."

"My mask," I said, suddenly realizing that neither of us had it.

He looked around like it might be at his feet. "Must have dropped it back there. Sorry about that."

I worried someone would see it lying on the lawn, would trace it back to me. I felt myself sweating in my costume. "Will someone find it?"

"Sure, maybe." He put his arm around me. "Don't worry about it. I'll get you a new one."

I didn't believe him. *Don't cry*, I told myself.

"Goddamn, it is cold out." He rubbed his hands together. "Did I tell you about the time I drove from Fort Mac to Calgary with no heater? Socks on my hands, a bottle of bourbon at my feet." It was almost the same story he'd told my mom when he first arrived, a story that sounded like a folk song. "Alcohol does not keep you warm," he said. "That is a myth."

I didn't say anything and it seemed like we sat there a long time, me kicking my legs through the air and him humming that tune to himself.

"Can we go home soon?" I said.

He looked at me as though surprised I was there, as though he'd forgotten I existed. Or maybe it was the word *home*. Maybe he didn't think of it that way.

My dad and I walked back to the house holding hands and my mom met us at the door. She threw her arms around us, me first, then him. "How was it?" She peered happily and worriedly into my painted face. "You had a good time?"

She didn't notice that I'd lost my mask and I guess she felt he'd proved himself, because that month she let him move in with us. He stayed almost a year. And when he left the next September, I missed him and believed it was my fault, but I didn't cry about it. A few years later, I did what all teenagers do, and I hated him. Then I tried to become him. Now he calls every once in a while and we talk like friends, just two men with the same name.

I am less in need of him now that I know Ken, my sponsor at AA. For a while there, Ken phoned every morning and every night to check in on me. I cried to him like a lost child—he has seen me when things were bad, way worse than anything my girlfriend has seen.

For years, Ken and I met every week, at a coffee shop or sometimes at the laundromat near my place. On days when I didn't want to talk, when I was tired of all that moral inventory, we played Go Fish while my clothes spun in the dryers. Or we drove around and I sang along to the radio, Ken telling me I was lucky to be a decent guy 'cause I sure couldn't carry a tune.

Ken's getting older now and he has a bad heart, so these days I'm the one who calls to check in. I wish he didn't smoke so much and he wishes he'd been there when his daughter was a kid. Neither one of us talks about God or anything of that nature, neither one of us uses the word *love*. But before we hang up we say to each other, "Have a good day, buddy," and that always helps.

Welcome to Paradise

We planned to spend the summer making boys fall in love with us. We would go down, get some, hook up. We'd never done any of these things. We'd never done anything. We'd never even been kissed.

"But I've been this close," said Lielle, her face an inch from mine, so near I could smell her watermelon lip gloss.

We were in Lielle's backyard, at the bottom of the pool that her dad never bothered to fill. The tank sat like a huge, mint-green bowl behind the house and we were always in the deep end. I don't have any photos of that summer, but I imagine I looked wide-eyed and flayed—every minute I spent with Lielle, in our universe of two, felt scorching, like the sun was burning off a layer of my skin. We drank iced tea mixed from crystals, bleached streaks in our hair with Sun-In. It was August and the days stretched out as empty as that pool. Sometimes I just lay against the tile and listened while Lielle practiced swearing in English.

"To *be* fucked or *get* fucked?"

"Either," I said. "Both."

We longed to live together, in our own house, in another country. I suggested Israel because Lielle spoke the language and I'd heard about floating in the Dead Sea. But Lielle said the Dead Sea was just a tourist trap, and the mineral crystals cut the soles of your feet, and the salt water stung your crotch. Not Israel, she said. That's boring. Somewhere completely amazing like India or Greece. Someplace where we could buy a huge house just for us. "We'll paint the walls gold," said Lielle.

"And we'll have a pet tiger," I said. "To guard the door."

We were fourteen, and we meant it. Or at least I did. But since we didn't have our own house, we hung out in the suburban homes we shared with our parents—me with my mother and her with her father. Lielle's house, with its three-car garage and floor-to-ceiling windows, was nearly always empty. Her mother lived in a settlement in the West Bank, apparently with a woman. Her dad was opening a new dental practice and was hardly home. He hadn't brought much to Canada after his divorce and hadn't had the time or inclination to buy chairs or tables or cushions once he'd arrived. Every wall was a glaring white.

Even in her own room, Lielle hadn't put up any posters. The walls of my room were pocked with holes from the pins I'd used to display posters of cats snuggling, Janis Joplin in lopsided sunglasses, Johnny Depp as Edward Scissorhands. It was my own pop-culture autobiography, as embarrassing now as a collection of bad tattoos. Lielle's room, absent of calicos and movie stars, seemed bereft—but also bright, astonishing.

When this emptiness got to us, we would climb each sun-hot rung of the pool's ladder and wander from the big, gated houses of Lielle's neighborhood. We hopped on the CTrain for a few stops, not bothering to buy tickets, then walked the winding streets, past playgrounds and grocery stores and gas stations. We crossed rushing city highways, teetered along medians in the road, found ourselves calf-deep in the yellow prairie grass that grew between Calgary's subdivisions. Drunk from the sun, we rested on someone's lawn, sprawled under a weeping willow. I taught Lielle more words. *Shit-head, shit-faced, shit-talk, shit-storm.*

When we arrived at my house, with its cluttered rooms and full fridge and the bossy notes my mother left me on the kitchen counter, it was like a promised land. We always had a snack, eating whatever we could see. Once we shared an entire tub of ice cream and passed a carton of orange juice back and forth. Then we lay on the soft, well-treaded broadloom, our arms wrapped around each other. Lielle breathed warmly on my neck and I could smell her watermelon lip gloss. She said, "Good night, shit-face," and we fell asleep.

At my house, we would sleep, eat, draw elaborate blueprints for the house we'd one day share, or go for walks. *Going for a walk* was code for going to the strip mall to smoke cigarettes and hit on the Little Caesars Pizza delivery guys. Cody and Brodie. Their rolled-up sleeves and tattooed biceps seemed to embody masculinity and we adored them obsessively—at least, Lielle did.

In preparation for seeing them, we sat on the edge of the bathtub and shaved our legs, then faced the mirror and applied Wet 'n' Wild eye shadows and flavored lip glosses. Then we put on shorts and cropped tops—Lielle always lent me her clothes—and strolled down the back alley behind Little Caesars like we hung out beside Dumpsters all the time. We must have done this a dozen times, but the day I remember most was the one that led to our crimes.

Cody and Brodie were in the parking lot, smoking and sitting on flimsy chairs they propped against a wall scrawled with graffiti. A girl named *Kat* had tagged her name everywhere and her scribbles were faded, almost illegible, a ghost of a presence. *Kat was here.*

"Hey." Lielle did most of the talking, her harsh accent making her seem older. "What's up?"

"I'll show you what's up." Cody wore a baseball cap and the brim shadowed the top part of his face—it was impossible not to watch his mouth when he talked. "Come sit on my lap."

Brodie just nodded and laughed at whatever Cody said. He didn't wear a cap and had a face like a movie star—all cheekbones—and a braid that hung down his back.

They made pizza deliveries in their own beat-up vehicles— Cody drove a Pontiac Sunbird and Brodie a pickup. We longed for one of them to offer us a ride somewhere—anywhere—as this would have given us an adventure to dissect for weeks. But Cody and Brodie mostly ignored us. They talked to each other in a mysterious shorthand or wrestled in the blinding sun, gripping each other by the waist and neck, tugging at each other's shirts.

"I can take you, I can take you," Cody said—he was eighteen, younger than his friend—and he gave Brodie a kick on the shin and called him a *dirty Indian*.

"What'd you say, white boy?" Brodie put Cody in a headlock and they tumbled to the pavement, scraping their knees, grappling and grunting, scratching each other until they bled.

"Oh, my god!" Lielle giggled. "Don't hurt each other!"

We believed they were showing off for us, proving their strength. We were pretty sure Cody liked Lielle and Brodie liked me. When they finished fighting, Lielle asked Cody if we could bum cigarettes off him, and he tossed his pack over to us.

Brodie rolled his own and never shared, but once he used his Zippo to light my cigarette. He leaned toward me, the flame cradled in big, callused hands.

"Thanks."

"No problem," he said. "So what's your name?"

"Hannah."

"Hannah-banana," Cody interrupted, smiling in that mocking way. "I like your yellow hair."

The first puffs always made me dizzy, but so did the way Cody and Brodie appraised me, smoke curling from their mouths. It occurred to me that maybe I was the pretty one, the one they might want.

"How old are you, Hannah-banana?" asked Cody.

"Can we go?" said Lielle.

"Why?" he said. "Where do you have to be?"

Then she turned and walked away, her cigarette dropping ash on the ground. I stayed where I was, leaning against the wall, and contemplated for an entire second the possibility that I might not follow her. Then I ran to catch up.

It was midafternoon, the hottest part of the day. My tank top stuck to my skin and my shorts were so tight I worried they'd give me a yeast infection. The streets were empty—it was Wednesday and most people were at work, in some other universe of air-conditioned cubicles and elevators and water coolers. The asphalt baked in the sun and smelled of tar. Most of the lawns we passed were crisp and brown. Others were freakishly green: aerated and fertilized, sprinklers spraying them all day.

"I'm thirsty," I said. "Let's go back to my house."

"I'm sick of your house." Lielle kicked at the gravel along the edge of the road. "Let's go to someone else's house."

"Whose?"

"Fuck if I care," she said, using the vocabulary I'd taught her. "Anyone's."

We had a month before high school started, a month before we'd be pulled apart: Lielle would attend a private school on the other side of the city and I would take the bus to public school. And after high school, Lielle would go back to Israel for two years to serve in the IDF. Her mother had been a junior officer in the Israeli army, and Lielle had shown me a photograph of her mom as a young woman in uniform, a beret pinned to her shoulder, a gun gripped in her hands. I tried to imagine myself, with my bony elbows and tangled hair, serving in the Canadian army. Or my mother—who always had laundry fluff clinging to her sweaters—holding a gun.

"What if you die?" I asked.

"Yes." Lielle nodded. "A person can die."

Between us, there was an unarticulated promise to remain best friends—despite high school, despite the army, despite death. But promises can be forgotten. We needed something—an adventure, a tragedy—to wed us together.

We walked down the street awake to possibilities. Most houses in my neighborhood were one or two stories, with beige or a sickly pink siding that was fashionable. Some people had swing sets on their arid lawns, or basketball nets bolted above the driveways.

We passed houses with cars parked out front or where windows and blinds were open. We wanted places that seemed closed up, empty and dark. Once we looked for them, they appeared, blooming like bruises on the bright skin of the street.

We found it, as perfect as though it had been promised us.

The curtains were drawn closed, the windows shut, the driveway a bare slap of concrete. It was a single-level, with faded green siding and a red door. Marigolds grew out front—heavy on their stalks, bowing as though to welcome us.

We walked by twice to be sure the place was empty. Without speaking, Lielle and I turned a corner and took the unpaved back alley. Behind the house was a wooden fence with a gate. Easy to unlatch.

We were trespassing already, in this backyard covered with patchy grass, the ground dusty and pale from lack of watering. Lettuce was going to seed, its edges burned from the heat. Maybe the owners had gone on holidays—to a cabin, or to visit family in another city, or to somewhere exotic like Greece or Morocco. I mouthed the word *Morocco* under my breath, because I liked the way its syllables folded into one another.

"What?" whispered Lielle.

"Nothing."

A stone path cut through the yard to the back porch. We tried the door: locked. We paused on the little cement stoop. Lielle said, "Let's try the windows."

She stood on her toes to reach the first-floor panes but they were locked. Then she tried the basement window. I was beside her, saying, "Oh, shit, oh, shit, oh, shit," even though I didn't quite believe we'd go through with it.

The basement window slid open.

"Rip the screen." I was suddenly, briefly courageous. "Use this." I took my key from my pocket and thought of my house—with iced tea in the fridge, Oreos in the cupboard, and innumerable other reasons not to break the law.

Lielle used the key to puncture a hole in the mosquito screen, then tore through it in a jagged line. She crouched in front of the window. "Do you hear an alarm?"

"No."

"A dog?"

"No."

"Okay." She nodded toward the gash in the screen. "You go."

"Why me?"

"I found the way in. It's your turn."

I wanted to burst into tears. I wanted to smack her face. I wanted, most of all, to go home. But I couldn't do that now—not in *this* now, the present we'd so recently created for ourselves.

"Okay." I took a breath like I was about to dive into deep water, then slid through the window feet-first. My T-shirt rode up and the ledge scratched the skin on my ribs.

"Come on." Lielle was hopping from one foot to the other like she had to pee. "Hurry up."

"Will you relax?" I shimmied the rest of the way through the window, and the torn ends of the mosquito screen scraped the back of my neck and caught my hair. I landed on something soft that broke my fall, a box that seemed to contain clothes or blankets. I blinked, willing my eyes to adjust to the dark. "I'm in!" I called to Lielle, but there was no answer.

My hands reached out and felt the cold cement floor. I stood up, brushed myself off, tried to stand on the box—of towels? winter jackets?—to see back out into the fresh air, the sunlight. The cardboard sank again under my weight and I couldn't reach the window ledge. "I'm in!" I yelled louder.

Nothing.

I sank down in the dark and imagined that box contained a yellowing wedding dress, or a wig collection, or the pelts of animals that the owner of the house had killed and skinned. The basement was cold and quiet. I shivered. "Lielle?" I whispered.

Then her head—shadowed and back-lit by daylight, ghostly

in the underground dark—appeared through the window above me. "What are you doing?"

"Where were you?"

"I was waiting for you at the back door." She said this slowly, like I was the one who spoke English as a second language. "Go upstairs and unlock it."

"I'm not going upstairs to unlock the door."

"That's the way it's done. Don't you watch TV?"

"I am not opening the fucking door for you. I can hardly see anything."

Her head disappeared and I was again abandoned. I was about to scream when her legs came through the window, then her hips. She shimmied through and fell on top of me, her elbow knocking me in the face.

"Jesus, *ow.*"

"Sorry."

She was, without realizing it, holding my hand. Our clammy skin stuck us together—we were married in our fear. We walked through the basement like that, tripping over boxes and old unplugged lamps and other objects covered in dust, stuff I couldn't distinguish. We knocked things over and whispered, "What-was-that-*oh-my-god*-what-was-that?" We found a narrow staircase and climbed it on our hands and knees.

When we opened the door at the top of the stairs, we were in the kitchen. The room was dim because the blinds were drawn, maybe to keep out the heat. Lielle let go of my hand, felt her way along the wall, and switched on a light. "Ta-da!" she said.

We burst out laughing. I bent over and clutched at my crotch—thought I'd pee myself—and that made us laugh more. We were hysterical, terrified.

When we caught our breath, I looked around the kitchen. The marigolds out front had led me to expect something homey, a kitchen that belonged to an elderly couple, maybe, like my neighbors, the Korens, who had pictures of their nieces and nephews on the fridge, meat in the freezer, cups and saucers for tea in a china cabinet.

But this kitchen—this kitchen belonged to someone who lived alone. Sunlight dish detergent by the sink. Beige linoleum designed to look like tile. The radio tuned to Country 105, emitting a grainy background hum. A grimy coffee percolator on the counter and one spider plant (dead) on the windowsill. On the fridge was a magnet that read *Welcome to paradise!* with an off-kilter drawing of a palm tree. The magnet didn't affix anything to the fridge. It sat alone on that white expanse.

Lielle turned on the tap, then left the water running and trailed her hand along the counter. "This place is weird." Her voice was full of excitement and a dangerous, creeping disappointment. "What do we do now?"

I was still thirsty, so I opened the fridge. Inside there was a bottle of French's mustard, half a loaf of bread, a container of store-bought lemon icing, and a liter of 2 percent milk. I grabbed that, even though I didn't like milk. Usually it grossed me out: the creamy taste, the white it left at the corners of my mouth, that smell of rot and reproduction. At home, I always refused it. But there—in that strange, sad, thrilling house—I drank it straight from the carton.

Even now I like ghost towns and abandoned houses, places that seem to be haunted, buildings with dark, locked rooms. While visiting friends and family, I find myself assessing their homes in terms of security. I look for open windows. I examine door hinges and latches and the flimsy locks on gates. I look for a way in. When I find it, I look for a way out.

My partner joked that this habit came in handy when we were looking to buy our own place. "She's an expert in home security," Sasha said to our realtor, keeping a straight face.

And our daughter, the child who came later, the child I kept— *kept*, as though anyone ever belongs to anyone else. We try to give her privacy. Though I once went through her pockets and opened her desk drawers. This was out of genuine concern, motherly instinct, but it sickened me. After, I tried to put everything back the way it was, the way she had it. As unchanged—undamaged— as possible.

I have no idea how long Lielle and I were in that house with its empty fridge and dirty countertops. Probably less than ten minutes. We went out the back door, and left the milk on the counter, the light on, the tap running. My legs felt weak, but as soon as we were outside, I started to run.

We ran until we got to my street, four blocks away, and that's when I threw up. The milk tasted sour in my throat. It landed in a white puddle on the road, looking pure and untouched against the pavement. Lielle wiped my face with her sleeve and said, "You okay?"

My being sick didn't ruin our afternoon. We linked arms and stumbled the rest of the way home like a couple of giddy drunks.

My mom looked up from the mail she was sorting and said, "What's with you two?" then asked if Lielle wanted to stay for dinner.

"Sure," she answered as we pounded up the stairs to my room. "Thanks!"

When we got to my room and shut the door, Lielle said, "Check it out."

From her pocket, she pulled out the palm-tree magnet. It was made of clay, probably bargained for and purchased on a touristy beach. I almost vomited again. I imagined the owner as a man, middle-aged. Softening around the middle, yellow stains under the arms of his buttoned shirts, his yearly vacation planned with care.

"You stole his magnet?" I said.

"Oh, god, Hannah-banana." Lielle gave me a light slap across the face. "*Welcome*," she said, "*to paradise!*"

And that was enough to pull me back in. For Lielle's sake, and for mine, I laughed along with her. And that's what we called it, our code for breaking in: going to paradise.

A few years later, Lielle served in the IDF. She liked basic training: sleeping in a tent, learning to shoot a gun. She emailed me a photo of her with two girls on either side, all of them in the same mud-green uniform. They were laughing and had their arms around each other. One of the girls had acne and aviator sunglasses and blew a kiss to the camera.

The army is like summer camp, Lielle wrote, *except with guns.*

She told me that the food was decent. That she now had muscles she hadn't realized existed. That an acquaintance of hers, a boy she'd kissed on a beach in Eilat, was dead.

Then I didn't hear from her for months, until she wrote to say that she was in Intelligence, doing observation. She had her own shift and her own turf: day after day, she watched four hundred meters of the security wall on a closed-circuit monitor. *My eyes get dry cause I forget to blink.* The same Gaza streets, the same faces on a grainy screen. She said her job reminded her of "going to paradise." (*Remember that? I can't believe we did that.*) She told me she'd given nicknames to the people she saw every day—old women in headscarves, boys playing soccer—even though her supervisor had warned her not to become attached.

She said she was having trouble sleeping now. She said she was getting *so fat*. She said she hoped to travel when her army stint was done. *Maybe India*, she said, *or something*.

We mostly limited our crime spree to my neighborhood, with its bungalows separated by low hedges and easy-to-hop fences. It was trusting and well tended. People had small lawns and friendly neighbors. There was always an unlocked window or a key under a mat.

We learned to assess, in seconds and without discussing it, which houses were good targets and which to avoid. We learned to pick locks using bobby pins and a small screwdriver. We learned that people forget to secure their back doors, or their garage doors, or their balconies. We learned that the body is malleable when it needs to be: it can fit through tight spaces, reach high ledges. We weren't so unlike *Kat*, the girl who'd graffitied her name behind Little Caesars. We too wanted to leave a mark, to own something by wrecking it. That desire was satisfied every time we climbed through a window or jimmied open a door, every time we walked in and took a breath of someone's private air.

I taught Lielle the word *shit-mix* and we tasted every bottle of liquor that people kept in their homes. Amaretto, Limoncello, scotch, vodka, gin, crème de menthe. Once we found some weed and a pipe, but the high just made us more paranoid than usual. Lielle thought the owners of the house were hiding behind the couch, which didn't seem far-fetched at all. Even empty houses feel occupied. And once, it did happen that a man emerged from the bathroom, a towel around his waist, in a house we'd assumed was empty. This was the only time we broke into a house in Lielle's neighborhood. The place was practically a mansion, the floors covered with lush white carpet that muffled every step.

"Hey," said the guy, when he saw us jumping on his bed.

For each spring I took on his mattress, I noticed something about him: bulky shoulders, tufts of hair around his nipples, moisture streaking down his freshly shaved face. A face distorted by rage, warped like I was looking at him from underwater.

"Hi," said Lielle, cheerful, as though we belonged there.

My insides were liquid. He would call the police; I would be arrested; my mom would have to pick me up from the station. But then Lielle grabbed my shirt and yelled, "Run!" and we leapt off the bed, made it out the door and down the stairs, outside, back toward the safety of the empty pool.

"Fucking kids!" we heard the guy yell as we crashed down his staircase. "You stealing, fucking kids—"

He was wrong. Stealing wasn't the point, though Lielle did take something from every house we broke into. She never stole electronics or CDs or jewelry or money. She took something personal. A postcard. A miniature spoon from Disneyland. A green button torn off a coat. A family photo. A tiny vial of perfume. She kept these things in her bedroom, on her desk or hanging from her walls.

I never stole anything. That was my one rule. I looked at the pictures that people kept in frames or in piles at the back of desk drawers. I ate their food, lay in their beds, tried on their clothes. I sat on their couches, watched their televisions, spooned yogurt from their containers. I went through their drawers and cupboards and closets, never looking for anything in particular, just looking. I found old tubes of lubricant, pornographic decks of cards, rusted nail clippers, disintegrating Kleenexes, old photographs of children who were perhaps now dead or abandoned or grown up—in any case, not children anymore. I read diaries and letters and overdue credit card bills. I peed in other people's toilets, and washed my hands with the sweet-smelling soap they must have stolen from hotel rooms. I dried my hands on their towels, used their lotion, and studied the medicine in their cabinets.

I learned through all this that inside another person's house, you're on borrowed time, loaned to you from another life. You have to be careful. You have to wear a watch. An hour feels like four minutes. Four minutes feels like a decade. You will begin to believe you live in that house. Its corners, its dust, its furniture, its dishcloths—they will begin to feel like your own.

By the end of August, my neighborhood was put on alert. The police called every house and left a recorded message on people's answering machines: *There have been a series of break-ins in your area. If you notice anything suspicious, please call the Calgary Police Department's nonemergency line.* I listened to the message three times, then hit delete. But my mom heard the news from our neighbors, Mr. and Mrs. Koren.

I'd never known their first names—hadn't even considered that they had first names. They were a retired couple who used to babysit me after school when my mom was at work. Mr. Koren would usually be in the living room, caring for his plants. Mrs. Koren and I sat in the kitchen, which was smoky from her cigarettes and warm from the oven. She usually had a batch of biscuits baking, or a pot of homemade barbecue sauce on the stove.

She always let me pick out a game from the Kids Room, which was on the main floor, wood-paneled, with a shelf of toys and a single bed in the corner. I loved that room, though Mrs. Koren never let me linger in there. She only sent me in to pick out a board game because she liked to play something while she made dinner. She taught me how to play cribbage, euchre, and gin rummy. We also played Snakes and Ladders, Yahtzee, and Monopoly. My favorite was Clue, because you could be any character you wanted; I always picked Colonel Mustard and Mrs. Koren liked to be Miss Scarlet.

Mrs. Koren never let me win the way my mom did. She sat at the plastic kitchen table, ashing her cigarettes into an old canning-jar lid, and said things like, "You think you're smart? You think you can beat this old lady?" She fed me plates of sugar cookies, candies from a dish, and sweet pickles directly from the jar.

When I was too old for a babysitter, my mother occasionally sent me over to the Korens with a banana loaf and instructions to "make sure they're still breathing." She made me shovel their walk when it snowed. Sometimes Mrs. Koren would call through her screen door as I left for school in the mornings. "You should come by someday. We'll play a game of rummy."

I meant to visit her, but never did. After a while, whenever I ran into her, the guilt made me fidget and pretend not to see her. Anyway, the Korens spent less and less time in town because they bought a trailer and used it almost year-round.

But now, years after I'd spoken much to either of them, Mr. Koren was on our front stoop, saying, "Heard anything about those break-ins?"

"Break-ins?" My mom had a distracted, overworked air about her. "What break-ins?"

"The police called." Mr. Koren's hair was whiter than I remembered. "Seems it's a problem around here."

Mr. Koren explained that he and his wife would be out of town for a few weeks and were worried about security while they were away. "Maybe you can keep an eye out." He looked at me when he said it. "I know you're home for the summer."

"Sure." Was I blushing? Blinking too much? Too little? I tried to hold his gaze. "Yeah, no problem."

"Good." Mr. Koren gave me a wink. "Keep your eyes peeled, kiddo."

After the conversation with Mr. Koren, we decided it was too risky—we'd have to stop going to paradise. So we went back to the bottom of the pool, though its green, shimmering walls felt like a cage now. And my house wasn't much better. There we watched daytime TV, particularly talk shows where people exposed their strange, depressing, private lives. We dressed up in the clothes that hung in my mother's closet, wearing her pleated skirts and shoulder-padded sweaters and pointy pumps, then put them back the way we'd found them. We played Would You Rather and Truth or Dare.

"I dare you to take off your shirt and run up the street screaming, *I'm left-handed! I'm left-handed!*" said Lielle.

"I don't want to take off my shirt."

"Why? Because you don't have a bra."

"Because I don't want to."

Lielle tossed her body backward and sprawled on my bed. "Forget it."

I went back to reading a *Cosmo* that Lielle had brought over, learning how to "achieve" glossy hair and skin that has a "summer sparkle." The magazine was mesmerizing even as it made me suicidal.

"Your neighbors' place is so close to your house." Lielle looked through my open bedroom window. "You can see right into their living room."

"'Super Foods, Super Sex,'" I read aloud. *Cosmo* was promising me the biggest, best orgasms of my life, if I incorporated flax and blueberries into my diet.

"Do they ever watch you?" Lielle leaned on the windowsill, her body half outside the house. She was wearing the shorts I'd worn when we went to visit Cody and Brodie, along with a T-shirt she'd altered herself, cutting the neck and sleeves off with scissors. "They can probably see you getting dressed and stuff."

"They're not like that. They're old."

I flipped to an article called "Ten Surprising Ways to Make Him Want More," which advised women to invite their boyfriends out for ice cream and then lick the cone suggestively.

"Maybe we should invite Cody and Brodie for ice cream," I said.

"It seems like they're never home." Lielle stared at the neighbors' brown-sided bungalow. "Do they go away a lot?"

"I guess so."

"Where?"

"I don't know. A swamp or something."

"We should go there."

"To the swamp?"

"No, shit-ass. To their house."

I'd spoken to Mr. Koren once before they left on their trip. He was in their backyard, opening the door and the windows to the trailer, taking the curtains off their rods and shaking them out. "You got to give it air," he said.

I was lying on a towel in the backyard suntanning. When Mr. Koren spoke, I looked up at him through my sunglasses, annoyed by the interruption.

"We go down to the swamp every year," he said. "It's our favorite spot."

"Oh, yeah?" I had no idea what he was talking about. I was bad at geography, and hadn't heard of the Everglades.

"You ever seen a swamp? It has alligators, and flowers of every color, and insects the size of my head." He spoke as though I were a four-year-old child. "They could eat you right up."

I could tell he meant this to be amusing. "Cool," I said, or something like that.

But it didn't matter where they were, or what the name of the swamp was. The point, as Lielle said, was that they weren't home.

"I don't think we should go over there," I said. "I don't think that's a good idea."

"Hello," she said. "The driveway's empty."

"We're not breaking into their place."

"So they live next door. What's the difference?"

What was the difference? Next door or down the road—they were all my neighbors. There was, of course, the sticky issue of the law—but if we'd already broken it a few times, what was once more? And what was the law anyway, if not rules that were decided without my input, rules I'd never agreed to follow?

These were sorts of things I asked myself that summer. And once you start asking those sorts of questions, it's hard to stop.

Getting in was easy. We slid my library card between the door and the frame, and the Korens' lock unlatched. As always, we went to the kitchen first, but were disappointed. The fridge and cupboards were full of what we called old-person food: canned meats, jars of pickles, digestive cookies, flat ginger ale, dried prunes. The liquor cabinet was disappointing too. I'd imagined that Mr. Koren might be a whiskey drinker, but all we found was a dented can of Molson in the fridge. Lielle popped the tab and we passed the beer back and forth. "She used to keep a lot of candy around," I said, but we couldn't find any.

The kitchen table—plastic and meant for a patio—was covered with a handmade table-runner. The brown plaid couch in the living room had an indentation where Mr. Koren sat and watched TV. The lace doilies on the furniture were the same as I remembered, but the house had fewer plants. Mr. Koren used to grow a collection of potted flowers and ferns and exotic things I didn't recognize—so much life that the air felt warm and marshy. Now there were only some cacti and succulents, things that could survive in the owners' absence.

"It smells funny in here," said Lielle. "Like mothballs."

That's when I remembered the Kids Room. It was on the main floor, down the hall from the kitchen. When I opened the door, it was exactly as I remembered. The single bed and shelves of old-fashioned toys and games.

"Cool," said Lielle. "It's like a movie set."

The board games were still piled neatly on a shelf: Yahtzee, Risk, Clue, the Game of Life. Boxes so old that the color had faded and the cardboard smelled stale. I took out the dominoes, which had uneven, hand-painted white dots. I poured them onto the floor and began standing them in line.

Lielle sat on the single bed, which was covered with a blanket knitted from wool that was the same mint green as the inside of the pool. She wrapped herself in it and the bed groaned when she stretched out. In the kitchen, she'd found a pack of Mrs. Koren's cigarettes and a book of matches. She lit one of these cigarettes, inhaled, and coughed violently. "These are kind of strong," she said.

I was lost in the rhythm of placing one domino after another. The house, the smell of that familiar tobacco—I'd returned to my childhood, to a time of quiet and focused play.

"They used to babysit me." I imagined Mrs. Koren calling to me at any moment from the kitchen, telling me to hurry up. "We used to play board games."

Lielle had gotten used to the strong tobacco and smoked leisurely now. She reclined on the bed.

"I came over after school," I said. "And some Saturday afternoons."

"Whose room is this?" Lielle turned on her side and the bed complained again. "I thought you said this place belonged to old people."

"It does. This is the Kids Room."

"What kids? You mean grandkids?"

As a child, I'd never asked the question. This room had simply existed in the same way other things existed—my house, my parents—and it never occurred to me to wonder. *You go to the Kids Room and pick us out a game*, Mrs. Koren said, smoking the same brand of cigarette Lielle now held.

I stood up, careful not to knock over the dominoes, which now reached across the floor. I stepped over them and opened the closet. It was full of children's clothing: shirts, pants, tiny pairs of overalls. I picked up a pair of corduroys. They must have hung on that hanger for years because the metal had stained them with rust. The pants would have fit a child around four years old. From the look of them and the rest of the clothing— some was hand-stitched—the child must have been a boy. Where was he? When had he slept here? I'd never seen or heard of him, and there were no photographs on the walls.

"The Kids Room," I whispered to myself. Then, *"The kid's room."*

Lielle was wrapped in the blanket, half asleep. "What?"

"We shouldn't be here," I said.

"Duh."

"I mean it." Right then, I heard someone in the house. Or thought I did. Someone humming to themlselves. "Lielle, let's go."

She yawned without bothering to cover her mouth. "Now?" She stood up, still wrapped in the blanket. She moved through the smoke, the cigarette in one hand, to the bedroom's threshold.

I nodded toward the blanket that covered her shoulders. "You're taking that?"

"I know it's gross." She looked down at the green wool. "But I'll wash it."

"Lielle."

"What?"

"It doesn't belong to us."

She laughed. "Nothing belongs to us."

"We're not here to steal from them."

"What are we here for, then? To go through their closets?"

The child's corduroys were still in my hand.

"I'm not the one who goes through people's drawers." Lielle held the blanket tight around her shoulders. "I'm not the one who reads their mail."

"It's different."

"Is it?"

"Can we just go home?"

"You mean to your house?" Lielle arched one dark eyebrow. "Why don't you go hang out with Cody and Brodie? You like them."

"No, I don't."

Then she pressed the burning end of the cigarette into the blanket. "Yes, you do."

I smelled the singe of wool and imagined the blanket, the room, the entire house swallowed by fire. "No," I said. "I don't." Then I stepped toward her, wanting to smack her, push her, tear the blanket from her shoulders. Instead, I kissed her—hard, fast, on the mouth.

She pushed me away. "Fuck you." Then she dropped the cigarette and the smoldering blanket slid off her shoulders.

"Wait." I reached for her hand—now I didn't want to leave. Outside this room, we'd be back in the ordinary world, where time passed. We would grow up; we would separate; we would die. "Lielle, wait."

But she walked past. Her foot kicked over one of the dominoes, then the rest fell in their inevitable way.

After the Korens', I locked myself in my room. Anytime the phone rang, I held my breath. I hoped it was Lielle, even though

I didn't want to talk to her. I also thought it might be Mr. or Mrs. Koren, home suddenly and coincidentally. Or it might be the police.

But nothing happened. I read the *Cosmo* Lielle had left behind.

The next day I put on her shirt, her shorts, her watermelon lip gloss, and walked over to Little Caesars. I hoped, in some delirious way, that Lielle would be there. Instead I found Cody, in his ball cap, leaning against that wall scribbled with the name *Kat*. I wondered how old *Kat* was now, where she'd gone, if she still lived nearby.

"It's you," said Cody, as though he'd been waiting for me, as though I'd been promised him. "Hey, Hannah-banana."

He passed me the burnt-down cigarette that had been hanging from his mouth, and I brought it to my lips. The filter was wet from his saliva. I inhaled, exhaled, and then—it happened fast—he was pressing me up against *Kat*'s wall, his breath hot on my skin. He'd tilted his cap back so that I saw his eyes—they were blue—and he kissed me. He crushed his erection into my stomach.

"I should go home," I said.

"Where's home?"

I gave him the Korens' address; I told him my parents were out; I said I'd meet him there later, after his shift was done.

Then I walked away with the stub of his cigarette still in my hand. It had burned down to the filter, was smoldering still, singeing my fingers.

Two days later, my mom and I came home from grocery shopping and found Lielle in our living room, watching TV.

"How did you get in?" my mom asked. "Did we leave the door unlocked?"

"The window," said Lielle.

My mom gave Lielle a blank, almost tranquil look—I wonder what she sensed that summer. Did the air in our place feel strange and foreign to her too? I wondered how long Lielle had been in our house and what she'd stolen from me.

"I made some popcorn," said Lielle. "Hope that's okay."

She stood to help my mom with the bags of groceries. I heard them talking in the kitchen and it was easy to pretend I didn't live there. To pretend I was a ghost.

"So guess what?" Lielle found me in my room. "We filled the pool."

"Why? Summer's over."

"My dad got a new girlfriend, so he wants to show off." She rolled her eyes. "Anyway, do you want to go swimming?"

"No, thanks." I wanted her to hate me the way I hated Cody. That seemed easier. But she crouched beside me and reached into her pocket. She pulled out the *Welcome to paradise!* magnet.

"I thought we could leave it on the porch or something," she said. "With a note that says we're sorry."

I took the magnet and felt its weight in my hand. It was ugly and cheap and badly made. I handed it back to her. "Keep it."

I wanted her to have it as a record, a souvenir, like the small collection I'd acquired: her *Cosmo*, her lip gloss, the cropped top she'd lent me. I'd thrown away the stub of Cody's cigarette, but Lielle's things were hidden at the back of my sock drawer. I'd begun to worry over the fact that my mother sometimes came into my room without knocking, to ask me to close my window, or to come down for dinner, or to help with the dishes. I'd never minded before, but now when she came in I would scream, "This is *my* room!" I was impatient with her, and it never occurred to me that she might be lonely. I worried she might enter my room while I was away and inspect my things, looking for—what? She probably had no idea, only intuited some loss, some difference in me, some secret life I kept from her. She'd started saying things like, *I'm concerned.*

I was concerned too, but for different reasons. Why had I kissed Lielle? And would she forget it ever happened? Forgetting must be easy—that's why the Korens preserved that room. And that's why I kept Lielle's watermelon lip gloss, as if lip gloss could keep time at bay, could protect us from whatever fate that kid had found.

Lielle didn't look at me, just turned the magnet over in her hands. "Don't cry," she said. And when I didn't stop, "Come on, shit-face. Don't."

I wanted to tell her what had happened with Cody, how it was nothing like *Cosmo* had promised. I wanted her to wipe my eyes with her sleeve and say, *It's okay,* and then it would be. I wanted us to sit at the bottom of a pool that would never be filled. To go to paradise and never get caught. To live together in another country, in our own house, a house with gold walls and a tiger guarding the door.

Todd

When Eddie woke from alcohol-fueled dreams, the bird was on the edge of the mattress. Black feathers, black feet, black beak. Eddie figured he was dreaming. He closed his eyes—there was a heaviness behind them, an aftermath from the Jim Beam he drank last night—but when he opened them, the crow was still there. *A bird in the house,* but Eddie couldn't remember the rest.

It must have flown in the bedroom window—he left it open because he still slept best when he felt the cold air and heard the noise of the street.

The crow made a sound like a rusty hinge opening. Eddie reached for one of its brittle legs but his arm was too slow and the crow hopped easily away. "You fucker," he whispered. He liked animals, had a dog growing up until she got a tumor that hung heavily from her leg, but he hated crows. They were street birds. Dirty. Thieves.

"Listen, man." He sat up in bed. "You can't be here."

The crow cocked its head as though confused, as though Eddie were the intruder. Maybe he was. He'd only moved in yesterday, proud to sign the lease. Right now all he had was a mattress thrown on the floor, his patchwork quilt, a few mismatched dishes, and a scratched pot. The bathroom sink was rusty and two of the stove's burners didn't work, but he planned to buy a fold-out couch for Abby when she came to stay.

The crow picked at a corner of the quilt, tugging a loose thread. Then made a low whine and watched him with a wary eye that reminded him of his daughter. The crow's eyes were blue like Abby's, something he'd never seen in a bird before. Maybe it wasn't a crow. Maybe it was a raven or a rook. But what was the difference? They all meant bad luck.

He spent the morning chasing the bird through the apartment, flicking a towel at it, and arrived late for work. His job was to install cable boxes and phone lines, and that meant he wore a name tag, rang doorbells, and slipped soft covers over his shoes before walking into strangers' homes—Yaletown high-rises, North Van mansions. He was quiet and polite and tried not to show his teeth when he smiled. He liked to tread over people's thick carpets and stand in their bright sunrooms. "Have a good one," he said each time he left.

When he finished work and got back to the apartment, he kicked off his shoes, heard them land with an echo against the door, then took a beer from the fridge. It was good to have his own place. If only he had a chair to sit on and maybe a CD player instead of that shitty tape deck. And a girlfriend, someone who found his jokes funny. Mostly he wished Abby were here, at the kitchen table. He didn't own a table yet, but when he did, she would sit there doing her homework.

What kind of homework would she do? He knew kids used computers now and he didn't have one. He also wasn't good at math and worried about how he'd help her. But these were small things—what was important was that he had cleaned himself up. And that his daughter still phoned him late at night, when her mom was asleep. "Hi," she'd say. "It's Abby." As though he might have forgotten.

No matter how bad things had gotten in his life, he always kept minutes on his phone so she could call to play the Question Game. It had no rules, no winner or loser, no beginning or end.

"What's your favorite fruit?" he might say, to start them off.

"Grapes. But only the green kind." She whispered so her mom wouldn't hear. "What vegetable do you hate most?"

"Cauliflower." That was an easy one. "What do you want to be when you grow up?"

"A bobsledder," she said. "What do you want to be?"

"A sea monster. Do you like sweaters or sweatshirts?"

"Sweatshirts. 'Cause they're not scratchy."

He collected this information, but knew nothing about the life she lived with Tara in Coquitlam. He was only a half-hour drive away but didn't own a car and, anyway, wouldn't have been welcome. So he didn't know the names of Abby's friends, or of the songs she listened to over and over, or even whether her hair was long or short now. And what could he tell her about his life? Not the part about sleeping in shelters or under cardboard. Not the part about buying drugs from a guy named Kit Kat. Not the part about emptying Tara's bank account.

So he and Abby played the Question Game, or they talked about the future: she was ten years old now and lived with her mom and grandparents, but she planned to move in with him when she was twelve and legally allowed to choose. "When I live with you, will we go to the aquarium?"

"Every day," he promised.

Now he poured Corn Pops into the same bowl he'd used for breakfast—Corn Pops were Abby's favorite. Or they had been a few years ago. When Tara was out, Eddie and Abby used to pour so much cereal into their bowls that the milk became thick and syrupy with sugar. This was one of their very-secret secrets.

He poured milk in now, and that's when he heard a grating sound from the bedroom, like a car driving over gravel. The crow. He'd forgotten about the crow. It flew into the kitchen and landed lightly on top of the fridge.

He banged his spoon on the counter and the bird fluttered to the other side of the room, then screeched at him—a sharp, startled squawk. Eddie threw a handful of Corn Pops at it, and they clattered over the counter and onto the floor. Then the crow picked one up and held it in his beak, as if to mock Eddie's inadequacy.

This couldn't be happening. Eddie was a human being—top of the food chain. Not only that, but he was a human being with a job and a debit card. A human being with a daughter who had his same blue eyes, a daughter who whispered into the phone that she missed him.

He strode to the entranceway and picked up one of his shoes. He would beat the thing to death.

But when he got back to the kitchen, he saw the crow stamping its small black foot to crush a Corn Pop to powder, then pecking the pieces off the floor. It ate quickly, nervously, watching Eddie with one of its blue eyes.

The fucking thing was hungry. And Eddie remembered being hungry.

He took the other bowl out of the cupboard, half filled it with cereal, poured in some milk. Did crows like milk? He would find out.

"Here." He set the bowl on the counter. "Have some."

For twenty minutes, the bird took tentative steps toward

him, jumpy shuffles that reminded him of the meth-heads on Hastings—except the crow looked normal, looked right. Finally it settled on the bowl's rim, and, before eating, executed a little bow. Eddie was in an empty kitchen, eating Corn Pops from the box and drinking beer from a can, but suddenly felt like he was in another country, at a dinner with a sober and elegant guest. "*Bon appétit*," he said, using French he'd learned from his buddy Marc, a Quebecois who knew how to swallow swords. And the crow seemed to answer him. It gurgled like an old man gargling mouthwash.

Each night he came home from work with something new— apples, pepperoni—and the crow greeted him at the door, cawed, and curtsied. Eddie felt disoriented like when his daughter was born—five pounds seven ounces, with bright blue eyes and a head of dark hair. He'd been terrified to hold her, scared he'd drop her, worried that her quick, irregular breathing meant her lungs were collapsing. He was only eighteen when she was born and she was a creature he didn't understand at all. She seemed fragile as an egg. He vowed to do his best, to at least keep her alive, and he learned to change diapers and give her a bottle. He rocked her to sleep by holding her against his chest so she could feel his heartbeat.

After the curtsy, the crow took three prim steps to the left, its talons clicking on the floor. Then it bowed a second time, deeply and formally, and Eddie bowed back. Sometimes they greeted each other this way for five minutes, bowing back and forth. It reminded him of the first time Abby smiled. She was six weeks old, so small he could hold her with one arm. Just a week earlier, her eyes didn't focus properly, but suddenly she looked at his face and smiled. Christ, she looked so fucking cute, wrinkling up her face and showing those pink gums. He'd smiled back and she smiled a second time. They did that, smiling at each other, for what seemed like hours.

He learned that the crow liked banana but not avocado, cheddar but not Swiss. It devoured cans of Spam and of gray, mushy cat food. It loved raw eggs, rejected all fruit, left Doritos alone unless they were softened in water, and was fond of his culinary specialty, omelets with onion and bacon. Once Eddie brought home a grocery-store rotisserie chicken and the crow ate half the carcass, including the bones.

Over dinner, Eddie took one bite—of toast or pizza or whatever—and tossed one to the crow, who leapt and dove to catch the food in its mouth. "Hell, yeah!" Eddie found himself cheering like during a hockey game.

After dinner, while he hoped for Abby to call, they had tugs-of-war with an elastic band. Or Eddie crumpled a piece of paper, rolled it along the floor, and the bird chased and pounced.

After about a week, Eddie gave the bird a name. He had no idea whether it was male or female, but he called it Todd, after his first roommate, a guy he'd worked with laying floors. Instead of tug-of-war, they'd done a lot of coke, but living with avian Todd wasn't so different from living with human Todd.

As with any roommate, Todd did things that pissed Eddie off. Almost every evening he came home to find garbage—orange peels and coffee grounds and candy wrappers—scattered on the floor. And the bird liked to steal stuff: Eddie's watch, his nail clippers, even his nipple ring—once he woke to the bird pecking at it, trying to tear it out. He also found lettuce in his sock drawer and crackers in his shoes. And he couldn't figure out why Todd hated his leather wallet. The bird repeatedly bashed it on the floor as if to kill it.

And there was the bird shit. On the floors, in the shower, on the walls. Powdery white streaks on the legs of Eddie's jeans.

But now he knew that crows weren't black: they were iridescent blue and purple and pine green, like oil spilled on concrete. And it was calming to watch as Todd built a nest in the bedroom, busily and tenderly arranging scraps of paper, old receipts, Post-it notes, socks borrowed from the laundry pile.

They both liked the *White Album*, would shake their tails to "Ob-La-Di, Ob-La-Da." And at night, they slept side by side— Eddie on his back, Todd with his beak tucked under a wing. The bird gave off a dry, yeasty smell and trilled softly in his sleep. Do birds dream? It was a question for Abby the next time she called.

"Yeah," she answered. "But only half of their brain sleeps at a time. I did a project on it. They probably only have half a dream."

He wanted to tell her about the crow, wanted to say, *I have a very-secret secret*. But if Tara found out, she'd just use it as more evidence against him.

"Were you asleep?" Abby asked. "What were you dreaming about?"

"Not sure," he said. "Probably that I was flying."

"Maybe you were a velociraptor," she said. "I've dreamt that lots of times."

They talked this way until one or both of them drifted off. And in the mornings, Eddie woke with small, hot feet on his skin. Demanding breakfast, Todd stood on his shoulder and plucked out his hair, one strand at a time.

He went to the library and learned that crows mate for life, though some make brief forays with other partners. They have a language system, can count to six, and are able to see more colors than the human eye. To navigate they learn the layout of the stars, watch the sun's movement across the sky, sense the Earth's magnetic field. There's even a theory that they find their way by listening to the groan and crack of tectonic plates, the gathering of ocean waves, a volcano's underground rumble. They can hear the explosion of meteors in space.

He wanted to tell Abby this, but she hadn't called in weeks. Which was normal, he guessed, 'cause she must be busy. He knew she took dance classes and had schoolwork and sometimes had sleepovers at other girls' houses.

In those weeks, Todd grew bigger and walked with what Eddie thought of as a dealer's strut. The bird lost his downy feathers, and stiff, glossy ones grew in to replace them—once Eddie woke to find a spray of molted feathers through the bedsheets, as though he'd spent the night wrestling a dark angel.

Todd's blue eyes changed too, darkened to the color of the plums Eddie used to steal from a yard on East Twelfth. And a few weeks after that, Eddie came home from work to find that Todd had laid an egg.

It was the color of an olive, speckled with gray like it had been spray-painted. The crow sat lightly on top of it, eyes half closed, feathers puffed out.

"Todd." Eddie crouched down. "So you're a chick."

The bird snapped her beak at him, offended by his bad joke.

Would the egg hatch? It needed to be fertilized—Eddie knew all about that—but maybe Todd had a boyfriend who flew in the open window and visited while Eddie was at work. And if it hatched, what was Eddie supposed to do? He shouldn't even have one crow living here—if the landlord found out, he could be evicted. If Tara found out, she'd say he was mentally ill.

He had to get rid of the bird. Take Todd outside, with her nest and her egg. Leave her in a park, maybe.

Todd snapped at him again, then opened her beak wide and

showed her small pink tongue. She was hungry. She probably needed more calories now. Probably couldn't feed herself while keeping the egg warm.

He went to the kitchen, got one of the jars of applesauce he'd bought for her, and fed her with a spoon. She thanked him in her usual way: chattered and gurgled, as though cheerfully gossiping about people they both disliked.

"Yeah, okay." He settled in beside her. "You're welcome."

Abby called three days later, in the middle of the night. "What's your favorite song?" Her voice pulled him from sleep.

"Something by the Beatles. Maybe 'Here Comes the Sun.'"

Streetlight shone through the window and he could see Todd in her nest. She hadn't moved in days and there was a bare spot on her belly now, which she pressed to the egg. One of the bird's eyes was closed, the other open. Half of her brain was sleeping and he wished he could tell Abby. But he said, "What's your favorite color?"

"That's your question? You already know the answer."

He did. Yellow.

But he was tired of trying to keep the game going. "Guess what?" He would just say it. "I live with a crow."

"What?"

"A crow. You know, a bird."

"It's, like, alive?"

"Yeah," he said. "Alive." Then he told her about waking up with the bird on the mattress. He told her about the nest, the egg. "Her name is Todd," he said. "You'd like her. She's funny and she plays soccer."

Abby was so quiet that he thought she'd hung up. That she'd gone to tell her mom that he'd lost his mind. That she'd never call again.

But then she said, "They're descended from dinosaurs."

"What?"

"Birds," she said, "are dinosaurs that can fly."

"Do you know how they navigate?" he asked. "By looking up at the moon and the sun. By measuring the curve of the Earth."

"For real?"

And he felt like a parent. Like a person who knew things and could care for her.

"For real," he said. "And did you know they can hear earthquakes before they start?"

"No."

"They can hear tectonic plates moving. They can hear rain before it falls."

Todd spent each day warming the egg, her bare brood-patch pressed to its smooth surface, and Eddie had that easy feeling you get when you crack open a beer. Even when he was on his hands and knees in the alley behind his apartment, looking for worms and slugs because he'd read they were necessary to a crow's diet, he felt good.

This lasted until he got back from work one evening and saw that Todd had abandoned her nest. He found her wandering distractedly through the kitchen, her nails clicking on the counter.

"Hey," he said. "What's going on?"

He went into the bedroom: the egg was still there, nestled in the torn-up paper, but it had gone cold. He tucked it under his shirt, held it against his heart. It started to warm up but what was he supposed to do now? He couldn't take an egg with him to work.

He went into the kitchen and turned the oven on low—maybe he could use it as an incubator. But this was the first time he'd used the oven, and it gave off a smell like burning oil, sent gray smoke into the room. "Shit." He waved away the smoke, hoping the alarm wouldn't go off.

Todd was in the kitchen with a Triscuit in her mouth, hiding it under the dish-drainer mat. She stepped back, cocked her head while inspecting her work, then pulled the cracker out and started again.

"Todd?" He held the egg in front of her. "What the hell?"

She ignored him. Tucked the Triscuit under the mat again, and seemed satisfied that the cracker was well hidden now.

"Hey." He held the egg right under her face, but she looked away. She scratched her head with one of her talons.

She must have figured out that there was no point, that the thing wouldn't hatch. Eddie went back to the bedroom, swept up the nest, and put it and the egg in the garbage. But when Abby phoned that night, he didn't tell her any of this.

"What are you going to do?" she asked. "When the baby's born?"

"I'll look after it," he said. "And so will you, when you live here."

He knew that she liked information, so told her that when the bird was born it would be called a "nestling," and when it learned to fly, a "fledgling." He said it would be smaller than her hand, bald and openmouthed. "Just like when you were born," he said. "You used to fit right in my pocket."

"No, I didn't!"

"Sure you did. And you had blue eyes that took up half your face."

He promised that she could name the new bird, and when she lived there, it would sleep in her bed.

"What about my friends?" she said. "Will I have to switch schools?"

"What do you mean?"

"If I move? Will I see Shyla anymore?"

He didn't know who Shyla was. Her best friend? A neighbor's dog? "Don't worry about that," he said. "You'll like it here."

"What will I tell Mom?"

"You'll tell her that you want to move in with me. That you're old enough to decide for yourself."

"But I mean, what will I tell her? She might be mad. Or kind of cry."

"That's why I got this apartment," he said. "So you could be here too."

"I know."

"Isn't that what you want?"

"I guess so."

"You guess so?"

"I don't know. Yeah. But—"

"But what?"

"It's just—"

Great. Now he'd made her cry.

"Christ, Abby," he said. "Forget it, okay?"

The next morning he called in sick to work and stayed in bed.

Todd flew up to him and tried to climb onto his shoulder, but he batted her away. "Leave me alone, buddy."

The bird flew into the kitchen and he heard a thud, then a sound like marbles scattering—she had spilled or broken something in a fit of hurt feelings. Eddie felt like he had a hangover and closed his eyes. When he opened them, the crow was on the mattress. Black feathers, black beak, black feet. She dropped something from her mouth. A Corn Pop.

"I'm not hungry, Todd."

But the bird made a disapproving *tsk-tsk* sound, then picked up the cereal in her beak. She used one of her long toes to scrape at his face—"Screw off," he said, and she dropped the Corn Pop into his open mouth.

Then she flew back to the kitchen, returned with more cereal, and he gave in this time. Opened his mouth and let her feed him. Her beak knocked his teeth and he tasted her bad, wild breath.

What the hell was he doing? Tara was right—there was something fucked up about him, something not normal.

"Go away." He swatted at the crow. "You can't be here." Which was what police officers and business owners and even librarians used to say to him. But the bird stayed, hopped closer.

"You can't be here." He slapped at her, his hand brushing her feathered face, and she croaked and stumbled on the mattress. Huddled and shivered like she was cold. "Come on, Todd." He climbed out of bed, picked her up, threw her toward the open window. "Get out."

But she flew back toward him, kept loving him like an idiot. So he smacked her for real this time, bent her wing feathers. "I said, get out." He slammed his fists against the wall, stamped his feet, and she puffed out her neck feathers, thrashed away from him. "Get out!" he screamed. "Out!" She shrieked and shrieked, circling his head—he heard the frantic flap of her wings. He swung with his fists and she slammed into the wall. Dropped to the floor.

Her wings beat the floorboards. Her eyes were open.

"Oh, Jesus." He fell to his knees. "Todd."

He crawled toward her and picked her up. She was so light—Abby had explained that the bones were hollow, and he pictured them made of delicate glass pipes. He'd fucked up; he'd fucked up. She seemed smaller, shrunken, and he held her to his heart.

"No," he said. "No."

Her quick, ragged heartbeat. Her crumpled feathers.

He couldn't even do this. Couldn't even care for a street bird. What would he tell Abby? That he was sorry. So sorry.

She shuddered in his hand. Then made a low, tuneless sound,

like she was asking a question. And he tried not to cry, tried not to keen. Tried to quiet himself so she could listen for an answer, so she could find her way. He touched the bird's broken wing-feathers, settled her against his chest, and hoped this would calm her. Hoped she'd forgive him. Hoped she was listening to tectonic shifts, or meteors, or the hush of rain before it falls.

Flight

She took the ferry, then three buses, to get into Vancouver. On the third, she fell asleep with her head against the window, the stop-start rhythm of the bus lulling her into dreams. She woke to a screeching sound and opened her eyes expecting to see people wounded, screaming. But the other passengers read newspapers or talked into their phones or slept with their heads tilted back, mouths open.

The guy next to her pointed to the window. Outside, the sky was moving like a wave of black water. Crows. They cawed and roiled overhead.

"They do that every night." The guy's hair hung to his eyes and his teeth were edged in black. "Roost overnight in Burnaby and come to town during the day. They commute."

She pressed her face to the window and her breath fogged the glass.

"Did you know crows can find their way home from anywhere? They're smarter than we are." The guy turned to her. "You new here?"

"Yeah."

"From where?"

When she was younger she used to tell people she was an alien from Pluto. "From the island. Victoria."

"Nice." When he smiled, there were so many lines around his eyes that his face looked like a cracked window. "Welcome."

Last week she'd met a man at the mall, got into his car—a silver Acura—and went down on him while her best friend, Marina, waited nearby. The man was tall, wore too much gel in his hair, and had teeth that were glaringly white. He'd approached them in the food court while she and Marina were dipping fries into a chocolate milkshake.

Marina was more experienced, but she had a boyfriend who skateboarded and kept rats as pets, and she didn't want to cheat on him. "The secret is, don't use your teeth," Marina whispered as they followed the man out to the parking lot.

"Got it. No teeth."

Then Marina grabbed her sleeve. "Are you sure? Maybe we should just go."

But they were already at the car and the man had unlocked it with his key-chain fob. It was the same make of car her parents drove and that seemed reassuring, like he must be an okay guy if he drove that car.

The outside of the Acura was clean, but inside the floor was sticky against her bare knees—probably spilled pop or coffee. The parking brake dug into her ribs and she kept her eyes closed. It seemed to take hours. A couple of times she scraped him with her teeth.

Then he finished, uttered a wet groan, and gave her $40. She climbed out of the car, aware of Marina's wide eyes on her. "What happened?" said her friend. "Are you okay? What happened?"

She untangled her hair with her fingers, shook her head. Her legs felt shaky. "Gross," she said. "Super gross." Then she made a barfing sound so Marina would laugh. "I need a juice or something."

Some secrets stay with you, like when that weird Mormon kid in grade four showed her the scars on his arm. They were behind the school, in a gully that became soggy and waterlogged each winter. He'd lifted his sleeve to show thick red crosshatched marks. She reached out and touched them and that's when he ran away. "Leave me alone!" he screamed, as though she were the one who'd hurt him.

But this man in an Acura—this was over as soon as she stepped from the car. She linked arms with Marina and went into the mall. Bought an Orangina and matching glittery halter tops. Then she put the rest of the money—she still had almost $20 left over—in the pocket of her jeans. She didn't touch it, but knew it was there, a secret against her hip.

And now she had no friends, no plans, and the $20 was nearly gone—she'd spent half of it on a ferry ticket. So when the guy on the bus asked, "Where you headed?" she shrugged her shoulders. And when he said, "You hungry?" she realized she was. She was sixteen and always starving.

He pulled the cord above her head to ring the bell, and they got off at the next stop. It was raining, the drops falling down the neck of her hoodie. The guy took her to a restaurant in Chinatown where everything was a shade of red: the booths, the plasticized tablecloths, the menus, the sweet-and-sour sauce. He pulled out a chair for her. "The spring rolls here are fucking awesome," he said.

His name was Eddie and he was thirteen years older than she was, but he didn't know that. He thought her name was Rachel and that she was twenty-four years old. That's what it said on the

ID she carried in her bag and that's what she told him. "Rachel." A dreamy look on his face. "That's a pretty name."

He looked older than twenty-nine but acted younger, and she wondered if he too was lying about his age. But then he told her, over spring rolls and steamed rice and ginger chicken, that he was a recovered addict, that there were whole years he couldn't remember. Chunks of time had been scooped out of his life like ice cream.

"Addicted to what?"

"Heroin. Morphine." He sounded both ashamed and pleased. "I smoked a lot of crack."

"That explains your teeth?"

"Shit." He laughed. "I'm getting my teeth fixed. That's a promise. I work for Telus now and they have a dental plan."

"You install phones?"

"Phones. Cable. Internet. It's awesome. What about you?"

"I'm a hairstylist." Delivering a lie so smoothly sent a warm feeling to her stomach, like when she and Marina passed a bottle of vodka back and forth.

"Cool," he said. "So you cut hair and stuff?"

She held up a piece of her own hair, which she hated—it was a boring brown and her mother had recently forbidden her to bleach it. "Cuts, dyes, perms." This wasn't entirely untrue. Last week she'd cut her own bangs and now they sat short and uneven on her forehead.

"I like talking to you, Rachel," he said. "I like looking at you too."

Earlier that morning she'd woken to the smell of cinnamon from the kitchen. Her dad was making oatmeal and had added apples and walnuts to it, like he did every morning.

She'd already packed her backpack—taken out her schoolbooks and replaced them with her Discman, her one-eyed bear, and extra socks. She put on her jeans, her hoodie, her wooden earrings. The $20 was still in her pocket—the bill had rubbed against her body for two weeks and now seemed as soft as her own skin. In social studies she'd used a pen to draw a dollar sign on her hand. *Forty dollars for my mouth*, she wanted to say, every time she smiled.

She passed through the kitchen. "I'm not hungry."

"No way, monkey," said her dad. "You have to eat something."

How do you look your dad in the eye when he had the same haircut as the man in the Acura? Now every man she saw had that haircut: her teachers, her soccer coach, even the Chinese guy who owned Al's Corner Store but whose name, it turned out, wasn't Al.

She sat at the table and her father set down a bowl of oatmeal— it looked like baby food—and she thought she might be sick.

"Hurry up," said her mother, pouring herself coffee—she never had to eat breakfast. She wore her blue RN uniform and clunky white sneakers that squeaked as she walked. "You need to be out the door in eight minutes, sweetie."

Sometimes it felt like a mistake, like she'd stumbled into her parents' lives in place of another, better girl. And that was likely true. She was the result of $30,000 in fertility treatments, her life started in a petri dish. Other zygotes in the dish didn't survive, but her cells had replicated. And now her parents rented an apartment on Quadra Street because they'd spent their down payment acquiring her. Had she been worth it? She wished she were prettier or had a talent or a knack for kindness. She wished, for her mom's sake, that she were tidier. She wanted to come from nowhere, to owe nothing. To rise up like Adam from the dirt on the ground.

But even Adam had a parent. Even he was beholden.

She ate a few bites of the oatmeal, then scraped the rest into the garbage. She wanted to hug her parents, but was afraid she'd

cry, afraid she'd worry them. " 'Bye!" she screamed as she threw
on her backpack and stepped out the door.

She walked to school but didn't go inside the building. She
wanted to ask Marina to come with her: *Let's go to Vancouver. I'm fucking
serious.* But Marina was obsessed with her boyfriend and wouldn't
have left for even a day. So she walked down Cook Street, then
Pandora, and at Douglas waited for the bus. It took practically a
hundred years to get to the ferry terminal and she missed the
eleven o'clock boat. "It's a two-hour wait, hon," said the woman
behind the glass. The woman reminded her of her mother.

"That's okay," she said. Then she used that twenty dollars,
money born of her own flesh, to buy a ticket for the next sailing.

When she reached Vancouver, she called home from a pay phone
and left a message to say she was staying over at Marina's. Then she
phoned her best friend's house and Marina's little sister answered.
"Is Marina there?"

"Who's calling, please?"

"Kiki, you know it's me."

"Marina's busy. Ryan's over."

"Put her on anyway."

"Where were you today?" said Marina when she finally picked
up the phone. "You missed the shittiest gym class ever. Dodge-
fucking-*ball.*"

"I'm in Vancouver."

"No, you're not."

"Yeah. I am."

"How did you get there?"

"I flapped my arms and flew. What do you think? I took the
ferry."

"Are you serious?" Was that admiration in Marina's voice? "Why?"

"I told my parents I was staying at your place. So if they call, just say I'm in the bathroom or something."

"When are you coming back?"

"I don't know."

"You are coming back, right?"

"Oh, my god." She looked around the ferry terminal, at the empty benches, the freshly mopped floor. "You should have come with me. This city is so wicked."

Eddie paid for dinner. As they left the restaurant, he touched the small of her back. "Do you want to come over? I want you to come over."

What did she owe him? He'd bought her dinner; he'd been nice. She let him hold her hand as they walked down East Pender and they didn't talk until they reached his building. He led her up two flights of stairs and stopped outside a door with a chipped paint job. "My place isn't much, okay?" he said. "But it's not forever."

When he unlocked and opened the door, there was a big, panting dog on the other side. A Rottweiler with a string of drool hanging from its mouth. "Jake, this is Rachel. Rachel, meet Jake." Then Eddie got down on the floor and let the dog lick every inch of his face. This guy was too open, she thought, too bighearted.

"I found him behind the Nesters'," he said. "Practically starving."

"Do you always take in strays?"

"Yeah, I guess. Last year I even lived with a crow."

"Like, a bird?"

He smiled up at her from the floor. "Jake likes you," he said, scratching behind the dog's ears. "I can tell."

This morning she'd woken up to her dad making oatmeal, and now she was in a stranger's apartment, drinking whiskey. She and Eddie shared the same cup, passing it back and forth. They sat on a couch with mismatched pillows and, worried she'd be cold, Eddie covered her shoulders with a threadbare quilt of corduroy, fleece, and smooth gold satin squares.

"My mom made it for me when I was born," he said, running his hand over the faded patchwork. "Even when I was fucked up all the time I made sure not to lose it. And to wash it by hand. The stitching is really fragile."

He didn't touch her, but he stared at her, his eyes glassy. She expected his weight against her, his sweaty palms on her skin. Instead he flipped his hair from his eyes and said, "Hey, you should give me a haircut."

"What?"

"Yeah, why not? I was gonna get it cut anyway."

"I don't have my stuff with me," she said. "I need my own scissors and clips and stuff."

"No excuses." He got up unsteadily from the couch and went to the kitchen, then came back with a pair of scissors. "Come on." He held her hand and pulled her into the bathroom.

He took off his shirt, exposing the knotty muscles of his arms, his soft middle, and a piercing in his right nipple that looked red and new.

"No, I've had it for years," he said when she asked about it. "It just never healed right 'cause I did it myself."

He knelt in front of her. She draped a towel over his shoulders and made a big show of asking what style he wanted, talking about his hair's texture, the thickness of the follicles. She was proud of the word *follicles*. Then she scrubbed his head in a bathroom sink streaked with rust. His wet hair was soft between her fingers, the water warm on her hands.

She started cutting, hoping for the best. She didn't want to take too much off, didn't want him to look like that guy in the Acura. Hair fell to the floor in wet tufts that skidded around her socked feet. She tried not to look at herself in the mirror. Her vision was blurry and she kept seeing her parents' faces reflected in her own. Her dad's almost-green eyes. Her mom's thick eyebrows and the shadow of veins below her skin.

When she was finished, she rubbed Eddie's head with the towel, ostensibly to dry his hair, but mostly to mess it up so he wouldn't notice how uneven the cut was. The left side was too short, patches nearly gone above his ear.

"There," she said when she was finished. "Done."

He stood up and examined himself, turning his head from side to side. He gave a low whistle. "Jesus Christ." He found her eyes in the mirror. "Are you drunk or something?"

"What?"

"This haircut." He turned toward her, and she was eye-level with his piercing—dried blood clung to edges of the metal. "What the hell?"

He must know now that she wasn't a hairdresser, that she wasn't Rachel. And who was he? What was he capable of?

"Sorry." She put her hand on the counter to steady herself. "I fucked up."

"Hey." He gripped her shoulder. "Are you gonna cry? Do not cry."

"I won't," she said. "I don't—"

He turned back to the mirror. "Whatever. It's no big deal." He gave a wink, as though playing a trick on himself. "Good thing I'm so handsome."

She woke with a fly buzzing above her face. She was fully clothed, on a fold-out couch, under a frayed quilt. She batted the fly away. Where was she?

Then the dog came over and ran his long tongue up her arm. Of course: the ferry, the bus, the haircut. She remembered very little—

whole hours had been wiped away as if by an eraser—but she remembered stumbling to the bathroom, saying, *I don't feel well.* Remembered that Eddie had tucked her in on the couch, under this quilt.

Now he was in the kitchen—she heard eggs popping in the pan. He'd opened the window, maybe so the smell of cooking oil wouldn't linger in the apartment. She heard the sound of crows crossing the city.

"Jake found you, huh?" He walked into the room with the same cup they used last night, except now it was full of coffee. He sat on the edge of the couch and gave her a sip. The coffee was creamy and sweet, the only way she liked it.

"You into omelets?" he said. "They're my specialty."

They ate sitting on the couch, sunlight streaming in the window and hurting her eyes. He talked about the future: he planned to stay on at Telus and go back to school in the evenings. He would finish high school, then apply to Langara College.

"Maybe you want to hang out again?" he said. "What are you up to tomorrow?"

Tomorrow. Next week. Next year. He talked about the movies they would see, the meals they would eat. He told her he liked his haircut now, that both his parents were dead, and that her eyes reminded him of the ocean, but not the ocean around here. The kind of ocean you see on postcards. "Let's go away sometime," he said. "Fly down to Mexico. I'd like to see you on a beach."

She looked out the small window above his bed at the gray sky and asked every question that came into her head. The name of his first girlfriend and how it felt to inject heroin and how modems worked. Have you ever seen anyone die? Have you ever paid for sex? Do you ever pray? Has your heart ever stopped?

"Jesus." He ran his hand through his bad hair. "You're a funny one, Rachel." But he answered everything: Yes, he'd seen his dad die and a few friends too. No, he'd never paid for sex. Maybe his heart had stopped once or twice, but he didn't know for sure. And yeah, he used to pray every night before bed. "I was raised that way," he said. "But then one day I got tired of talking to the sky. It's nicer to talk to people."

When he'd answered every question she could think of, she kissed him—because she owed it to him, and because she wanted to. His mouth tasted like the coffee in the mug.

"What about you?" he said, his face close to hers.

"What about me?"

"Do you ever pray?"

"I used to," she said. "But my parents aren't religious or anything. I just did it on my own."

"What changed?"

"My friend Marina's Catholic and she took me to the cathedral. That just made everything seem complicated."

"What about your parents?" he said. "What are they like?"

Her parents. They thought she was at Marina's and wouldn't start worrying about her until later tonight. And if she stayed here until tomorrow, next week? She would be Rachel, twenty-four years old.

"They're normal," she said. "My parents. They don't know me at all."

Eddie put his arm around her. "I bet they miss you."

Then he called Jake over so the dog would show her tricks: sit, shake, jump, dance.

They ate leftover Chinese food, drank coffee with whiskey poured in, snacked on Corn Pops straight from the box, lay naked on Eddie's single bed. "I could do this for a year straight," he said. But she was telling time by when the crows flew over the city: once in the morning, once in the evening.

After the second darkening, she put on her clothes. "I'm going out for smokes. You want anything?"

"You smoke?" He was in the bathroom cleaning his piercing, that wound that never healed. "Maybe you can grab me a Pepsi?"

She quietly shouldered her backpack, stepped into the hallway, and clicked the door shut behind her. She ran down the stairs to the street and nearly knocked into a woman on roller skates, a cigarette dangling from her caved-in mouth. "Watch where you're going!" shouted the woman, pigtails flapping behind her like wings.

Where was she going? Home. Her dad will make oatmeal; she'll go to school; Marina will probably break up with the boy who keeps rats.

Tomorrow. Next week. Next year. She'll finish high school, barely passing math and biology, and will graduate without any distinction at all. Then she'll move to Vancouver, for real this time. She'll study at UBC but drop out after one semester, disappointing her parents forever. To make rent, she'll lie about her experience and get a job editing internal documents for Scotiabank. She'll use words like *derivative* and *high-risk investment* seriously when talking to coworkers and ironically when talking to friends. Like everyone else, she'll fail to predict the financial crash. And that same year, when she really will be twenty-four, she'll run into Eddie on the SkyTrain.

At first she won't recognize him—he'll have had his teeth fixed. But then, holy shit, it's that guy from that weekend when she was sixteen. She'll have told the story since then, made it funny, no longer a secret. *I got on the ferry with five bucks in my pocket, wearing this slutty halter top, thinking I was so badass.*

"Rachel." Eddie will look at her and a smile will shatter his face. "How are you?"

Who is he? What is he capable of? She'll know he would be

heavy in her life, would anchor her to the ground. And in the end, what would she call it? Gravity? Love?

"That's not my name," she'll say, even though she'll remember the omelet he made her when she was sixteen and hungry, even though she'll want to open her arms and hug him. "My name's Samantha." And it will feel like a lie. "I don't know you." Like giving herself a small, keen wound. "You're thinking of somebody else."

The Ark

I knew the answer. *Pick me, pick me.* I wore my Sunday dress: blue like the sky, with puffed sleeves and a lace collar. I still remember how it felt to spin in that dress, then watch it settle around me like a cloud.

I stretched my hand so high that little grunts escaped my throat. But Miss Robb's eyes passed over me, scanned the other children fidgeting with their fancy church clothes or picking their scabs.

We didn't sit in rows like in real school; we sat on the floor in a half-moon around Miss Robb. She sat in a chair, above us, ankles crossed—I remember the shimmer of her pantyhose.

"Miss Robb," I pleaded. "I know! I know the answer."

"Toby?" Miss Robb always called on Toby. "What do you think?"

Toby's spine straightened. Eyes widened. He was holding a plastic figurine of a giraffe, one of the animals Miss Robb used to illustrate lessons about the Garden of Eden or Noah's ark. He squeezed the giraffe's neck. He hadn't heard the question.

"Love." Miss Robb pulled a Kleenex from the sleeve of her sweater and dabbed at her delicately runny nose. "What is love?"

Toby shifted his weight and reached inside the hole in the knee of his pants to scratch his grass-stained skin. He must have fallen and skidded on his way to church, because he also had a bruise above one eye. He was the kid who fell out of trees, who cried often and easily, who popped wheelies in the church parking lot instead of standing calmly beside his parents and brother. He'd once punched Kipp Fitch in the stomach.

"It's——" Toby turned to me for help, but I kept my eyes forward. "It's love."

"Love is love?" Miss Robb had a habit of thoughtfully touching her hair-sprayed bangs. Her nails were always painted pink and were never chipped. "Interesting. But where does love come from?"

I couldn't take it anymore. "God!" I nearly shouted. "God is love!"

My arm dropped once the words were out. Relief at giving the correct answer. At six years old, I believed that giving correct answers was essential. Otherwise, no one—not Miss Robb, not my parents, not even God—would like me.

"Very good." Miss Robb gave me a tight smile. "Both of you."

That's why I hated Toby. Because I was the best, and he was the worst, and yet people grouped us together like a pair on the ark.

And it wasn't just Miss Robb. Our families lived on the same block, so we carpooled to church, all of us crushed into the Burkes' minivan—me seated with Toby and his older brother Jerome. Our parents socialized outside of church, visiting for barbecues on the back deck or organizing what our parents called *activity days*. How many hours of my life did I spend in roller rinks or bowling alleys with Toby and the rest of the Burke clan? Forced to stand by while he skidded around the waxed floor in his bowling shoes and let balls thunk heavily on the wood? Our parents were busy drinking beer, so it was Jerome who had to thwack his little brother upside the head. *Give it a rest, Toby.* Jerome, who only threw strikes or spares.

Even Toby himself seemed confused—he thought we were friends, when in fact we were enemies. He brought me gifts: two twists of Twizzlers he'd tied in a knot, a purple stone he'd found in a park, an eraser in the shape of a troll. He would slip these into the pocket of my blue Sunday dress so subtly that I wouldn't notice until I got home, pulled off the dress, and the offerings dropped to the floor and glared at me. I wanted to throw them out but instead hid them under my bed, tucked beneath a corner of the carpet that had lifted away.

The worst was Story Time, when Toby sat next to me, too close. We were all at Miss Robb's feet, in that half-moon, as she read to us from her *Illustrated Bible*. She rested it on her knee so we could see the panels: Mary and Joseph surrounded by lambs and donkeys, or Jesus walking on placid water, or the angel Gabriel floating like a helium balloon.

Story Time should have been one of my happiest moments. I loved the illustrations, I loved the musicality of Miss Robb's voice, and I loved the expectation of what came next: we would all file out of the Sunday school room and into the main church, past the tidy wooden pews, toward Pastor Guthrie. His white mustache had two yellow stripes that extended from his nostrils—the discoloration came from smoking cigarettes, but I believed that God had bestowed a golden mustache upon him to match the cross that gleamed behind the altar. All the children would kneel in front of him and he would place a light hand on each of our heads. What can I say about Pastor Guthrie? Only that he was genuine—his blessing made you feel safe. Then the service would be over, and we would get to have cookies.

But all of that was ruined because Toby sat next to me during Story Time and he smelled like Bazooka gum, like the gel his mother combed through his hair, like a sweater left out in the rain.

He even ruined my favorite story, the one about Joshua and Caleb, who were rewarded for their faithfulness while everyone else was punished for their wickedness.

If the Lord is pleased with us, he will lead us into that land, a land flowing with milk and honey, and will give it to us.

Toby tapped my shoulder but I kept my eyes on the illustration, on Caleb's outstretched arm. I nudged him away, but he tapped again. And again. When I glanced toward him, I was confused—Toby held a small animal in his hand, something soft and tender. Defenseless. Then I understood: he had unzipped his fly. He was holding his penis.

I gasped, turned away. Focused on Miss Robb's nylons.

Because my servant Caleb has a different spirit, and follows me wholeheartededly.

I held that word in my mind, the way I used to hold Kraft caramels in my mouth, hoping they would never dissolve. *Wholeheartedly.* It sounded right, sounded pure, sounded perfect. I would live my life—I decided it then—wholeheartedly.

How old were we when we built those small replicas of Noah's ark? Miss Robb was still Miss Robb, not yet Mrs. Lopez, so we must have been nine or ten. Miss Robb said, "Leanna, you'll work with Toby."

"Yes, Miss Robb." I hoped my voice conveyed my dismay but

also my forbearance, my charity. Toby was beside me—we must have been younger, only seven or eight, because he still wore that suit with the hole in the knee.

"Please get started," said Miss Robb to the class. "I'll be back in a few moments."

We were left to make arks out of construction paper, popsicle sticks, markers, swatches of fabric. There was so much that didn't need to be said: that we should gather our materials, then sit quietly and work. That once we finished our arks, they would be displayed in the classroom and admired by our parents. And that my ark would be the best.

"What should we use?" I picked up a swatch of material, blue to match my dress. "For the sails."

"The ark had sails?" said Toby.

I couldn't believe his stupidity. "It was a boat."

"Not all boats have sails." Toby picked up a pair of scissors that were gummy with glue and flashed them in front of my eyes. "Ferries have motors."

I began gathering popsicle sticks, sheets of paper. "Fairies don't exist."

"Do so. I've been on one."

I clenched my fists, accidentally crumpling the blue paper. "Noah's ark had sails."

Toby grabbed a chunk of my hair, and, with those gummy scissors, cut an inch off the end. My hair. I'd washed it that morning, brushed it thirty-six times per side. Tears rushed to my eyes. But I did not, *would not*, give him what he wanted—a reaction. I continued to gather popsicle sticks, squeezing them until my hands hurt.

"We'll build the body out of these." My throat thick. "Because the Bible says Noah used wood."

"Fine." Toby seemed to deflate like a week-old balloon. "You start, okay? I'll be right back."

"Where are you going?" As if I cared.

Toby snapped the scissors at my face, but when I flinched, he only laughed. "None of your beeswax," he said.

At our wedding, people hugged us and cried. *Such a beautiful couple,* people said, pressing their damp cheeks to my face, smudging my makeup. *You two are just perfect.*

Toby and I sat at the head table, held hands under the table-cloth. His grip warm, familiar, nearly crushing the bones of my fingers. When people tapped their glasses, a soft tinkling sound that rose like a tide, we would lean toward each other and kiss, sometimes for longer than seemed proper.

But why didn't my memories match anyone else's? It was as though they believed we'd always been these people—as though I'd worn a white dress my whole life, as though Toby had never been a bruised and bruising boy, had never smelled weird, had never scared and annoyed me.

Only Jerome made sense. He swayed in front of the microphone during his speech, slurred about how much Toby and I used to hate each other.

"All three of us would be in the back of my parents' van," he said. "Them on either side of me. They'd fight the whole way, didn't matter where we were going. Leanna would tell Toby to quit staring at her. Toby would tell Leanna to shut her ugly mouth. Leanna would tell him he was ugly. Toby would say, *Good one.* Leanna would get all righteous and say he better be respectful or she'd tell. *Tell who?* Toby would say. *Jesus?*"

When Toby left the room, the air shifted—an exhalation, a settling of molecules. I inspected my hair. He hadn't cut enough that anyone would notice, so I decided not to tell my parents. The last time I'd told on him—when Toby pinched my arm so hard it left a welt—Jerome dragged him to our house and shoved Toby through our doorway.

"What do you say?" Jerome stood behind Toby, arms crossed. He was four years older, impossibly grown-up. "Come on. We don't have all day."

Toby looked so small in his torn suit.

"It doesn't matter," I said. "It didn't hurt that bad."

"Toby has something to tell you," said Jerome. "And we will stand here until he opens his mouth and says it."

So we did. Stand there. Toby started to cry, gulping tears that he tried to swallow. He sounded like a drowning victim, but Jerome didn't put an arm around him or pat his back. Jerome already had power in his body, sureness about the way he placed his feet. From then on, when I prayed, I envisioned God looking exactly like Jerome—tall and blond, with a face that seemed to be made of finely cut glass. Even my parents, who stood in the entryway, were somehow frozen in place, unable to stop this display.

Toby finally choked out the word, "Sorry."

"What was that?" said Jerome. "I don't think I heard you."

"I'm sorry," Toby said, louder.

"I know." I only wanted it to stop. "It's okay."

Jerome looked at me, a brief stare that stilled me. "What else, Toby?"

Toby took a breath. "And it will never happen again."

Then he turned and ran from our house, tore up the street. Jerome nodded to us, and my parents spoke to him as though he were an adult: "Well, thank you for coming by," and "We'll see you on Sunday?"

I couldn't live through that again. It had left me shaken for weeks, unable to hate Toby with my usual purity and heat, my usual wholeheartedness. And it had made me clumsy and nervous around Jerome. He was the usher at the church, trusted with keys to the front door, tasked with arriving early and greeting parishioners as they arrived. Now I tripped on the church steps when I saw him, became tongue-tied when he handed out the week's bulletin. And when our families went skiing together, Jerome holding my mittened hands and helping me to balance on the bunny hill, I kept crossing my skis and landing in the snow. I could barely pull the thin mountain air into my lungs.

So I tucked my hair behind my ear, and set to work glue-gunning popsicle sticks together. I don't remember how long I worked, only that when Toby came back I'd burnt the ends of my fingers and had nearly completed the bones of the boat. He stood beside me and I could feel the reverberations of his body: he was breathing hard, keyed up.

"Leanna." He tugged on the sleeve of my dress. "Come see something."

"I'm busy."

"*Leanna.*"

"No."

"Please?"

I'd never heard Toby say *please* before. And even when Jerome or their father was nearby, I'd never seen Toby look so scared. So I let him take my hand, pull me from the Sunday school room, down the hallway.

He brought me to a door I'd never noticed before, a door that opened to a dark staircase. We walked slowly down the stairs and I saw that it was a basement like at home, like every basement I'd ever seen. Full of crap nobody wanted to deal with—old stained coffee cups and rolled-up altar cloths and bank boxes held shut with stiff, crackly tape. This was probably my first disappointment with the church, my first moment of doubt: this building was no better than any other.

The only light down there came from a small octagonal window. Dust got in my eyes, my nostrils. I was trying to love dust because Miss Robb said we were all made from it. I sneezed.

"Bless you," whispered Toby.

He walked ahead of me, as if he knew his way, toward an old furnace that sat silent in the summer.

"Where are we going?" I said.

Toby didn't answer. He crouched beside a shoe box on the floor. When he opened the lid, a dark thing moved inside.

I stepped away. "What is that?"

"I found it down here," said Toby.

I moved closer and crouched to see. A bat. Black eyes, tufts of orange fur on its forehead. Wings folded like umbrellas.

Toby lifted it from the box and placed it in my hands. It was small and soft, a mouse with wings. I could feel its terror—it shivered. Then it stretched out its wing, unfurled it like the sail of a boat. A transparent membrane, delicately veined—like a leaf, like lace.

"I love it." The words just came out. I held the bat closer to my face, smelled the dust on its fur. Then it opened its mouth, showing a row of tiny teeth, and screamed. A sound of agony.

"It's hurt." I saw that its wing was torn, ripped like the knee of Toby's pants. "What happened?"

Toby shrugged. "Don't know."

"You found it down here?"

"It's for you."

"We should tell Miss Robb."

But then we'd have to explain why we'd left the Sunday school room, why we were in the basement. So we dealt with it on our own. Toby tried to feed the bat part of a Fig Newton that he'd found in his pocket. Then we stroked its head and sang one of the songs Miss Robb had taught us:

> *Without Him I would be nothing*
> *Without Him I'd surely fail;*
> *Without Him I would be drifting*
> *Like a ship without a sail*

The bat breathed in fast gulps. I suggested the one thing I knew could heal. "We should give it a name."

Did I suggest it or did Toby? One of us thought of that long-ago man who lived wholeheartedly, who was welcomed into the Promised Land. Caleb.

I remember how it felt to bestow a name upon that bat, the way Adam might have—to define the small mystery breathing in my hand. Naming was a declaration of love. The bat belonged to me, and I would save it.

Toby and I squeezed our eyes shut and prayed. *Please*, we said. *Please help.*

I outgrew that dress with its lace collar; I outgrew Miss Robb and her stories. What is love? When I was sixteen, it was a Europop song. *Baby don't hurt me, don't hurt me no more.*

I was beyond love, above it, because everyone and everything had disappointed me. Miss Robb married and had children and grew frumpy and old—she no longer had perfect bangs and pink nails. And my parents were idiots. Jerome told me that our families had spent so much time together because his parents felt sorry for us. That the Burkes had paid for all the bowling and skiing outings—the french fries and hot chocolate, the gas, the admission tickets.

He told me this when we still hung out in their basement,

which had a small trampoline and a pool table. He'd taught me how to dust blue chalk over my pool cue and into the crease of skin next to my thumb.

"It wasn't a big deal." Jerome nudged my cue to help me line up my shot. "It was charity."

When I heard that word, *charity*, I felt sorry for my family too. And I despised us. Despised my father for losing every job he found and declaring that it wasn't his fault—his boss was a moron or his coworker had something against him. Despised my mother for the way she fell for pyramid schemes and believed that selling face creams or vitamins or little decorative amulets would save us.

And Jesus. Impossible to count the ways He had let me down. So I stopped talking to Him. Silence was easy; it happened all the time. My mom stopped talking to my dad for days on end; I had stopped talking to my best friend in Grade 2 because she'd stolen my barrette; Jerome stopped talking to me because he'd grown bored of hanging out with a kid. And now I stopped talking to Jesus. A day went by, then a week, then months. Nothing happened—no pestilence, no punishment. I only realized later, decades later, that God's silence was a heartbreak to me. That my body felt like a sail with no wind filling it out.

And Toby? He grew into those hand-me-down suits. Tall and broad-chested like his brother, he arrived at church without baggy sleeves or holes in the knees of his trousers. His hair was streaked with sun—he now spent his excess energy outside on basketball courts, playing for the school's team. He also became an usher at church, taking over from Jerome, who passed on his keys. Now Toby arrived early each Sunday morning to turn on the lights, check the thermostat, place the hymnals. Toby shook our hands when we passed through the door. Toby passed the collection plate. Toby stood for the entire service, ready to assist anyone who needed help.

At sixteen, Toby was the only one I didn't hate, the only one who hadn't disappointed me—because my expectations had been so low. But Toby had forsaken me. When he stood at the church door and I approached, his gaze grazed the top of my head and his smile emptied. As though he'd never written me love notes, never prayed with me in the basement of this church, never showed me his flaccid penis. As though he'd never chosen me.

Usually I ignored him too, but once, I dared him to look at me. Dared him to deny me. "Hi, Toby," I said. "How's it going?"

"Hello, Leanna."

Nausea rushed through me like a wave. "No one calls me that anymore."

Toby turned away from me, toward a young family who were arriving. "Hello! Welcome." He reached to shake the adults' hands, and the children clamored to be near him. But I—my body—blocked him from moving toward them, from lifting the children into the air, from spinning them until they were delirious and sick.

"I'm Lea now."

"Okay." He delivered a perfectly pleasant smile and the family passed by, their bodies moving around us like water. "Thanks for letting me know."

"You're welcome." When I stared at him, his face went red like the time he'd punched Kipp Fitch. "Anything else I can do, Toby?"

"I actually go by Tobiah now," he said.

"Really? *Tobiah?*"

"Your parents are inside." He moved to let me past. "If you're waiting for them."

"I'm pregnant." I hadn't told anyone else yet because my body was still hiding the fact. Only the skin around my eyes had darkened; I wore a mask all the time now. "*With child.*"

Toby looked at me then. We were both thinking about sex—he knew I'd had it and I knew he hadn't—but it was more than that. He must have sensed the violence in me. I wanted to grab him by the throat and drag him to the basement. For ten anxious weeks, pregnancy had left me exhausted most of the time, enraged the rest, and I wanted to punch someone, to feel flesh give way under my fists. I wanted to hurt Toby. *Tobiah.* I wanted to make him remember me; I wanted to make him cry; I wanted us to hold hands and pray. *Please help.*

Our prayers worked. Or is this just my memory of it? My brain telling me a story? The bat flew from my hands.

And then? Did we walk up the staircase together?

We must have returned to the classroom and continued building our ark. We must have glued our popsicle sticks together, carefully traced and cut our sails. Because Miss Robb came back with a plastic basin full of water. She was flushed from carrying it, and some had sloshed onto her blouse. She apologized for taking so long. "But it's worth the wait," she said, "because I have a surprise." She raised her lovely eyebrows. "We're going to sail our arks," she said. "For real."

Then all the children took turns putting their arks on the water. Every single one of them sank, paper turning soggy. "Oh, dear," said Miss Robb.

Then it was our turn. Toby and I each held one side of our boat and lowered it to rest on the water's delicate membrane.

Our ark—I remember this for certain—could float.

With child. I said the words, and my insides started to roil—I felt seasick. I marched into the church, ignoring Pastor Guthrie's nicotine-stained smile, ignoring Jerome's noncommittal nod, ignoring Jesus pinned naked to his cross. I sat in the wooden pew beside my parents and ignored them too. I flipped to the first reading.

Partway through the sermon, my lower back was singing with

pain. I stood, walked to the back of the church, down the hallway that led to the Sunday school rooms. I could hear children laughing or screaming or crying. I needed to be alone. I opened the door that led to the dark basement, and sat on the steps.

The basement was still lit by that one octagonal window—dust floated through the air. Then I fell. The memory is just an image, like from the *Illustrated Bible*: my body at the bottom of the stairs. Then Toby above me, helping me to my feet. Toby hugging me like he'd never forsaken me. Holding me and saying, "Leanna. Leanna, are you okay?"

What is love? We were in one of those pews—Toby had the keys to the church and this was the only place we could find privacy. Toby's heart pounded against my hand. Was it fear of me? Or rage? Or adoration? When we were on that pew, he couldn't stop saying how much he loved me. We did not have sex but we kissed, and Toby pressed both his hands to my breasts. They had been sore during that brief pregnancy, tender as bruises. Now they were numb.

Everything was forgotten. Forgiven. For Toby, my body was pure. I was Leanna.

But I remembered. I remembered the waxy smell of the empty church. I remembered splinters from the wooden pew in my back. How many times had Jerome and I come here? Four? Five? Jerome pouring sips of sacramental wine into my mouth.

I also remembered sitting in this pew after my fall, bleeding. Toilet paper stuffed into my underwear. I told my parents I didn't feel well, that I needed to go home.

Three or four days later, I was in the bathroom, the door locked, and could hear the TV downstairs—my parents were watching *M*A*S*H*. I sat in the empty tub and something slipped out of me, something smaller than a bat. The child was perfect: toes, fingers, eyebrows. Delicate eyelids made of skin so transparent that I could see the blue veins underneath.

Caleb. I was sure he was a boy. I named him as soon as I held him to my chest.

Here is what I believe: The bat was healed. Flew from my hands. Toby and I sat on the basement floor, and the bat circled above us, never hitting a wall or any of those piles of dusty boxes and books—bats use echolocation, I would learn later in school.

Caleb circled and circled until he found that octagonal window, the only source of light, and flew free.

For years, I remembered. Even when I got married, I couldn't forget that I was taking Jerome's name too. But then I had a stroke of luck: I got pregnant again. Again and again. My brain hardly worked for years and I forgot everything, even the names of my own children. It was a joke in our family, me calling one by the name of another.

"I'm Sarah." My daughter would roll her eyes. "*That's* Rebekah."

"Take out the garbage," I'd say, "whoever you are."

Toby would place a kiss on the back of my head. "My wife," he'd say with a laugh, "the idiot."

I lived in fog, a beautiful fog like in paintings of winter, of ocean. Memories passed by like clouds on the other side of a window. Some were friendly, familiar: The bat's stunning, sliced wing. Toby holding gummy scissors.

When they were still small, my children liked to curl up around me in the hour before bedtime, their bodies warm and protective. I read them the story of baby Moses, the story of the Red Sea, the story of Joshua and Caleb.

None of you will enter the land I swore with uplifted hand to make your home, except Caleb son of Jephunneh and Joshua son of Nun.

My youngest daughter cried at this. She wanted to change the ending so that all the Israelites could enter the Promised Land. She wanted a more forgiving God. "Why?" she asked. "Why is God so mean?"

I didn't know the answer. There was no answer.

Toby appeared in the doorway, knelt and took her tear-streaked face in his hands. "In His wisdom, God knew what was best for them." His voice was perfectly calm, perfectly correct. "They were unfaithful, honey. So they were punished."

He kissed her hair and she clutched his shoulder. She trusted him more than anyone else in the world.

"God isn't mean," he said. "God is love."

"I remember this one time." Jerome swayed at the microphone, paused so long that I felt afraid of what he might say. "This one time, I couldn't stand it anymore, so I put my hands over both of their mouths. And they bit me."

The audience, our family and friends, laughed. Toby squeezed my sweaty hand under the white-linen table. And when Jerome looked at us, I remembered being sixteen, begging and negotiating with God, asking only for Jerome to look at me again, to talk to me. And when he didn't. When he didn't, I lost my faith.

"They bit me," said Jerome, "at the same time."

Then he turned back to our guests. He lifted his glass and liquid sloshed onto his suit jacket. "If that's not love," he said, "what is?"

That wooden pew. The pain in my lower back. Standing during the sermon, walking to the back of the church, down the hallway that led to the Sunday school rooms. I opened the door that led to the dark basement, and sat on one of the steps. I would not vomit. I would not vomit now, here, in this church. I breathed in fast gulps.

The door opened behind me. Light on the staircase, showing the dust. A shifting of molecules.

"Leanna. You okay?"

The door closed and it was dark again. Toby stood over me.

"Hey, Toby." I clutched my stomach. Took a breath. "Remember that bat?"

"Of course."

Two words, and I knew that Toby was still the boy who'd tugged on my sleeve, who'd said *please*, who brought me here to show me a pure-hearted thing. So I stood up, nauseous, unsteady. He was a few steps higher than me and I reached for him. We were companions, always had been, and there was no one who would be more faithful to me. No one who would love me so wholeheardedly.

I held out both hands to him, knowing we would build our own ark in this world. But he didn't catch me. He moved calmly away, one step higher. And I lost my balance, fell down the stairs, fell so fast that my brain didn't keep up. My brain didn't keep up for years. It still reached for him, still felt relief, still believed in this story: that this was love, that it would save me.

STEVE AND LAUREN:

Three Love Stories

The Hole

They had been living in the house for three years when Lauren noticed it. While vacuuming the living room, she moved the coffee table to one side and saw a hole in the floor, big enough that she almost caught her foot in it. She turned off the vacuum—a Kenmore Gentle Sweep they'd received as a wedding gift—and got down on her hands and knees. She touched the frayed carpet and splintered floorboards. She peered down and saw blackness.

It struck her as strange that there was a hole in the floor, because the house didn't have a basement. One reason they'd purchased this property was that the foundation was built on solid rock. The city sat on a fault line and Steve said that houses built on rock would fare better in an earthquake. He had done research.

She returned the coffee table to its place, careful to set each leg in its divot. She would mention the hole to Steve that evening.

But when he came back from the Science Fair he'd judged all weekend—as a new teacher, he was expected to participate in many extracurricular activities—he told her he'd run into Amanda and Quinn, who'd just returned from a month in Honduras.

"I'm surprised they could afford it," Lauren said while she helped unload groceries from a cloth bag. She thought about Honduras and pictured colorful houses, beaches with bright water, and guerrilla soldiers in fatigues. "Was there a coup there recently? Was that Honduras?"

"I invited them over sometime. Thought we could barbecue."

Was she thinking of Nicaragua? *Nicaragua.* That was a nice word, full of pleasing sounds. She worked as a rep for a condo developer, which was more than a full-time job, but one day she planned to take a night class and learn Spanish or French, one of those elegant European languages. She had so many ambitions, resolutions unfulfilled. She'd once taken up sewing, and now bolts of fabric sat unused in a closet. And there was a whole list of books she meant to read: *The Master and Margarita, Anna Karenina.* She'd planned to be one of the few people to actually get through *A Brief History of Time,* but for years it had gathered dust on her bedside table.

"Maybe you can make that cake thing," said Steve. "The chocolate-orange one."

"Sounds good." She poured them each a glass of wine. "We haven't seen those two in forever."

Steve and Lauren didn't vacuum often. Steve believed that a clean house was the sign of a wasted life, and Lauren, though naturally a tidy person, had come to agree. So the hole remained hidden. Busy at work, Lauren forgot about it until she next had one of those nights: the kind where she lay awake, listening to Steve's breath, knowing she would be exhausted in the morning. She was thinking about nothing (a brand of eye shadow she wanted to try, a twinge in her neck that never went away), and then she remembered the hole.

She climbed from the bed, walked quietly down the stairs, and went to the living room. She pushed the coffee table against the entertainment center, turned on a lamp—one they'd bought at an antique shop in Chemainus—and saw that the hole had grown. It was big enough to swallow her entire head. She crouched down. The hole seemed to be filled with nothing at all—no light, no shadow.

She recalled that Steve sometimes mentioned dark matter (or was it dark energy?) and claimed that most of the universe was invisible to even the most advanced telescopes and satellites. When Steve told her these things, he used his teacher voice and Lauren became the bored student. It wasn't that she didn't care about dark matter (okay, maybe she didn't care about dark matter or dark particles or whatever—maybe she felt that if something is undetectable, it isn't worth talking about); it was the pedagogic note in her husband's voice that made her feel trapped and helpless. It reminded her of being in grade three, seated in front of Ryan Ogle, who blew on her neck to annoy her, whose breath was warm and wet, both horrible and welcome to her.

A slight, sweet smell rose from the hole. The air felt cool on her face.

Lauren went to the kitchen and made herself a cup of mint tea and took a spoonful of liquid magnesium supplement—she'd read in a magazine that this was a natural cure for insomnia. She flipped through the business section of the previous day's paper. Then she went back to bed. Suddenly chilled, she slid under the covers and pressed herself against her husband's body.

The next morning, Steve switched off the lamp that Lauren had left on. (He was better at turning off lights and reusing Ziploc bags, and he never let the water run while brushing his teeth.) He didn't say anything about the coffee table, still pushed aside, or the hole, which had continued to grow. As Lauren watched her husband stride across the living room, she worried he might trip and tumble into it. She imagined a strange, abrupt widowhood. The bouquets and gift baskets that would arrive.

In six years of marriage, Lauren had never imagined life without her husband. She had not indulged anxious thoughts (what if he died? got sick? what if he left her?) because there was no point in worrying about possibilities that might never occur. Steve had told her that some scientists believed the universe was infinite, or maybe there were infinite universes, and every possibility was being played out in every moment. So in one universe, Steve was slipping through the hole. In another, he was leaving her because he'd fallen in love with Amanda. In yet another, they were all dead.

This was exactly why she avoided that kind of thinking. It wasn't healthy.

Steve calmly walked into the kitchen. He didn't root around for his tape measure to assess the damage. He didn't mention stopping by Home Depot to buy materials and make repairs. But it was Monday, and he was always distracted and tense on Mondays—he still got nervous about being in front of a class. Lauren didn't want to bug him by bringing up the abyss in the living room. Besides, it wasn't a big deal. They planned to install hardwood anyway.

Over the next week, Lauren sneaked down to the living room each night. The cool air emanating from the hole reminded her of the basement in her childhood house, where her parents had stored the camping gear, the tools, the boxes of clothes and books they planned to get rid of but never did. Sometimes she played amid the junk: paint samples, an old hide-a-bed, a crushed top hat and broken wand from when her older brother was into magic. Sometimes the basement flooded, tepid water seeping from the cracks in the walls, and the whole family spent hours down there with buckets and mops and rubber boots. These floods had been some of the best days of Lauren's childhood—there'd been a sense of absurdity and family togetherness—and she was quietly disappointed when her father installed a sump pump.

Then one afternoon she came home from school and heard sounds coming from the basement. Her parents weren't home yet. She pressed her ear to one of the heating vents and heard a girl's nervous giggle and her brother's soft, insistent, coaxing voice— noises that made her feel sick to her stomach. She never played in the basement again.

But now something like gravity pulled her toward the hole. She could peer into that nothingness forever, hours slipping by without her knowledge. She felt full of fear and a dark desire. She could jump. Into what? She imagined a still, bottomless lake. Or a windless field of tall, unmoving grass. She imagined that her parents' bones were down there, heaped and rotting. She waited for something to appear from the hole: a swarm of flies, a crow, a dove. Nothing came.

But the smell grew stronger—like some tropical fruit (what did they grow in Honduras?) beginning to soften. And the hole continued to grow. After a few weeks, she and Steve had to step gingerly around it when they walked through the living room or settled on the couch to watch their shows. (They liked reality programs about home decor and fashion design, though Steve had sworn Lauren to secrecy about this.) And when Amanda and Quinn came over for dinner, they skirted the hole's edges, pressing their backs to the wall as they passed through to the deck.

Against her better intentions, Lauren drank too much wine that night. She laughed too loudly and told the same story twice—about the time she and Steve saw a black bear on the side of the highway, and Steve thought it was just a really big raccoon. Their friends didn't stay late, and when Lauren went to hug Amanda goodbye, she nearly pulled them both to the floor.

"I gotcha." Steve put his arm around her in an embarrassed, apologetic way. "There we go."

Later, after Lauren made her unsteady way upstairs (they could do the dishes in the morning), she looked in the bathroom mirror and saw that her wine-stained mouth was a dark hollow in her face. She opened it wide, closed it, opened it again. She started to cry.

Steve (she hadn't even heard him come in) put his hand on her shoulder. "What's wrong?"

Lauren turned away from him, hid her face, but he pulled her to his chest. "You're just drunk, sweetheart."

"Don't you see it?" She took his hand, led him downstairs, pointed to the hole in the floor. "Don't you see that?"

"What?" Steve turned to her and cocked his head in his guileless way. "You mean that hole?"

Lauren was crying—*weeping*, really, which was a dramatic word, the kind they used in the novels she read in her book club. She was weeping so hard that she couldn't speak.

"Of course I see it," he said, using that patient and patronizing teacher-voice. "What do you want me to say?"

He tried to put his arms around her and she pushed him—not hard, just a nudge. He nearly lost his balance and a small scream caught in her throat. She thought for a second he would fall in, or fall out—just *fall*.

She grabbed his arm.

"Sweetheart?" His mouth was stained too. As he spoke, blackness stretched across his face. "What do you want me to do?"

"We should go down there. We should see what's down there."

"Really?" Steve looked at her like she was one of his students, a child who meant well but needed to be corrected. "Is that really what you want to do?"

Yes. That's what she wanted to do.

"Lauren? Honey? I'm not sure it's the *best* idea."

The temperature in the room had dropped a few degrees, and a cool breath drifted over her skin. She stepped to the edge, her stocking feet over the hole's crumbling lip.

"Lauren?"

She remembered being six years old, at her first swimming lesson. Taking one step down the pool's ladder, then another. The water a cold shock at her ankles, her knees, her thighs.

"Let's go up to bed." Steve took her hand, held it so tight it hurt. "I think you're just tired."

She'd ended up in the deep end, flailing, choking.

"You're right." She let him pull her back. She wiped her eyes, though the tears wouldn't stop. "I'm sure you're right."

Steve gathered her in his arms and carried her upstairs, the way he'd done on their wedding night. (That had been a joke, of course, to carry her over the threshold—a way of both embracing and repudiating tradition, done in the same spirit as when they'd hyphenated their names.) He laid her on the bed, peeled off her T-shirt and jeans, and they made love under the warm sheets.

She woke the next morning hung over and worn from weeping. Steve was still asleep—he was so tired since starting at that school—and she went downstairs to get a glass of water.

In the kitchen, she washed last night's dishes, then made pumpkin-millet waffles and a pot of coffee. When Steve came downstairs, he kissed the back of her head and lingered to smell her hair. "This looks great, babe."

She handed him a plate with two buttered waffles. She wasn't hungry, but he ate happily, and she admired him for it. He looked at the news on his laptop, and told her what was happening in Tunisia, or maybe it was Syria. He got another waffle. She sipped her coffee.

Behind them, a black mouth opened wider and wider. Steve and Lauren held hands across the table, and the morning—one of many mornings, infinite mornings—passed in its sweet and usual way.

The Watch

Steve first met Jennifer before class in the staff room, while he made himself a cup of Earl Grey tea.

"Are you boiling water?" she asked. "Is there enough for another cup?"

There was only enough for one cup, but he insisted she have it. She drank a kind of sweetened coffee that came in a small tin and was probably full of chemicals. His wife would have been appalled, but Steve found this disregard for good health—and even good taste—to be novel and charming. While he boiled himself more water, he introduced himself as the guy who teaches science, and Jennifer Walton said she'd recently been hired to teach math and Spanish. She was blond and had an athletic build that gave her a robust, all-American look, though she was from Vernon, British Columbia. He noticed her strong arms and wrists as she sipped her frothy drink. She was so different from Lauren, a petite, nervous brunette, with delicate bones and a fluttery manner.

"I've never taught at a middle school before," she said. "The grade nines scare me already. You can smell their hormones when you walk in the door."

He assured her that you get used to the smell.

She laughed. "Good to know. See you at lunch?"

He nodded and glanced at the time—he had his morning routine down to a science—and saw that his watch had stopped. That had never happened before. The watch had belonged to his father, and was as sturdy and well built as the old man had been. Recently, Lauren had replaced the stiff leather with a silver strap more suited to Steve, and presented it to him a couple of days after their twelfth anniversary, which had passed with little fanfare. The gift was one of his favorites, combining Lauren's care for him—she understood how much he missed his dad—with her aesthetic talent.

Steve shook his wrist, and that solved it. Time started up again.

At a staff meeting a month later, when Jennifer sat beside him (she smelled crisp and fresh like the outdoors, probably because she cycled to work each morning from her rented apartment in Fairfield), his watch stopped again.

And it happened the following day when she asked him to join her for lunch at the Mediterranean deli near the school. This was where the staff went to buy lunch—the students stuck to the school cafeteria or the nearby Wendy's.

Lunch on a Tuesday. That was innocent enough. Plenty of people have lunch together; Steve had eaten lunches with people he didn't even like. So he agreed, and they sat at a table near the back and ordered a dish of hummus and baba ghanoush to share, a plate of warmed pita, and two Greek salads. He encouraged her to try the Turkish coffee.

"I've always wanted to see Istanbul, haven't you?" she said. He hadn't. But in her company, the idea of traveling to an enormous foreign city didn't seem intimidating—it seemed exciting.

"Yes," he said. "Absolutely."

He asked what she would do with her two months off during the summer, which was still eight months away. She had another job lined up as a guide in the Parliament buildings, showing tourists around the grand rooms and staircases. She wouldn't take more than a couple weeks of actual vacation because she was saving to buy a condo.

Steve, by contrast, hoped to do very little. "I like to garden and do yard work. Take my kids camping," he said. "That must sound boring."

"Not at all." She rested her chin on her hand. "That sounds lovely."

"I go for runs." Steve said this to impress her, though it must be obvious he'd let himself go lately. It had been a busy year. Lauren had started a new business as a real-estate stager; she talked almost nonstop about curtains and lampshades, and made repeated trips to IKEA in Vancouver, leaving him to deal with the kids. Ruby and Cameron were five and three, respectively, and had so much energy that Steve sometimes shunted them outside, where they literally ran circles around the backyard. Cam, the youngest, once did so until he threw up. On top of this, Steve's father had died this year, and Steve had spent hours sorting through his dad's possessions and acting as the executor of his will. Steve hadn't found time to grieve yet, though he had the sense that he ought to.

When he thought about the summer, he mostly looked forward to sleeping.

"I'd like to take the kayak out too," he said. "Do a few hikes."

They heard, distantly, the first end-of-recess bell. Steve looked at the time, hardly believing that fifty-five minutes had passed so quickly, and saw that his watch had stopped. He would have to take it to be repaired.

"We should get going." Jennifer zipped up her sweatshirt—she dressed like a gym teacher, but made jeans and T-shirts, hoodies and ponytails, look appealing. "I don't think I can finish this coffee. Do you want some?"

It occurred to him that sharing a cup with a woman who was not his wife—putting his lips to the same rim as she put hers—was something he hadn't done in a long time. "Are you sure?"

"I'm a caffeine addict who can't drink real coffee." She laughed. "It's embarrassing. Usually I stick to Coke."

He picked up the small clay cup. She had stirred in several packages of sugar, and the liquid inside was thick and dark and sweet.

Tuesday lunch became their routine. He learned that she had a boyfriend in Calgary, a two-and-a-half-year, long-distance relationship. She encouraged him to tell her about Lauren and the kids, and never seemed bored by his reports of the insanity, delight, exhaustion, and terror of fatherhood. He asked where she'd learned Spanish, and she told him about her exchange in Madrid. She asked him for advice on how to deal with Tyson Mapplebee, a fourteen-year-old who'd made remarks about her body in front of the class. She cried when she told Steve about it, sitting at that small, flimsy table in the deli. "I sent him out of the room, but by then I'd completely lost control. You know how kids get. They were staring at me. Waiting for me to freak out."

"Tyson probably has a crush on you," said Steve. "Not that it makes it okay."

He reached across the table and touched her arm in a way he hoped was light, comforting, friendly. She looked down at his hand and frowned, so he withdrew it. But she just wiped her eyes and said, "Your watch is wrong."

He shook his wrist. "I don't get it. I just had the battery changed."

"I'm sorry about this. I'm sorry to be so *emotional*." She laughed at herself, then looked around the deli. "I guess we're lucky no one else is here." She meant any of the school staff. Other teachers sometimes joined them for lunch, which was always a disappointment to Steve. "What would they think if they saw us sitting at a table together," she said, "and me in tears?"

For months, he didn't tell anyone about the fact that his watch stopped working every time he saw Jennifer Walton. Not his wife, of course, but not Jennifer either.

It wasn't until December, right before Christmas break, that he mentioned it. He and Jennifer were both looking forward to the time off work, but were also apprehensive about the holiday. She was going to Calgary to see her boyfriend, to finally make up her mind about him. And Steve would be celebrating his first Christmas without his dad, who (he told Jennifer, and she listened with that look of thoughtful interest that he adored) gave extravagant gifts, sang old love songs in a deep baritone, and spent most holidays with a glass of scotch in his hand. Steve felt enormous loneliness when he thought about Christmas without his dad, and felt the same thing when he thought about two and a half weeks without Jennifer. So he suggested something out of the ordinary.

He told his wife about an end-of-term dinner—though from his vague explanation, Lauren probably understood he was going out with several colleagues—and met Jennifer at a small Indian restaurant across the bridge, at the other end of town. They ate butter chicken, rice with raisins and coconut, and spinach daal.

They drank beer, felt celebratory—*school's out!*—and then, by accident, as though by tripping and falling into it, acknowledged their feelings for each other.

"What do we do now?" said Jen.

They held hands across the table—relieved, exhilarated, full of expectation—and Steve told her about the watch. He explained that every time he saw her—*like clockwork*, he said, feeling witty—it stopped.

She shook her head, amazed. She didn't laugh, or question it. "That's exactly how I feel," she said.

In that moment, he felt sure that his dad would have liked her. His father had loved Lauren, of course, but he wouldn't disapprove of Jennifer either.

Steve marveled at his luck to be sitting across from her, to be holding her hand. Then he marveled at that watch: its simplicity, its complexity, its longevity. He marveled that someone had invented a mechanism that could tell time, that could guide him through his day. And the fact that it could be worn on your wrist was almost a miracle!

But if there were ways to gauge time and space and gravity, why was there nothing to help him now? No scale to measure competing, worldly joys: the weight of duty, the tidal force of desire.

Jen undid the watch's clasp and slid it off his wrist. "It's beautiful," she said, and ran one finger over its face. She knew it had been a gift from his wife, and she held it carefully. He liked this about her—she was a discreet, gentle person. A person you could trust. Which was good, because so was he. He didn't want to leave Lauren. He didn't want to wreck his life. And his kids, my god. The previous night, Ruby had announced that she planned to change her name to Nouille, the French word for "noodle." He couldn't hurt those kids.

He wanted a break, that was all. It wasn't his marriage or his children that he wanted to escape. It was his schedule.

It was eating breakfast in the car, running kids to school and preschool, arriving at work to the ringing bell. It was socializing with other couples who had children, visiting his widowed mother each Saturday, caring for the pets (one cat, two hamsters) and their accoutrements (a litter box, a wood-chip cage). It was the email in-box, the class prep, the marking, the arguments with Lauren, the (much worse) silent not-arguments with Lauren. It was her moods and cycles, her habits. (Lately she'd started putting yogurt on her face—something about the lactic acid and her pores.) It was worrying that her business would fail and they would be thousands of dollars in debt. It was worrying that her business would succeed and she would leave him. It was loving her but not having the energy to tell her so, or even to touch her. It was seeing the hurt in her yogurt-smeared face.

His was (Jen herself said so) a lovely life. He just wanted a respite from it. He wanted to meet Jen in a hotel somewhere, in a foreign city, a city they'd never seen, a city that existed only for a weekend.

Two days. Forty-eight hours. That was all he wanted in the world.

Jen slipped the watch back over his wrist, and her fingers on his skin made him dizzy. She fastened the clasp and asked again, "What do we do now?"

He didn't know the answer. He didn't even know what time it was. His watch had stopped, and anyway, he wasn't looking at its face. He was looking at the strap, a simple metal band. It was heavy on his wrist. It was a gift.

The Nap

One afternoon they broke into a house with a long drive-way and neglected garden. Steve smashed the latch on the screen door and picked the lock. Lauren had no idea he could do that. They'd met each other only a few months earlier and this was their first vacation together.

The hinges were rusty. Steve kicked open the door.

They wanted to make love—that was all they did in those days. They'd been driving up-island to a bed-and-breakfast they'd booked for the weekend, sharing a bag of chips and listening to eighties pop that made them nostalgic. Then Lauren shifted in the passenger seat and licked Steve's neck, and he pulled over.

"This is no good," said Steve as he unclipped her seat belt. "You deserve a bed. You deserve to be properly loved."

She was a sucker for this kind of talk, so she didn't say anything as he pulled her toward that locked-up house. It was a simple cottage, just a few rooms—probably someone's summer home.

They knew little about each other, and nothing about what

lay beyond the door. But Steve took Lauren's hand and they stepped—full of fear, full of longing—into the strange house.

Lauren groped for the light switch, flicked it on, and gasped, delighted with the modern but earthy interior. It was simple, tasteful. Exactly what she would have done. "I love it," she said.

Steve quickly found the bedroom and they didn't turn on the lights or bother to remove all of their clothes. They made love in a dark room, on top of a bed that smelled of mildew and dust. Afterward, arms wrapped around each other, they fell asleep.

Lauren was the first to open her eyes. Her muscles were achy and stiff. She'd always had a tense body, a body that worried for her, but this brittleness was new. She stretched her arms above her head, and noticed the ring on her finger—a gold band with no jewels. It was simple, tasteful. She did not remember getting married.

She lay on the bed and listened to Steve's breath. She knew the rhythm of his exhalations as though they were her own. She shook him, this stranger who had become her husband. "Hey. We fell asleep."

They climbed groggily from the bed, their eyes sleep-crusted, their mouths dry. It felt like jet lag.

"I'm always like this after a nap," said Lauren. Then she noticed the way Steve looked at her.

Her appearance shocked him. She was hunched, gray, with folds in the skin of her neck, clusters of age spots on her cheeks. Time had passed. Nearly fifty years.

"Forty-eight," she corrected him.

He stared at her, his mouth open. "What's happened?"

"It's not like you look so great," she said. "Where's your hair?"

The room had become theirs, and it was clear from the framed pictures by the bed that they'd raised children. A son and daughter.

"Yes," said Lauren, suddenly recalling. Cameron was a pediatrician. He was married to a woman who used an old-fashioned loom to weave $300 scarves that she sold on the Internet—what kind of job was that? And their daughter was a freelance writer who lived in Montreal. They worried about her. Ruby. She was such a lonely, guarded woman. She owned two parrots and talked to them as though they were human. She'd once told her mother that the birds would outlive her and Lauren had said, "That's not true. That's not possible." She couldn't believe that her daughter would die. Just like she couldn't believe that this grown woman, Ruby, had once locked her tiny mouth to Lauren's breast.

"They visit during holidays," said Steve. It was coming back to him. This was their property, purchased when the kids were in school. Since that afternoon when they broke in, they'd fantasized about coming back. So years later, when they saw this house on the market, they bid on it immediately. It had been their summer home until they retired; now they lived here year-round.

They left the bedroom and entered the kitchen. The fridge was full—evidently, they'd become vegetarians, probably at Lauren's insistence—but neither of them was hungry. In the cupboards they found a matching set of dishes. Lauren moved quickly to the next room, in her busy way, but Steve lingered over the dishes: white and blue bowls and plates. A creamer, a serving platter, a set of salt-and-pepper shakers. He held each object in his hand, feeling the weight of the ceramic, tracing the hairline cracks.

As he held his favorite mug, he noticed his hand. He knew that over time, a person's chromosomal telomeres shorten. This can lead to damaging mutations, to strange errors in the replication of cells. Crucial proteins are no longer produced; DNA is not repaired. This can be expressed as something dramatic: a disease of one kind or another. Or it might be felt as a quiet, eerie loss of function—a waning. The joints of his fingers were stiff. His arm was weak. The mug, stained from years of coffee drinking, felt heavy. He set it on the counter.

He knew there were limits and that each species has its duration. Mayflies survive only a couple of minutes. Wild blueberry bushes live for thirteen thousand years. It is the usual, necessary, beautiful course of things. So why did he feel such grief?

Lauren came back into the kitchen. "You took up photography."

Steve had no memory of this, but the chemistry of darkrooms had always fascinated him.

Lauren showed him a series of prints he must have taken of her. Photographs of when she was pregnant, when she was uncharacteristically chubby, and one where she was lying on a green lawn, laughing. She had been so beautiful. Why hadn't she known it at the time?

"Look at me," she said, meaning the photo. But Steve examined his wife, and her face still pleased him. Age had softened her. In some of the photos—particularly one taken in this kitchen, years before—she looked hollowed and drawn.

Steve held this last photo and said, "Were you ever unfaithful to me?"

Lauren couldn't remember. "No. Never." She considered asking him the same question, but wasn't sure if the answer mattered.

Steve again picked up that mug.

Lauren was suddenly irritated (it was just like him to get sentimental over a few cracked dishes), so she left him standing by the kitchen counter. Her knees throbbed as she climbed to the attic.

There were no windows. She slid her palm along the wall to find the light switch.

This floor must have been their office; she opened a pine filing cabinet. Steve had been a middle school teacher and had won city- and province-wide awards. There were newspaper clippings that had been proudly, carefully saved. Lauren had been many things:

a clerk in the Sears window-treatments department, a sales rep for a condo corporation, a small-business owner, a large-business owner, and, on occasion, a corporate keynote speaker. A keynote speaker—what kind of job was that? She couldn't remember being so confident, so audacious.

She leafed through old tax returns. What had it been like to sell window coverings at Sears? It had been fun, she thought. Then she had to sit down, because the memories came back in a rush. Waiting for the bus in the mornings, an umbrella over her head. Wearing those too-tight, fake-leather heels. Discovering a gift for salesmanship, the secret joy it gave her. Having a donut and black coffee in the mall's food court each afternoon. Carrying binders full of curtain samples, the weight straining her arms.

She was glad that was done. What a relief. But then again, if she could, she'd do it all over. Everything. Her whole life. She'd live it again, just for the small but real pleasures of a donut and coffee, of holding her daughter in her arms, of making money, of sleeping late, of waking up.

She carried a stack of returns down to the kitchen—slowly, concerned about falling on the stairs—where she found Steve, staring at a sugar bowl.

She showed him their tax returns, which they'd always filed jointly. They looked at the paperwork and tried to piece it all together.

Here's what they did not remember: The time Steve locked himself in the attic for six hours and refused, for no reason he could explain, to come out. The time Lauren smashed several of those blue and white dishes against the countertop, one by one. Their honeymoon in Hawaii. The hundreds of times they read *Bartholomew and the Oobleck* to Ruby before bed. The fall Steve took from his bike, the year Cam dressed as a penguin for Halloween, the time Ruby spilled grape juice on Lauren's favorite raw-silk throw.

Here's what they did remember: The time Cameron was colicky and Lauren was so tired she hallucinated. The time Ruby had her stomach pumped. The winter of the record snowfall, when Cam and Ruby built a snow fort in the backyard. The elaborate breakfasts Lauren prepared, the brand of chocolate bar Steve liked, the agony of trying to wake a teenage Ruby before noon. All four of them dancing in the living room to Prince's *1999*.

Life seemed so solid once, but now had melted like Dalí's watch and slipped through their fingers. They read over their tax returns, looked at the photos, and decided they'd lived a good life, without tragedy or scandal. Did this make them a success? Had it been the goal? Was it enough?

The sun had gone down and the house was dark. They loved it here, though still had the feeling they were getting away with something. They looked at one another in that old, conspiratorial way. They knew a little about each other, and nothing about what lay beyond the door. But Steve put down the sugar bowl, and took Lauren's hand. Then—full of fear, full of longing—they left the way they'd come in.

ACKNOWLEDGMENTS

Earlier drafts of several of these stories appeared in *Zoetrope: All-Story*, the *Iowa Review*, *Lucky Peach*, the *Virginia Quarterly*, and the *The Walrus*. Thank you to the editors of these magazines for their support.

Some of these stories required research and I am indebted to many sources. I couldn't have written "Girlfriend on Mars" without reading the wonderfully strange *Mars 1999* by Brian O'Leary. I couldn't have written about crows and birds of prey without reading *H Is for Hawk* by Helen MacDonald, *Crow Country* by Mark Cocker, *Mind of the Raven* by Bernd Heinrich, *In the Company of Crows and Ravens* by John M. Marzluff and Tony Angell, *Corvus: A Life with Birds* by Esther Woolfson, and the North American Falconers' Association's *A Bond with the Wild*. Most of all, I couldn't have written about the Hawk Man or his birds without having taken a class at The Raptors in Duncan, BC, where knowledgeable and dedicated staff educate the public about these incredible creatures.

A kernel of inspiration for the story "Last One to Leave" came from Corrie ten Boom's book *The Hiding Place*; I read the book as a child and never forgot the idea of being thankful for the fleas. Peter Trower's work was essential to the writing of "Last One to Leave," especially his essays "From the Hill to the Spill" and "Sojourn at Junkie Log." I'm grateful to Harbour Publishing for the way they preserve BC's history, and to Lorna Jackson, whose inspired teaching at the University of Victoria showed me how to look to history when imagining fiction.

Many thanks to Serhy Yekelchyk, professor at the University of Victoria, who generously agreed to read an early version of "Hard Currency" with an eye to historical accuracy. His help was invaluable, and any remaining errors in the text are entirely mine.

I began the story "Flight" in Aaron Golbeck's Downtown Eastside Studio Society workshop, and am so appreciative that Aaron and the PEERS participants welcomed me to those sessions.

Chris Erhard Luft recorded an audio version of "Steve and Lauren: Three Love Stories" in his Vancouver studio. Recording and producing the audio took an enormous amount of work; the fact that Chris found time for this project is a testament to his passion for the arts.

I did much of the work on these stories while I was a writer-in-residence. Thank you to the board of Historic Joy Kogawa House, especially Ann-Marie Metten, who is an organizational genius and a supportive friend. Thanks also to the teens and to the members of the Taiwanese Canadian Cultural Center who attended my workshops in Vancouver; I'm honored you spent your time with me. A huge thank-you to Jackie Flanagan, Caitlynn Bailey-Cummings and the steering committee of the Calgary Distinguished Writers Program at the University of Calgary, a program that changed my life and introduced me to so many valued friends. Thank you also to Fundación Valparaiso, for their support during my residency in Mojácar, Spain.

To my agent, Tracy Bohan, thank you for your long-sighted

and passionate work on my behalf. And thank you to Jacqueline Ko of the Wylie Agency, who has been tireless in her work for me in the U.S. Thank you to Maria Rogers, Steve Colca, Dave Cole, Erin Sinesky Lovett, and everyone at W. W. Norton, especially my editor, Jill Bialosky, whose insightful editorial feedback pushed me to deal with those niggling weak points in my stories. Thank you to Steve Myers and everyone at Penguin Random House, Canada, especially Nicole Winstanley, my editor and ideal reader, whose faith in my work makes all the difference.

Thank you to JoAnn McCaig, Kelsey Attard, and everyone at Freehand Books—I have the best job a writer could ask for. To the staff at Munro's Books, I'm so grateful for your support. Thank you especially to Jim Munro, who has been my friend as well as a strong advocate for my work. Thank you to Ben Schwartzentruber for his support while I began work on this manuscript, and for his inspiring love of books.

I am grateful to my community of fellow writers who offered advice and edits and much-needed camaraderie: Marjorie Celona, Rhonda Collis, Naomi K. Lewis, Kat Main, Susette Mayr, Aaron Shepherd, Jeanne Shoemaker, Sarah L. Taggart, Aritha Van Herk, and Samantha Warwick. A huge thank-you to the Unmentionables— your feedback, support, and companionship are essential. Most of all, I need to thank Diana Svennes-Smith, who helped immeasurably with each story in this collection. Her quiet confidence in my work allowed me to finish these stories at a time when I had lost faith in them. Diana, thank you for your friendship and for sharing your editorial vision and wisdom with me.

My family has had such a positive influence on the creation of these stories. My mum, Pauline Willis, helps me in so many essential ways, including by acting as a sounding board and proofreader. My dad, Gary Willis, understands the peculiarities of the writer's life and I so appreciate our conversations and his advice.

My aunt, Charis Wahl, read an early version of this manuscript, told me—kindly, honestly—that it wasn't working, and helped point the way forward.

Kris Demeanor makes me laugh and makes me breakfast, and I'm grateful every day for his commitment to thoughtful art, his intelligence, and his openheartedness.